"Poor, gutted, jam-packed Earth couldn't afford largescale enterprises that didn't have a high chance of a high profit. The geegee made spaceflight cheap, but not that cheap. It was the asteroids that counted."

Yes, I recite in my mind, *that's correct: not the inner planets, but the flying mountains of the Belt—thousands of them, minerals right there for the taking, gravity so weak that hauling costs dropped to something a small entrepreneur might be able to meet. And Jupiter, there was the other factor that gave us the freedom of space.*

It wasn't foreseen. Predictions had to do with Luna, Mars, Venus, not naked rocks and a poisonous giant. But then, Columbus was looking for the Indies when he found America. I wonder what serendipities are waiting for us among the stars?

TALES OF THE FLYING MOUNTAINS

POUL ANDERSON

TOR

A TOM DOHERTY ASSOCIATES BOOK

To
Peg Campbell

Contents

Prologue

We the people of the spaceship Astra, *in order to accomplish man's first venture beyond the Solar System, guarantee survival, maintain justice and tranquility, promote the common welfare, and secure the liberty of ourselves and our posterity, do ordain and establish this Constitution for the governance of ship and personnel until such time as their mission shall be completed.*

Brave words. They recall to us the law of the Asteroid Republic, which in turn drew on the law of the United States of America. And so they hearten us, now when the worldlets have long vanished from our telescopes, when Earth is lost in the glare of that star among stars which Sol has become, and when Jupiter and Saturn soon will be.

Necessary words. Before, those who embarked on an exploratory vessel signed the articles of the expedition. Together with the traditional rules, including the captain's benevolent despotism, that was enough. But we are headed for new suns. It will take more than forty years (at 0.01 *g*·acceleration, turnover at midpoint) to reach Alpha Centauri. And of course we will not then go straight back. The probes which preceded us beamed far too much information, far too tantalizing, about the planets of that triple system. Lifetimes will be insufficient to study them. Meanwhile, things at home will be changing. So will things on and in *Astra*, until at last "home" means her. The crew may well decide that maser contact is all they want. They may leave Alpha Centauri, not for Sol but for some other star.

Thus we have not committed just ourselves, we have committed an unknown number of generations after us. It is legally, morally, and practically impossible for us to bind them to any rigid frame of our own ways. While standby authority must exist for emergency use, the ship in general has to be run as a democracy.

"Ha!" says Lindgren.

"What?" I ask. I've been arguing that we, the Advisory Council, won't necessarily count for much. Our little group can debate issues; we can arrive at a consensus; but will the Congress pay attention?

"He said, 'Ha,' " Missy Blades tells me. After a moment, thoughtfully: "I agree with him."

"Myself," Orloff remarks, "I might go so far as to add, 'Ho!' "

A chuckle runs through the room, a grin across the eight faces I see. Five of those faces are lined, skins dark and leathery from decades of the raw spatial sunlight that no helmet plate will quite filter out, hair whitened; but the bodies are lean, lithe, carelessly and colorfully dressed, and age seems only to have deepened the merriment and sharpened the irreverence of youth. These, the elder statesmen of *Astra*, were in their day the conquerors of the flying mountains and the great outer worlds. They never had time for solemnity.

Amspaugh, our president, did. Most of his life was spent in offices—wheedling politicians and businessmen, riding herd on functionaries and computers, digging tunnels through solid kilometers of official paper: the necessary organizational work of the Foundation, which in the end became his particular service to the dream which we have begun to live. As a result, while he is liked and respected, he does seem a bit pompous on occasion.

"Ladies," he intones. "Gentlemen. Please remember that Mr. Sanders is new to this circle, and in fact new to the whole practice of civil government. I think we're wise in coopting people from Engineering, Navigation—every nonelective department—but let's not haze them."

"Oh, that's okay," I say hurriedly. "It takes time for one like me to phase in to the private jokes."

Missy Blades reaches over from her chair and pats my hand. "You'll do, Winston," she says. "Not that I'm surprised. We didn't invite you without getting to know you pretty well first. You're here because of more than the good job you've been doing."

A compliment from her means considerable. I look through the viewport with pride.

This lounge (comfortable, almost luxurious; decorated in an unpretentious richness of dark colors, classic pictures, bookshelves filled with codices as well as spools; for music, at the moment, Nielsen's *Fynsk Foraar* rejoicing softly in the background) occupies the dome of a turret rising from the outer hull, so high that most of the atmosphere is below it. Hence our view straight outward is of stark splendor, a black sky blazing with stellar myriads and the shining belt of the Milky Way. If you come over to the port, though, and glance down the sheer metal of the turret, you will see a haziness that marks *Astra*'s exterior air. A cloud drifts by, dimming one of the lamps which, on their ornate posts, replace the sun we are leaving behind us. Strictly functional, a geegee unit shoulders above the near horizon. You can't see its contribution to the network of force, but you know that without this, the gas would whiff away into vacuum and a lethal sleet of radiation would smite us.

We spy a park, grass, flowerbeds, trees, surrounding a pool. Otherwise little has been done about terraforming the outside—or, for that matter, more than half the cavernous interior. Leave those jobs for the future, as population grows. What we have serves us well for the present.

Well, indeed. We sit warm, at ease, breathing sweet air, smoking, drinking, snacking as we feel like it. The artificial gravity is a solid one *g* underfoot, its vector so aligned that we cannot detect the slight pressure of our acceleration. Nor do we sense the monstrous outpouring of engine energy by which this mass is driven starward. Modern technology is subtle as well as powerful.

We are not yet at Bussard velocity, where we can begin scooping up interstellar hydrogen to burn in the fusion reactors. But we have enough fuel of our own to reach that condition, and afterward to brake at interplanetary speeds as we back down on Alpha Centauri. We have a closed biocycle—everything essential to life can be reclaimed and reused indefinitely, for millions of years if need be—which at the same time is expansible. Boats, machines, robots, computers, instruments, and in the microfiles virtually all the knowledge of all the human civilizations that ever were, lie waiting for us like Aladdin's genie.

Perhaps someday they'll find a means of cracking the light-speed barrier, and come take us or our descendants off a worldship that will then be obsolete. Maybe. The point is, that legend doesn't have to become real. It'll take longer this way, but already, as things are, the universe has been opened to us.

So I think, and rejoice that my work is part of the glory, until Lindgren speaks:

"Getting back to the subject, since our Congress was honestly and democratically elected, it is a true representative of the people aboard. Therefore it'll fall headlong over its big flat feet, enacting into law whatever this council recommends. Saves it doing its own thinking, you see."

I must show a bit of shock, though he has merely observed the obvious, because Amspaugh's chocolate features contract in a slight frown and he says, "You might have put it more tactfully, Sigurd."

"Why?" asks Lindgren, interested.

Amspaugh runs a hand across his grizzled woolly hair and has no ready answer.

"Let's buckle down to business," proposes Dworczyk. "Best way for our freshman member to learn how we operate. Besides, I've an experiment going in my lab that I want to check on as soon as possible."

"Very well." Amspaugh turns to me. "I suppose you know that our single agendum today is educational policy."

"I'd heard mention of that," I reply. "But, uh, what's the rush? The first babies are scarcely born."

"They'll keep that up, though," McVeagh reminds me.

Missy Blades murmurs: " 'And thick and fast they came at last, and more, and more, and more.' Right up to the legal limit of population, whatever that may be at any given time. It's still the favorite human amusement."

Amspaugh takes pipe and tobacco pouch from various pockets and fumbles with them. "The children will grow," he points out earnestly. "They will require schools, teachers, and texts. The noncontroversial basics pose no problem, I imagine—literacy, science, math, et cetera. But even while the pupils are small, they'll also be studying history and civics. Presently they'll be adolescent, and start inquiring into the value of what they've been taught. A few years after that, they'll be franchised adults. And a few years after that, they'll be running the society.

"This isn't a planet, or even an asteroid, where people simply live. The voyage is the ship's entire *raison d'être*. Let the ideal be lost, and the future will be one of utter isolation, stagnation, retrogression, probably eventual extinction. To avoid that, we're uniquely dependent on education.

"We'll only have a thread of maser contact with Sol, years passing between question and answer. We'll only have each other for interaction and inspiration; no fruitful contacts with different countries, different ways of living and thinking. Don't you see how vital it is, Mr. Sanders, that our children be raised right? They must have a proper understanding, not simply of the technology they need, but of the long-range purpose and significance."

Having stuffed his pipe, he pauses to light it. Orloff talks into the silence: "Basically, what we must decide is what the history courses should include. Once we know that, we have writers who can put it into textbooks, actors who can put it on tape, and so forth for every level from kindergarten through college. In the absence of outside influences, those teachings are likely to be accepted, unchallenged, for generations if not forever. So what ought they to be?"

"The truth," I blurt.

"What is truth?"

"Why . . . the facts . . . what really happened——"

"Impossible," Amspaugh says gently. "First, there are too many facts for any human skull to hold, every recorded detail of everybody's day-by-day life since ancient Egypt. You have to choose what's worth knowing, and set up a hierarchy of importance among those data. Already, then, you see your 'truth' becoming a human construct. Second, you have to interpret. For instance, who really mattered more in the long-term course of events, the Greeks or the Persians? Third, man being what he is, moral judgments are inevitable. Was it right, was it desirable that Christianity take over Europe, or that it be later faced with such enemies as Mohammedanism and Communism?

"An adult, intellectually trained and emotionally mature, can debate these questions with pleasure and profit. A child cannot. Yet unless you raise the child with a sense of direction, of meaning, you'll never get the adult. You'll get an ignoramus, or else a spiritual starveling frantic for some True Belief—a potential revolutionary. *Astra* can't afford either kind."

"The problem was foreseen," Orloff puts in, "but we purposely delayed considering it till we should have been en route for a while and gotten some feeling of how this unique community is shaping up."

"I see," I answer. "At least, I think I see."

"Details later," Amspaugh says. "What we must

arrive at is a basic educational philosophy." He gives me a long look. "The original circle of us know each other quite well. I think, by and large, we can predict what stand everybody will take. That isn't good. We need a wider range of thoughts. It's a major reason why we're inviting new members in, you the latest.

"So would you like to open the discussion?"

"Well . . . well, uh—" I haul my brain cells together. "All right," I respond, "you have to select and you have to judge. You have to state, 'This was bad and must never be allowed to happen again; that was magnificent and something you ought to emulate.' Agreed.

"But what's the difficulty here? The conventional issues on Earth and in the Solar System—they're abstractions out among the stars. Oh, I suppose we'd better give the kids horrible examples of things like war and slavery, to try and make sure those won't revive among them. And good examples, naturally, like the Magna Carta or the American Declaration of Independence or the Bill of Liberties, to make them appreciate what they've got.

"As for inspiration, though—good Lord!" I exclaim, warming to my theme. "What's wrong with the conquest of space for your central motif? Tell them about Goddard, Tsiolkovsky, Oberth, Esnault-Pelterie, Ley. Tell them about Sputnik, about Mercury-Gemini-Apollo, about Emett and how he wouldn't listen when they laughed at his gyro-gravitics, about Rotmistrov on Mars and Shuhara on Venus—about their own ancestors, who turned cold, airless, lifeless rocks into the Asteroid Republic! What better can you do?"

Another silence follows. I become embarrassed. Their gazes upon me are not unkindly, but some have grown sardonic. At length Missy shakes her wise old head.

"No, I'm sorry, Winston," she says. "That won't work. Too many other facts are floating around in our libraries, and a percentage of students will get interested enough to do a little research. If we've told them about the wonderful space rockets, and nothing about the nuclear warheads that most of those rockets were meant to deliver—in effect, we'll have lied to them, and they'll find that out and distrust everything else we've tried to teach them. Likewise for the interplanetary era. Maybe Joe Amspaugh is right and no such thing as absolute historical truth exists. But we must try to pass on as much reality as we're able."

"I'm not sure about that," says Conchita Montalvo. Like Luis Echevaray and myself, she is of a younger generation. A slight insecurity forces seriousness and a professorial style of talking upon her. (Alone, we laugh a great deal.) "As Mr. Orloff just reminded us, this is going to be an utterly isolated group. Isolated also from the turbulent, complicated, often cruel and crooked mass of humanity. Our children won't have much chance to develop antibodies, so to speak. Facts too gross could appall them in their innocence, could throw them over into cynicism or rebellion. Quite frankly, I don't know if we dare do anything but suppress certain data."

That startles the rest of us. We're asterites; our loathing of censorship is as automatic as it is for every other kind of officiousness. Lindgren opens and closes his mouth a time or two before he manages to ask, "What episodes are you thinking about?"

"Many," Conchita replies. "Someone mentioned Emett and the origin of the truly interplanetary age. How can you explain to an unsophisticated youngster what brought on *that* beginning?"

Nothing Succeeds Like Failure

"Oh, no!" Junius Harleman turned from the door-scanner. "It's him!"

"Who?" His wife looked into the screen. It showed a small, thin, unkempt man in a lurid aloha shirt, tentatively prodding the chime button on their porch.

"Quentin Emett," Harleman groaned. "You've heard me talk about him. That crank who's been besieging my office this past year. Now he's tracked me down to my home."

"We don't have to let him in, do we?"

"I'm afraid so. I can't simply brush him off. He's Senator Lamphier's cousin."

"Pity." Martha gestured at the television set which dominated the outmoded Neo-Sino décor of their living room. "And just when the Kreemi-Rich Hour is due on."

Harleman brightened a trifle. There might be worse fates than listening for a while to Q. Emett, Scientechnist. Like most middle-aged husbands, he had resigned himself to many things, privately admitting that his wife doubtless did likewise. "Well, I'm sorry," he said, "but an administrator's lot is not a happy one. Will you make some coffee? I'll get rid of him as fast as I can."

His paunch preceded him down the hall. When

he opened the door, a street light gleamed off his scalp, between strands of gray hair. The summer evening of Silver Spring, Maryland, rolled pitilessly over him. You could boil in that air, he thought, if you didn't drown first. The neighborhood was quiet, the only traffic at the moment one of the armored patrol cars which kept it in that state.

"Why, hello," said the chief of the National Aeronautics and Space Administration. "What brings you here?"

"I, uh, I think you know," answered his visitor.

"Well, this is hardly the hour for business discussions, Mr. Emett."

"On the contrary, uh, it, it is. You, uh, you're supposed to testify in Congress tomorrow, aren't you? And you expect a, a, a hard time, don't you?"

Harleman winced. Emett pressed his advantage with the fierceness of timidity that has at last nerved itself up: "You only hope your budget won't be cut further. Your whole agency might be dismembered. True? Well, I believe I, uh, I can help you. Mr. Harleman, I know you c-c-consider me a crackpot. All right. I won't try again to, uh, prove my ideas are sound *per se*. But it's occurred to me, uh, whatever your opinion of them as engineering, uh, well, they may have very practical uses in p-p-politics. If you'll hear my suggestion?"

Something went *click* inside Harleman. A tingle followed it, up and down his spine. "You know," he said, "you might barely have something there. I can't give you any promises, but—come in, come in."

Air conditioning enfolded them like a blessing as he closed the door. After introducing Emett to his wife, Harleman declared solemnly, "We have a confidential matter to discuss. Would you bring us coffee in my study, please?"

Thirty years before, a writer in the *New Republic* had called Congressman Ashley Stanhope (R.-S.C.) "Uncle Scrooge." The swear word stuck. He was in truth fanatically tight-fisted with what he described as the taxpayer's hard-earned dollar, except, of course, for always vital undertakings in his district. Before long, he started gleefully using the nickname himself. After seniority gave him the chairmanship of the House Committee on Space and Science, it became generally known as Murderers' Row. Every good liberal wondered, often aloud, when he would have the decency to die.

Though the room over which Stanhope presided was duly cooled, Junius Harleman sweated. He was almost glad of the absence of spectators—not because this hearing was secret, merely because news media and public alike were monumentally uninterested. The men who sat around the long table looked equally bored; all except Stanhope. Uncle Scrooge saw a chance to kill a federal agency. His ears virtually quivered.

After the oath had been gabbled, the old man spoke. Magnolia blossoms dripped from his lips. "Welcome, suh. Ah'm sure you're tired of appearin' befoah this group, and others, each yeah. Ah sympathize. We'll try and make this a short, easy session, ri-ight?"

"Thank you, sir." Since two others were already smoking, Harleman dared start a cigarette. Drawing the pungency into his lungs, he remembered he was overdue for an anticancer shot. "I quite understand that NASA must explain its plans and justify its requests for appropriations like any other bureau. I am prepared to do so."

"Well, now, that's mighty good of you, Mr. Harleman." Stanhope bridged the fingers of his liver-spotted hands. The wattles wagged beneath his chin. "Ah'm mighty pleased to see such cooperation. Believe me, it's a seldom thing. Too many of these bureaucrats seem to believe they have a divine right to their jobs and their projects."

"I have been a civil servant throughout my working life, sir," Harleman answered, and added automatically, "The entire thrust of my action orientation has been toward a meaningful decision-making dialogue."

Stanhope cocked one bushy eyebrow. *You're an incompetent hack,* he refrained from saying, *as witness the fact that you allowed yourself to be maneuvered into the directorship of NASA, a wretched blind alley where no one wants to be and which I intend to brick off.*

"Dialogue," he did say. "Ye-es, Ah think we might just do a little talkin' today. A little down-to-earth conversation. Down to Earth," he repeated with an audible capital. "Ah do believe it's past time we spoke about fundamentals. Ah mean, suh, the reason why NASA should be continued at all."

"Mr. Chairman," said the gentleman from Nebraska. "Point of order. Did not the same act which commanded this agency to dispose of its oversized Houston facilities and headquarter itself in Washington ... did not that act specifically extend its life for a minimum of twenty years?"

"Why, yes, Mr. Bryan, it did," Stanhope purred. "But legislation can be amended or repealed, can't it, now? And Ah do feel this committee should consider whether it oughtn't to put moah emphasis on the 'science' part of its function and distract itself less with the 'space' part."

I knew this was coming, Harleman thought, and braced himself.

"Let us be frank, suh," Stanhope said in his direction. "It's no service to you, either, to pree-tend that the space program's not in deep trouble. And not only our space program; the Russians, the West Europeans, the Asian League, ever'body's is falterin'. Befoah we go into such matters as the budget you propose to propose, why don't we take an hour or two and ask ourselves what produced this situation?"

And get your oratory into the Record and mail copies to your constituents . . . franked, Harleman dared not say. Aloud: "I am at your service, Congressman. I am as much in favor as you are of generating escalation of focus on multilinked problem-complexes."

Stanhope smiled tigerishly. "Thank you, suh. Now let's pree-tend foah about five minutes that Ah'm one of yoah agency's outright foes. You know it's very possible that Mr. Ruysdale will be a candi-date in the next presidential election, and you know he openly advocates abolishin' NASA. Suppose Ah take the position of one of the many people who agree with him. A hypothetical position only, you realize, Mr. Harleman. Only foah the purpose of hearin' youah counterarguments, which Ah'm sure are good."

As a matter of fact, Harleman thought, *they're lousy, and you know it and I know it and I don't really want to save NASA, just my own career, and you know that and I know that.*

For a moment he locked eyes with the old man. It was almost like telepathy. *If we go through the*

*motions, in the next three or four years we can help
each other achieve our ends. You can kill the further
development of astronautics; I can get the directorship of a viable agency. But the motions include a
ritual combat.*

"I'm familiar with the position you describe,
Congressman," he said. "Naturally, I consider it
untenable. But if you would like me to refute it for
your minutes, please do set it forth."

"Thank you, suh." Stanhope glanced at a bescribbled sheet of paper on the table before him.
"The points are really quite simple, as you know.

"Let's admit the *o*-riginal impetus of the various
national space programs was military and political rivalry. Well, that's fadin' out, foah a while at
least, along with the twentieth century itself. We'll
soon be enterin' a whole new millennium with its
special problems. Those problems are so serious
they're partly responsible for the decline of international tensions. Everybody's got too much to do
at home—what with overpopulation, poverty, un-
rest, exhaustion of resou'ces, pollution of environment, and growin' sho'tage of chemical fuels. Ah
might remark that the giant rockets have contributed a good share to those sho'tages and that
pollution. And what have they given us in exchange?"

Harleman drew breath. Stanhope gestured for
silence. "Oh, yes," he continued, "weather satellites,
communication relays, knowledge in biology and
astronomy and stellar physics and planetary structures. . . . Ah'm not a yut, suh, in spite of the image
certain people project of me. Ah'm aware of the
benefits. But Ah'm also aware that we're long past
the point of diminishin' returns.

"No place but Earth is habitable without the

most ee-laborate life support systems. No natural resou'ces out yonder are worth the cost of transportation heah. Each expedition we send out brings back less new knowledge; and the knowledge it does bring has less impo'tance; but the price tag hasn't been lessened any, no, suh. I have testimony from moah than one authority; we're about at the end of the line as far as improvin' the rocket goes. They talk and talk about 'break-throughs,' but the last one was the reusable booster, and that was a generation ago.

"We don't want to discontinue the useful programs, like relays and monitors. But those have long since become so standard that they've gone under the jurisdiction of othah agencies, like the FCC or the Weather Bureau. What's left foah NASA? A rare interplanetary exploration. The Lunar base, the orbital stations—but if we can get othah countries to close down theirs, and it looks like we can, then we'll be closin' down ours, at a mi-ighty big annual savin'.

"The fact is, except foah work in the immediate neighborhood of Earth, space is costin' us too much and givin' us too little. We can't affo'd that any longer, what with so many domestic problems cryin' out foah an answer, not least the problem the o'dinary citizen's got, keepin' enough money after taxes to suppo't his children.

"And let's be blunt, Mr. Harleman, maybe impolitely blunt, but we're talkin' as friends today, aren't we? Isn't it a fact that NASA's own personnel are aware of this? Aren't they quittin' in droves, not simply because of reduced appropriations, but because nothin' is left that appeals to any ambitious young man?

"Shouldn't we maybe try foah an international

agreement to suspend the whole futile scramble? Won't you confess that NASA has outlived its usefulness?"

Stanhope leaned back and waited, still smiling.

Harleman gathered in his wits. The ancient intimidated him. And so did the others, especially the liberals, like intensely staring Thomasson of Massachusetts. Their purpose in starving his agency was not to save money but to release it for welfare expenditures. That suited Harleman fine—if he could get a decent post disbursing part of that money. He wouldn't, if he made too much trouble now. On the other hand, they would feel there was something wrong about an administrator who did not put up a spirited fight for the bureau he already headed. Scylla and Charybdis . . . .

He bought a few seconds by stubbing out his cigarette, and several more by talking while he marshalled his thoughts:

"Mr. Chairman, distinguished members of this committee, I wish to express my appreciation of your foresight as well as your graciousness in offering me this opportunity to contribute to the illumination of those polymorphously reticulated interrelationships, sociological and humanistic as well as technological and economic, which determine the forwarding of a nonalienated and viable infrastructure. This is probably not the appropriate body before which to disseminate multigraphic and quantitative scientific and engineering presentations. Rather, it would appear evident to my perception of the situation that the aegis of this distinguished group is superimposed on the intricacy of era-characteristic fields of inquiry falling more under the rubric of basic philosophical justifications, while simultaneously concerning ourselves not to lose sight of the over-all necessity for action-oriented orchestration of innovative inputs."

Three or four representatives shifted in their chairs and glanced at their watches. Stanhope let his eyelids droop.

"In short," Harleman finished, gauging his moment, "we are about to start off on a whole new tack."

"Tacking in *space?*" Thomasson muttered.

"No one disputes that NASA has exhausted certain possibilities." For just an instant the buried dream flickered in Harleman, that he had known in the eerie rising of Sputnik One before dawn, and in man's first landing on the moon. He could not but add, quietly: "No basic reason for that, gentlemen. If we'd had more vision, if we'd worked only a little harder, we could have succeeded with the tools we had. We could have built larger and better Earth-orbital stations; supplied them from a colonized, really colonized moon; developed the nuclear-powered reaction drive to its true limits; built our giant ships in space and kept them there, so they needn't contaminate this planet and needn't fight their way up through its gravity well. We could have gone to the ends of the Solar System. By now, perhaps, we might already be thinking about the stars. Maybe then our young people wouldn't be playing at gangsterism and political radicalism. They'd have had better things to do."

Bitterness tinged his words, for he remembered how he had become estranged from his only son. But he saw he was losing them and sprang back in haste:

"Well, never mind. We confront an existing situation. We need a whole new approach. And I think we've found one."

Stanhope opened his eyes wide. "Indeed?" he murmured. "Might Ah ask what?"

"I'm delighted to explain. Have you heard of gyrogravitics?"

Stanhope shook his knaggy head. Carter of Virginia said, slowly, "Has to do with atomic theory, doesn't it.

"That's right," Harleman answered. "I don't claim to follow the mathematics myself, but I've had scientists give me a lay explanation. It grew out of the effort to reconcile relativity and quantum mechanics. Those two branches of physics, both indispensable, were at odds on certain fundamental questions. Is nature or is nature not deterministic—describable by differential equations? Well, you may have read how Einstein once declared he couldn't believe that God plays dice with the world, while Heisenberg thought cause-and-effect was nothing but the statistics of large numbers, and Bohr suggested in his complementarity principle that both views might be true. Later, building on the work of such as Dyson and Feinberg—" Harleman saw them drifting away again. *Damn! I spent too much time with Emett last night. That jargon of his soaked into my skin.*

"Well, the point is, gentlemen," he said, "in the newest theory, matter and energy are described by their properties from the equations, equations like those of a rotating force-field. Including gravitation."

Carter jerked to an upright sitting position. "Wait a minute!" he exclaimed. "You aren't leading up to antigravity, are you? I happen to know what the Air Force has been doing in that line for the past fifty years. It's no secret they've drawn absolute blanks. Antigravity belongs with witches on broomsticks. I could reach Mars easier by . . . by astral projection."

"Not antigravity, sir," Harleman told him. "Gyrogravitics."

"A change of labels doesn't——"

"Please sir. I've had some most interesting discussions with a Mr. Quentin Emett. Some of you may have heard of him: an independent investigator——"

"Means he hasn't got his Ph.D.," Thomasson said grimly.

"Well, yes, he does happen to lack a union card," Harleman replied, and saw a bit of approval in Stanhope. "The academic establishment doesn't like him. However, the academic establishment—" He shrugged and smiled at Stanhope. *Huge tax subsidies. Left-wing professors. Unruly students.* "Frankly, he probably wouldn't have gotten my ear if he weren't a close relative of Senator Lamphier. But I need hardly assure you, gentlemen, the senator is no nepotist." *He's the most majestic nepotist on Capitol Hill, as you know better than I. But you also know you're well advised to stay on the good side of him.* "He satisfied himself as to Mr. Emett's qualifications before sending him to me. In the course of talks occupying almost a year, I have likewise satisfied myself.

"Mr. Emett's ideas are unorthodox, true. He proposes to develop a generator which, by means of nuclear resonance rotations, will create fields that we can call gravitational, or antigravitational, or pseudogravitational, or whatever we like. I think 'gyrogravitic' is probably the best word, though if we can get this work authorized, the R and D effort should have a more suitable name such as, for example, Project Dyna-Thrust."

Carter sneered. "And you'll make your space-ships weightless and float them right off Earth, eh?"

"No, sir." Emett had carefully rehearsed Harleman. "Conservation of energy and momentum are not violated. In effect, a gyrogravitic drive should react against the entire mass of the ambient universe. You'll still need power to rise, or accelerate, or maneuver in any other way. But it'll be minimum power; you won't be throwing energy out in exhaust gases. The power plant can be minimal too; since you can hover free, or nearly free, you don't need a huge motor to raise you as fast as possible. Any energy source will do—fuel cells, batteries, nuclear reactors, I suppose even steam engines—though no doubt as a side benefit we'll get small, portable fusion plants. A ship like this would be almost one hundred percent efficient, silent, unpolluting, economical to build, capable of going anywhere. The capability would derive in part from interior gyrogravitic fields. These would provide weight though the ship be in free fall, cushion against pressure when it accelerates, ward off solar-storm particles, meteoroids, and similar hazards." Harleman ratcheted up his enthusiasm. "In short, gyrogravitics can give us the whole Solar System."

"So can sorcery," Carter grumbled, "if only we can discover how to make it work."

Harleman talked nominally to them all, actually to Stanhope: "My belief is, the United States can't write off its huge investment in NASA, and in any case, positively not overnight. Research must go on. One advantage of Mr. Emett's proposal is its modest cost. If we establish Project Dyna-Thrust, it should be feasible to discontinue various other activities and thus reduce the total budget—without feeling that we have broken faith with our predecessors or abandoned the Endless Frontier of Science."

More quasi-telepathy: *Give NASA this crank undertaking for two or three years. It'll provide the necessary excuse and cover for phasing out most of everything else. Let's not shock the voters and endanger both our careers by letting the end come too abruptly, too rudely.*

"Well, now, Mr. Carter," Stanhope said, "we might just go a little further into this. Mr. Harleman's testimony has barely begun, and already it sounds interestin'. Yes, mighty interestin', I must say. Ri-ight?"

Of course, Emett was not altogether alone in his hopes. Enough reputable physicists conceded some theoretical possibility of success—though no useful probability, understand, for at least the next five hundred years—that the idea could safely be described as "worth study." Enough personnel were willing to join in the effort that it could be organized. These tended to be far-out specialists who were skeptical of a space drive but who welcomed the chance to do basic research with expensive equipment; and graduate students desperate for thesis material; and engineers who didn't have what it took to hold down any top-flight job, but who would work with plodding competence wherever they were paid.

Harleman felt rather proud when he had finished rounding up that crew. It hadn't been easy. Therefore he was doubly hurt when Emett protested: "B-b-b-but I don't want that many!"

"I beg your pardon?" Harleman wondered if his

ears were failing him. These damned D.C. summers—
and so few occasions for running down to the
breezes of the Cape. . . .

"A, uh, a small team," Emett tried to explain.
"Selected, uh, by myself. We, well, what we need
is merely the, the, the use of different facilities—
computer time, for instance, and, uh, access to the
Astroelectronics Lab, and . . . well, these other people running around, they'll, they'll take up my
time finding work for them!"

"I see." Harleman stroked his cheek and looked
across his desk at the little man who jittered in a
visitor's chair. "I'm afraid you don't see, though. It
surprises me, when your original suggestion—that
this project would keep NASA going a while—that
was such a shrewd thought, I'm surprised you
don't realize that in government there is no such
thing as having too many people working under
you."

"There is! There is! Gyrogravitics is, uh, at the
s-s-stage nuclear physics was in . . . in 1930. . . . They
couldn't have used a, a gigatron and the whole
huge outfit which serves one—not then."

"Oh, yes, they could, Mr. Emett. Not directly,
perhaps; but as means for getting more funds for
the work they really wanted to do. Think. Government employees are also voters, and closer knit
than average. Prestige and influence are propor-
tional to numbers." Harleman sighed. "I guess I'd
better take charge till I can locate a suitable
subadministrator for you. But you understand this
means you'll have to accept a lower title and
salary."

"I d-don't care. Just let me do my job." Appar-
ently nature had designed Quentin Emett for precisely one thing. All else, like eating, was incidental.

It did not cross Harleman's mind till later that similar remarks had been made about such folk as Oberth and Von Braun. He was too preoccupied with phone calls, memos, interviews, conferences, and tables of organization. For a while, press and TV were after him, too. But Dyna-Thrust was not an especially good story: only a few men puttering around with abstruse calculations and unspectacular experiments. After the Christmas battles between the People's Union for Righteous Excellence and the Friends Upholding Closer Kinship had run their bloody course through the streets of various cities, the media never did get back to NASA. . . . Whenever he could steal a few hours, Harleman was angling for a new post in another agency, against the day when this one would be dismantled.

Thus he paid scant attention to Dyna-Thrust's progress reports. They were dull, difficult reading; and in truth, the whole thing was nothing but a sideshow. Other projects, like Stormwind, Aldebaran, and Paul Bunyan, survived yet and were larger, splashier, and costlier. Indeed, sufficiently many new ones were being proposed that the public relations office had trouble thinking up names for them. A giant establishment, like a giant redwood, dies slowly, and may keep on growing and branching in some degree to the very end.

Harleman knew that Emett's gang were discovering things. He hoped those things would justify enlarging their division next year. Other than that, he was too busy to care.

Until the day when the CIA man came.

That was in February. Snow lay dingy along Washington's streets. Cars moved through slush with soft, sloppy noises. The air was raw and wet, the trees leafless, the low gray sky might never have held any stars. Harleman shivered at the prospect of venturing out, and considered an excuse for eating dinner downtown. The Kreemi-Rich Hour would be on. He decided that what with Martha's latest medical bill the bank account couldn't well stand it, and returned from the window to his desk. Once more he was looking over data for preparing a budget request. As he would the following year, he thought, and the following year, and the following year. . . . Eight to go before he retired. . . . He welcomed the time of Alfred Wheatley's appointment.

"Come in, come in. Sit down. Cigarette? What can I do for you?"

He had expected some routine matter. The CIA had inquired of him before. It had never involved anything sinister, no espionage or subversion or drama, nothing but help in keeping track of details like the state of the art in other countries. He supposed the CIA had to produce reasons for its own appropriations.

Wheatley was different from its previous representatives. In physical appearance he could have been a lawyer or accountant or petty commissioner. But his eyes burned. He spoke in a high, taut voice.

"Mr. Harleman, what do you know about Soviet work on gyrogravitics?"

"What?" Harleman realized he was gaping. "Why . . . I daresay they're interested, like us," he hedged. "If I remember correctly, part of the theory is due to Russian physicists. But of course, my agency as such is no longer privy to classified information." He attempted a chuckle. "Not that the Russians would offer us a look at their secrets, would they?"

"Still, some of your people must have contacts,"

Wheatley said. "Like at that conference in Bucharest a few months ago, where applications of advanced physics to astronautical research were discussed. Several NASA men attended."

"Well . . . yes, no doubt. We try to keep abreast—Why don't you ask them directly?"

"That's being done. To get blunt, Mr. Harleman. I'm here more to give you a preliminary briefing than the other way around. Nothing classified . . . not yet . . . beyond Administratively Confidential. However, a leak would be most undesirable at this stage of the game." Wheatley spoke with emphasis.

"I understand," Harleman said, quite truthfully after his decades in government. His heart skipped a beat and started ticking faster. Could it be—could it be—?

Wheatley said: "We have intelligence that the Soviets are mounting a sizable effort in the field of gyrogravitic propulsion."

Glory exploded over Harleman. As through a shining mist and choirs of angels, he heard himself reply, "I'm not surprised, considering that the work I instigated has been reported in the open literature. Its progress has surpassed my expectations."

"We don't want the United States to fall behind."

"Absolutely not. The prerequisite expansion of infrastructure will demand——"

——bigger appropriations! More personnel! Larger offices! Advancement for everybody!

The object was not even a toy. It was too ugly, as well as small: some batteries, some haywired circuits, some less identifiable apparatus, cobbled in haphazard fashion onto a sheet of Masonite. It was grotesquely inefficient; waste power came out as a shrill whine and a weird bluish shimmer that made the whole thing look doubly unreal.

But it rose. At the end of its tether, it pulled on a spring with a force equal to 3.2 times its weight.

"W-w-we did it," Emett said to his crew. Tears coursed down his face.

"A lot of engineering left before you can raise a spacecraft," cautioned an assistant.

Emett brushed the words off as if they were flies. "Leave that to the engineers," he said scornfully. "We've done the real job."

Both Junius and Martha Harleman would have preferred spending a particular week, five years later, in their old home town. He could have gone fishing when he wasn't impressing the Lions Club and she could have traded Washington gossip for local with her former bridge companions. However, it was more or less incumbent on the head of NASA to attend the first International Gyrogravitics Conference. Besides, it meant several days off work that did not come out of annual leave; and neither of them had visited Paris before.

He found himself lonely and bored among the scientists. She thought it was inconsiderate that most clerks in the stores spoke French. Both were glad to return.

Still, they enjoyed a few high moments, especially the climactic banquet. Martha gloated over the dresses and jewels she saw. As for Harleman, well, it wasn't every day that one got to sit between two Nobel Prize winners, the man affable and the lady (he did not add to Martha afterward) good-looking. And then when the toasts came, and the head of the Russian project arose—using English, too!—

"—cannot be denied that the recent Soviet triumph, in the flight of *Vladimir Three* to the moon and back under piloting of Captain I. E. Novikov, it cannot be denied that this achievement of the great Soviet peoples drew inspiration, if not information, from the earlier flights of the American, ah, the American flights. We trust that the great Soviet peoples will return the inspiration through the fleet that this very evening they have launched on its historic mission—not to Mars, not to Venus, but to the moons of Jupiter!" After the excitement had died away a bit: "We trust also that the ease and economy of these flights, already at our present stage of cosmonautical gyrogravitics, will inspire the peoples of Western Europe, Asia, yes, Africa, Latin America, Australia, every continent, every fraternal people . . . we hope they too will be inspired to join in man's great conquest of the Solar System. I trust that my American colleague, Mr. Garleman, ah, H-H-Harleman, to whose far-seeing vision the world is so indebted, will join me in proposing a toast, not to any individual, however high the honors that are due Premier Bogdanovitch, Party Secretary Kuropatkin, and, ah, many others . . . no, I ask my American colleague to join me in proposing a toast to the genius of mankind!"

And Junius Harleman stood up before God and everybody, raised his champagne glass, and responded firmly: "To the genius of mankind! May it carry us to the stars!"

Meanwhile he looked across the table, straight into the eyes of his opposite number, and once again it was like telepathy. *You were in the same mess as me, weren't you? And you found the same way out, didn't you? Including the argument that if one side was working on such a project, yours dared not refrain, however screwball it looked.*

Don't worry. I'll keep quiet if you will.

Interlude 1

"Do you mean that the geegee was invented merely because a couple of bloated bureaucracies were bound and determined to keep going?" Lindgren says. "Why, that's not a dangerous disillusionment, it's a truism. Been one ever since Gray published his researches into the period."

"I am not speaking of children in the Asteroid Republic," Conchita replies. "By school age, they have already experienced so much rough-and-tumble give-and-take that the fact their ancestors were not omniscient saints comes as no surprise. I am worrying about children here, for whom this ship will be the only immediate reality."

"M-m ... if anything, I'm inclined to believe that makes it especially important that we level with them," Amspaugh says carefully. "For instance, if they don't know how bureaucracies work, they could easily fall into the same trap that Earth did."

"Besides," Dworczyk adds, "the Republic specifically disavowed that kind of government when it became independent. The kids'll find plenty to be proud of in their asterite forebears." McVeagh chuckles. "What's funny?"

"The thought of those unwashed, greedy, turbulent rock rats—what they'd think if somebody had

told them they were noble dreamers!'' McVeagh
laughs aloud.

"Hoy, wait,'' I protest. "You can go too far in the
opposite direction. None of the pioneers would
have survived if they'd lacked courage, intelligence,
good technical educations at a minimum, persis-
tence . . . and, yes, cooperativeness where it was
needed. They didn't uniformly leave home in search
of a material fortune. I've read old letters as well
as books. A lot of them wanted room to live and
grow, freedom, a better chance for the next generation.''

"The economic incentive was important, though,''
Lindgren argues. "In fact, without it, no coloniza-
tion would ever have taken place. Poor, gutted,
jam-packed Earth couldn't afford largescale enterprises that didn't have a high chance of a high
profit. The geegee made spaceflight cheap, but not
that cheap. It was the asteroids that counted.''

Yes, I recite in my mind, *that's correct: not the
inner planets, but the flying mountains of the Belt—
thousands of them, minerals right there for the taking,
gravity so weak that hauling costs dropped to something a small entrepreneur might be able to meet.
And Jupiter, there was the other factor that gave us
the freedom of space.*

*It wasn't foreseen. Predictions had to do with Luna,
Mars, Venus, not naked rocks and a poisonous giant.
But then, Columbus was looking for the Indies when
he found America. I wonder what serendipities are
waiting among the stars?*

Lindgren, who has strong lungs, continues. "Nevertheless, friends, in spite of the potential payoff, I
needn't tell you how hard and dangerous those
early days were. You might assign people to go out
into space, live like monks for years on end, risk

death in any of a hundred nasty forms, the way some countries in fact did. But the North American government didn't have that power. Aside from military personnel and, all right, I'll grant you a few dreamers . . . there was nothing to attract our ancestors except the hope of getting hog-rich.

"I don't think an honest historian can neglect greed as a factor."

"I might insert a footnote," McVeagh offers. "Probably the self-reliant individualism we asterites brag of didn't come about because anyone really wanted it. People simply had no choice. Scattered across airless cold worldlets, millions of kilometers apart, if they couldn't deal personally with whatever might befall—that was the end of them."

"Well, I suppose it can do no harm for our texts to trace the origin of our institutions, as long as a proper respect is shown for those institutions," Conchita yields. "After all, ruthless natural selection, over generations, did produce a more fit race."

"Come off it!" snorts Missy Blades. "You know better. Racism is proof of inferiority. The superior person doesn't need it. Besides, consider the average crewman on *Astra*."

"I should have spoken more precisely, no doubt," Conchita says. "The point I was trying to make—that I think our texts and teachers ought to make—is this: Selection produced a type of human being better adapted to space than the typical Earthling. Likewise for the two life styles. Therefore the revolution was both inevitable and desirable."

"Now that's been debated through several tons of scholarly prose," Amspaugh says. "The causes of the revolution, I mean. I would oppose trying to straitjacket our children's education with any single theory. Rather, I believe we can do best by describing earlier, similar events, like the American Revolution—putting our own into historical context, you see."

"But the similarities are so superficial, so misleading," Conchita retorts.

"Well yes," Amspaugh admits, "it was a unique war in several regards, including its origins. However, there are plenty of analogies to other colonial revolts——"

"I know," says Lindgren. "Earth's mercantile policies and so forth." He, like Amspaugh, fancies himself a student of interplanetary history. Mostly their debates are good. I go to the bar and mix myself a drink, listening as the former mine owner's big voice proceeds:

"However, what was the proximate cause? When did the asterites first start realizing they weren't pseudo-pods of a dozen terrestrial nations, but a single nation in their own right? There's the root of the revolution. And it can be pinned down, too."

" 'Ware metaphor!" cries someone at my elbow. I turn and see Missy. She's quietly joined me to mix a gin and bitters.

The viewport frames her white head in Orion as we return to the little cluster of seated people. She pulls a cigar from her tunic pocket, strikes it on her shoe sole, and adds her special contribution to the blue cloud in this room as she takes her chair again.

"Excuse me," she says. "I couldn't help that. Please go on." Which I hope relieves you of any fear that she's an Unforgettable Character. Oh, yes, she's old as Satan now; her toil and guts and conniving make up half the biography of the Sword; she manned a gun turret at Ceres during the war, and afterward was mate of the *Tyrfing* on some of the early Saturn runs when men took their lives between their teeth because they needed both hands free; her sons, grandsons, great-grandsons fill the Belt with their wild ventures; she can drink any ordinary man to the deck. But she's also one of the few genuine ladies I've known in my life.

"Well." Lindgren grins at her. "You know my pet hypothesis, Missy. The germ of the revolution was when the stations armed themselves. That meant more than police powers. It implied a degree of sovereignty. Over the years, the implication grew."

"Correct." Orloff nods his big bald head. "I remember how my governing commission squalled when our station managers first demanded the right. My superiors foresaw trouble. But if the stations belonging to one country put in space weapons, what else could the others do?"

"They should have stuck together and all been firm about refusing to allow it," Lindgren says. "From the standpoint of their own best interests, I mean."

"They tried to," Orloff replies. "I hate to think how many communications we sent to Moscow from our office; and those of the other nations must have done the same. But Earth was a long way off. The station bosses were close. Inverse square law of political pressure."

"I grant you, arming each new little settlement proved important," Amspaugh says. "But really, it expressed nothing more than the first inchoate stirrings of asterite nationalism. And the origins of that are much more subtle and complex. For instance . . . er——"

"You've got to have a key event somewhere," Lindgren insists. "I say this was the one."

A silence falls. No one seems to want to go directly back to the main topic of discussion. Or are we at the precise crux of it? Missy stares for a while into her drink, and then out to the stars. The Dippers are visible. Her faded eyes seek Polaris— but it's Earth's, not ours any more—and I wonder what memories she and it are sharing. She shakes herself a little and says:

"I don't know about the sociological ins and outs. All I know is, a lot of things happened, and there wasn't any pattern to them at the time. We just slogged through as best we were able, which wasn't really very good. But I can identify one of those wriggling roots for you, Sigurd. I was there when the question of arming the stations first came up. Or, rather, when the incident occurred that led to the question being raised."

Our whole attention goes to her. She doesn't dwell on the past as often as we would like. Thanks to antisenescence, we have a number of persons aboard who experienced those days of more than a hundred years ago. But mostly they were non-American space-folk, like Orloff, or Earthlings, like Echevaray (though he is young), who became citizens of the Republic later. None among us were as close to the core of things as Missy.

A slow, private smile crosses her lips. Again she looks beyond us. "As a matter of fact," she murmurs, "I got my husband out of it." Then quickly, as if to keep from recalling too much:

"Do you care to hear the story? It was when the Sword was first getting started. They'd established themselves on SSC forty-five—oh, never mind the catalogue number. Sword Enterprises, because Mike Blades's name suggested it. What kind of name could you get out of Jimmy Chung, even if he was the senior partner? It'd sound like a collision with a meteoroid. So naturally the rock also came to be called the Sword.

"They began on the borrowed shoestring that was usual then. Of course, in the Belt a shoestring had to be almighty long, and finances got stretched to the breaking point. The older men here will know how much had to be done by hand, in mortal danger, because machines were too expensive. But in spite of everything, they succeeded. The station was functional and they were ready to commence business when . . ."

The Rogue

It was no coincidence that the Jupiter craft were arriving steadily when the battleship came. Construction had been scheduled with this in mind, that the Sword should be approaching conjunction with the king planet, making direct shuttle service feasible, just as the chemical plant commenced action. We need not consider how much struggle and heartbreak had gone into meeting that schedule. As for the battleship, she appeared because the fact that a station in this exact orbit was about to start operations was news important enough to cross the Solar System and push through many strata of bureaucracy. The heads of the recently elected North American government became suddenly, fully aware of what had been going on.

Michael Blades was outside, overseeing the installation of a receptor, when his earplug buzzed. He thrust his chin against the tuning plate, switching from gang to interoffice band. "Mike?" said Avis Page's voice. "You're wanted up front."

"Now?" he objected. "Whatever for?"

"Courtesy visit from the NASS *Altair*. You've lost track of time, my boy."

"What the . . . the jumping blue blazes are you talking about? We've had our courtesy visit. Jimmy and I both went over to pay our respects, and we had Rear Admiral Hulse here to dinner. What more do they expect, for Harry's sake?"

"Don't you remember? Since there wasn't room to entertain his officers, you promised to take them on a personal guided tour later. I made the appointment the very next watch. Now's the hour."

"Oh, yes, it comes back to me. Yeah. Hulse brought a magnum of champagne with him, and after so long a time drinking recycled water, my capacity was shot to pieces. I got a warm glow of good fellowship on, and offered— Let Jimmy handle it. I'm busy."

"The party's too large, he says. You'll have to take half of them. Their gig will dock in thirty minutes."

"Well, depute somebody else."

"That'd be rude, Mike. Have you forgotten how sensitive they are about rank at home?" Avis hesitated. "If what I believe about the mood back there is true, we can use the good will of high-level Navy personnel. And any other influential people in sight."

Blades drew a deep breath. "You're too blinking sensible. Remind me to fire you after I've made my first ten million bucks."

"What'll you do for your next ten million, then?" snipped his secretary-file clerk-confidante-adviser-et cetera.

"Nothing. I'll just squander the first."

"Goody! Can I help?"

"Uh . . . I'll be right along." Blades switched off. His ears felt hot, as often of late when he tangled with Avis, and he unlimbered only a few choice oaths.

"Troubles?" asked Carlos Odónoju.

Blades stood a moment, looking around, before

he answered. He was on the wide end of the Sword,
which was shaped roughly like a truncated pyramid.
Beyond him and his half dozen men stretched a
vista of pitted rock jutting crags, gulf-black shadows,
under the glare of floodlamps. A few kilometers
away, the farthest horizon ended chopped off like
a cliff. Beyond lay the stars, crowding that night
which never ends. It grew very still while the gang
waited for his word. He could listen to his own
lungs and pulse, loud in the spacesuit; he could
even notice its interior smell, blend of plastic and
oxygen cycle chemicals, flesh and sweat. He was
used to the sensation of hanging upside down on
the surface, grip-soled boots holding him against
that fractional g by which the asteroid's rotation
overcame its feeble gravity. But it came to him
that this was an eerie bat-fashion way for an Oregon farm boy to stand.

Oregon was long behind him, though, not only
the food factory where he grew up but the coasts
where he had fished and the woods where he had
tramped. No loss. There'd always been too many
tourists. You couldn't escape from people on Earth.
Cold and vacuum and raw rock and everything,
the Belt was better. It annoyed him to be interrupted here.

Could Carlos take over as foreman? N-no, Blades
decided, not yet. A gas receptor was an intricate
piece of equipment. Carlos was a good man of his
hands. Every one of the hundred-odd in the station
necessarily was. But he hadn't done this kind of
work often enough.

"I have to quit," Blades said. "Secure the stuff
and report to Buck Meyers over at the dock, the lot
of you. His crew's putting in another recoil pier,

as I suppose you know. They'll find jobs for you. I'll see you here again on your next watch."

He waved—being half the nominal owner of this place didn't justify snobbery, when everyone must work together or die—and stepped off toward the nearest entry lock with that flowing spaceman's pace which always keeps one foot on the ground. Even so, he didn't unshackle his inward-reeling lifeline till he was inside the chamber.

On the way he topped a gaunt ridge and had a clear view of the balloons that were attached to the completed receptors. Those that were still full bulked enormous, like ghostly moons. The Jovian gases that strained their tough elastomer did not much blur the stars seen through them; but they swelled high enough to catch the light of the hidden sun and shimmer with it. The nearly discharged balloons hung thin, straining outward. Two full ones passed in slow orbit against the constellations. They were waiting to be hauled in and coupled fast, to release their loads into the station's hungry chemical plant. But there were not yet enough facilities to handle them at once—and the *Pallas Castle* would soon be arriving with another. Blades found that he needed a few extra curses.

Having cycled through the air lock, he removed his suit and stowed it, also the heavy gloves which kept him from frostbite as he touched its space-cold exterior. Tastefully clad in a Navy surplus zipskin, he started down the corridors.

Now that the first stage of burrowing within the asteroid had been completed, most passages went through its body, rather than being plastic tubes snaking across the surface. Nothing had been done thus far about facing them. They were merely shafts, two meters square, lined with doorways, ventila-

tor grilles, and fluoropanels. They had no thermo-
coils. Once the nickel-iron mass had been sufficiently warmed up, the waste heat of man and his
industry kept it that way. The dark, chipped-out
tunnels throbbed with machine noises. Here and
there a girlie picture or a sentimental landscape
from Earth was posted. Men moved busily along
them, bearing tools, instruments, supplies. They
were from numerous countries, those men, though
mostly North Americans, but they had acquired a
likeness, a rangy leathery look and a free-swinging
stride, that went beyond their colorful coveralls.

"Hi, Mike. . . . How's she spinning? . . . Hey, Mike,
you heard the latest story about the Martian and
the bishop? . . . Can you spare me a minute? We
got troubles in the separator manifolds. . . . What's
the hurry, Mike, your batteries overcharged?"
Blades waved the hails aside. There was need for
haste. You could move fast indoors, under the low
weight which became lower as you approached
the axis of rotation, with no fear of tumbling off.
But it was several kilometers from the gas receptor end to the people end of the asteroid.

He rattled down a ladder and entered his cramped
office out of breath. Avis Page looked up from her
desk and wrinkled her freckled snub nose at him.
"You ought to take a shower, but there isn't time,"
she said. "Here, use my antistinker." She threw
him a spray cartridge with a deft motion. "I got
your suit and beardex out of your cabin."

"Have I no privacy?" he grumbled, but grinned
in her direction. She wasn't much to look at—not
ugly, just small, brunette, and unspectacular—but
she was a supernova of an assistant. Make somebody a good wife some day. He wondered why she
hadn't taken advantage of the situation here to

snaffle a husband. A dozen women, all but two of them married, and a hundred men, was a ratio even more lopsided than the norm in the Belt. Of course, with so much work to do, and with everybody conscious of the need to maintain cordial relations, sex didn't get much chance to rear its lovely head. Still . . .

She smiled back with the gentleness that he found disturbing when he noticed it. "Shoo," she said. "Your guests will be here any minute. You're to meet them in Jimmy's office."

Blades ducked into the tiny washroom. He wasn't any 3V star himself, he decided as he smeared cream over his face: big, homely, red-haired. *But not something you'd be scared to meet in a dark alley, either,* he added smugly. In fact, there had been an alley in Aresopolis. . . . Things were expected to be going so smoothly by the time they approached conjunction with Mars that he could run over to that sinful ginful city for a vacation. Long overdue . . . whooee! He wiped off his whiskers, shucked the zipskin, and climbed into the white pants and high-collared blue tunic that must serve as formal garb.

Emerging, he stopped again at Avis' desk. "Any message from the *Pallas?*" he asked.

"No," the girl said. "But she ought to be here in another two watches, right on sked. You worry too much, Mike."

"Somebody has to, and I haven't got Jimmy's Buddhist ride-with-the-punches attitude."

"You should cultivate it." The brown eyes lingered on him. "Worry's contagious. You make me fret about you."

"Nothing's going to give me an ulcer but the shortage of booze on this rock. Uh, if Bill Mbolo should call about those catalysts while I'm gone, tell him . . ." He ran off a string of instructions and headed for the door.

Chung's hangout was halfway around the asteroid, so that one chief or the other could be a little nearer the scene of any emergency. Not that they spent much time at their desks. Shorthanded and undermechanized, they were forever having to help out in the actual construction. Once in a while Blades found himself harking wistfully back to his days as an engineer with Solar Metals: good pay, interesting if hazardous work on flying mountains where men had never trod before, and no further responsibilities. But most asterites had the dream of becoming their own bosses.

When he arrived, the *Altair* officers were already there, a score of correct young men in white dress uniforms. Short, squat, and placid looking, Jimmy Chung stood making polite conversation. "Ah, there," he said, "Lieutenant Ziska and gentlemen, my partner, Michael Blades. Mike, may I present . . ."

Blades's attention stopped at Lieutenant Ziska. He heard vaguely that she was the head quartermaster officer. But mainly she was tall and blonde and blue-eyed, with a bewitching dimple when she smiled, and filled her gown the way a Cellini Venus doubtless filled its casting mold.

"Very pleased to meet you, Mr. Blades," she said as if she meant it. Maybe she did! He gulped for air.

"And Commander Liebknecht," Chung said across several lightyears. "Commander Liebknecht. *Commander Liebknecht.*"

"Oh. Sure.'Scuse." Blades dropped Lieutenant Ziska's hand in reluctant haste. "Hardjado, C'mander Liebfraumilch."

Somehow the introductions were gotten through. "I'm sorry we have to be so inhospitable," Chung said, "but you'll see how crowded we are. About all we can do is show you around, if you're interested."

"Of course you're interested," said Blades to Lieutenant Ziska. "I'll show you some gimmicks I thought up myself."

Chung scowled at him. "We'd best divide the party and proceed along alternate routes," he said. "We'll meet again in the mess for coffee. Lieutenant Ziska, would you like to——"

"Come with me? Certainly," Blades said.

Chung's glance became downright murderous. "I thought——" he began.

"Sure." Blades nodded vigorously. "You being the senior partner, you'll take the highest ranking of these gentlemen, and I'll be in Scotland before you. C'mon, let's get started. May I?" He offered the quartermistress his arm. She smiled and took it. He supposed that eight or ten of her fellows trailed them.

The first disturbing note was sounded on the verandah.

They had glanced at the cavelike dormitories where most of the personnel lived; at the recreation dome top-side which made the life tolerable; at kitchen, sick bay, and the other service facilities; at the hydroponic tanks and yeast vats which supplied much of the station's food; at the tiny cabins scooped out for the top engineers and the married couples. Before leaving this end of the asteroid, Blades took his group to the verandah. It was a clear dome jutting from the surface, softly lighted, furnished as a primitive officers' lounge, open to a view of half the sky.

"Oh-h," murmured Ellen Ziska. Unconsciously she moved closer to Blades.

Young Lieutenant Commander Gilbertson gave her a somewhat jaundiced look. "You've seen deep space often enough before," he said.

"Through a port or a helmet." Her eyes glimmered enormous in the dusk. "Never like this."

The stars crowded close in their wintry myriads. The galactic belt glistened, diamond against infinite darkness. Vision topped endlessly outward, toward the far mysterious shimmer of the Andromeda Nebula; silence was not a mere absence of noise, but a majestic presence, the seething of suns.

"What about the observation terrace at Leyburg?" Gilbertson challenged.

"That was different," Ellen Ziska said. "Everything was safe and civilized. This is like being on the edge of creation."

Blades could see why Goddard House had so long resisted the inclusion of female officers on ships of the line, despite political pressure at home and the Russian example abroad. He was glad they'd finally given in. Now if only he could build himself up as a dashing, romantic type. . . . But how long would the *Altair* stay? Her stopover seemed quite extended already, for a casual visit in the course of a routine patrol cruise. He'd have to work fast.

"Yes, we are pretty isolated," he said. "The Jupiter ships just unload their balloons, pick up the empties, and head right back for another cargo."

"I don't understand how you can found an industry here, when your raw materials only arrive at conjunction," Ellen said.

"Things will be different once we're in full operation," Blades assured her. "Then we'll be doing enough business to pay for a steady input, trans-shipped from whatever depot is nearest Jupiter at any given time."

"You've actually built this simply to process . . . gas?" Gilbertson interposed. Blades didn't know whether he was being sarcastic or asking a genuine question. It was astonishing how ignorant Earthsiders, even space-traveling Earthsiders, often were about such matters.

"Jovian gas is rich stuff," he explained. "Chiefly hydrogen and helium, of course; but the scoopships separate out most of that during a pickup. The rest is ammonia, water, methane, a dozen important organics, including some of the damn—doggonedest metallic complexes you ever heard of. We need them as the basis of a chemosynthetic industry, which we need for survival, which we need if we're to get the minerals that were the reason for colonizing the Belt in the first place." He waved his hand at the sky. "When we really get going, we'll attract settlement. This asteroid has companions, waiting for people to come and mine them. Home-ships and orbital stations will be built. In ten years there'll be quite a little city clustered around the Sword."

"It's happened before," nodded tight-faced Commander Warburton of Gunnery Control.

"It's going to happen a lot oftener," Blades said enthusiastically. "The Belt's going to grow!" He aimed his words at Ellen. "This is the real frontier. The planets will never amount to much. It's actually harder to maintain human-type conditions on so big a mass, with a useless atmosphere around you, than on a lump in space like this. And the gravity wells are so deep. Even given nuclear power, the energy cost of really exploiting a planet is prohibitive. Besides which, the choice minerals are buried under kilometers of rock. On a metallic asteroid, you can find almost everything you want directly under your feet. No limit to what you can do."

"But your own energy expenditure—" Gilbertson objected.

"That's no problem." As if on cue, the worldlet's spin brought the sun into sight. Tiny but intolerably brilliant, it flooded the dome with harsh radiance. Blades lowered the blinds on that side. He pointed in the opposite direction, toward several sparks of equal brightness that had manifested themselves.

"Hundred-meter parabolic mirrors," he said. "Easy to make; you spray a thin metallic coat on a plastic backing. They're in orbit around us, each with a small geegee unit to control drift and keep it aimed directly at the sun. The focused radiation charges heavy-duty accumulators, which we then collect and use for our power source in all our mobile work."

"Do you mean you haven't any nuclear generator?" asked Warburton.

He seemed curiously intent about it. Blades wondered why, but nodded. "That's correct. We don't want one. Too dangerous for us. Nor is it necessary. Even at this distance from the sun, and allowing for assorted inefficiencies, a mirror supplies better than five hundred kilowatts, twenty-four hours a day, year after year, absolutely free."

"Hm-m-m. Yes." Warburton's lean head turned slowly about, to rake Blades with a look of calculation. "I understand that's the normal power system in stations of this type. But we didn't know if it was used in your case, too."

Why should you care? Blades thought.

He shoved aside his faint unease and urged Ellen toward the dome railing. "Maybe we can spot your ship, Lieutenant, uh, Miss Ziska. Here's a telescope. Let me see, her orbit ought to run about so. . . ."

He hunted until the *Altair* swam into the viewfield. At this distance the spheroid looked like a tiny crescent moon, dully painted; but he could make out the sinister shapes of a rifle turret and a couple of missile launchers. "Have a look," he invited. Her hair tickled his nose, brushing past him. It had a delightful sunny odor.

"How small she seems," the girl said, with the same note of wonder as before. "And how huge when you're aboard."

Big, all right, Blades knew, and loaded to the hatches with nuclear hellfire. But not massive. A civilian spaceship carried meteor plating, but since that was about as useful as wet cardboard against modern weapons, warcraft sacrificed it for the sake of mobility. The self-sealing hull was thin magnesium, the outer shell periodically renewed as cosmic sand eroded it.

"I'm not surprised we orbited, instead of docking," Ellen remarked. "We'd have butted against your radar and bellied into your control tower."

"Well, actually, no," said Blades. "Even half finished, our dock's big enough to accommodate you, as you'll see today. Don't forget, we anticipate a lot of traffic in the future. I'm puzzled why you didn't accept our invitation to use it."

"Doctrine!" Warburton clipped.

The sun came past the blind and touched the

officers' faces with incandescence. Did some look
startled, one or two open their mouths as if to
protest and then snap them shut again at a warning look? Blades's spine tingled. *I never heard of
any such doctrine*, he thought, *least of all when a
North American ship drops in on a North American
station.*

"Is . . . er . . . is there some international crisis
brewing?" he inquired.

"Why, no." Ellen straightened from the telescope.
"I'd say relations have seldom been as good as
they are now. What makes you ask?"

"Well, the reason your captain didn't——"

"Never mind," Warburton said. "We'd better continue the tour, if you please."

Blades filed his misgivings for later reference.
He might have fretted immediately, but Ellen
Ziska's presence forbade that. A sort of Pauli exclu-
sion principle. One can't have two spins simul-
taneously, can one? He gave her his arm again.
"Let's go on to Central Control," he proposed.
"That's right behind the people section."

"You know, I can't get over it," she told him
softly. "This miracle you've wrought. I've never
been more proud of being human."

"Is this your first long space trip?"

"Yes. I was stationed at Port Colorado before the
new Administration reshuffled armed service assign-
ments."

"They did? How come?"

"I don't know. Well, that is, during the election
campaign the Social Justice party did talk a lot
about oldline officers who were too hidebound to
carry out modern policies effectively. But it sounded
rather silly to me."

Warburton compressed his lips. "I do not believe it is proper for service officers to discuss political issues publicly," he said like a machine gun.

Ellen flushed. "S-sorry, Commander."

Blades felt a helpless anger on her account. He wasn't sure why. What was she to him? He'd probably never see her again. A hell of an attractive target, to be sure; and after so much celibacy he was highly vulnerable; but did she really matter?

He turned his back on Warburton and his eyes on her—a 5,000 percent improvement—and diverted her from her embarrassment by asking, "Are you from Colorado, then, Miss Ziska?"

"Oh, no. Toronto."

"How'd you happen to join the Navy, if I may make so bold?"

"Gosh, that's hard to say. But I guess mostly I felt so crowded at home. So pigeonholed. The world seemed to be nothing but neat little pigeonholes."

"Uh-huh. Same here. I was also a square pigeon in a round hole." She laughed. "Luckily," he added, "space is too big for compartments."

Her agreement lacked vigor. The Navy must have been a disappointment to her. But she couldn't very well say so in front of her shipmates.

Hm-m-m . . . if she could be gotten away from them. . . . "How long will you be here?" he inquired. His pulse thuttered.

"We haven't been told," she said.

"Some work must be done on the missile launchers," Warburton said. "That's best carried out here, where extra facilities are available if we need them. Not that I expect we will." He paused. "I hope we won't interfere with your own operations."

"Far from it." Blades beamed at Ellen. "Or, more

accurately, this kind of interference I don't mind in the least."

She blushed and her eyelids fluttered. Not that she was a fluffhead, he realized. But to avoid incidents, Navy regulations enforced an inhuman correctness between personnel of opposite sexes. After weeks in the black, meeting a man who could pay a compliment without risking court-martial must be like a shot of adrenalin. Better and better!

"Are you sure?" Warburton persisted. "For instance, won't we be in the way when the next ship comes from Jupiter?"

"She'll approach the opposite end of the asteroid," Blades said. "Won't stay long, either."

"How long?"

"One watch, so the crew can relax a bit among those of us who're off duty. It'd be a trifle longer if we didn't happen to have an empty bag at the moment. But never very long. Even running under thrust the whole distance, Jupe's a good ways off. They've no time to waste."

"What is the next ship due?"

"The *Pallas Castle* is expected in the second watch from now."

"Second watch. I see." Warburton stalked on with a brooding expression on his puritan face.

Blades might have speculated about that, but someone asked him why the station depended on spin for weight. Why not put in an internal field generator, like a ship? Blades explained patiently that an Emett large enough to produce uniform pull through a volume as big as the Sword was rather expensive. "Eventually, when we're a few megabucks ahead of the game——"

"Do you really expect to become rich?" Ellen asked. Her tone was awed. No Earthsider had that chance any more, except for the great corporations. "*Individually* rich?"

"We can't fail to. I tell you, this is a frontier like nothing since the conquistadores. We could very easily have been wiped out in the first couple of years—financially or physically—by any of a thousand accidents. But now we're too far along for that. We've got it made, Jimmy and I."

"What will you do with your wealth?"

"Live like an old-time sultan," Blades grinned. Then, because it was true as well as because he wanted to shine in her eyes: "Mostly, though, we'll go on to new things. There's so much that needs to be done. Not simply more asteroid mines. We need farms, timber, parks, passenger and cargo liners, every sort of machine. I'd like to try getting at some of that water frozen in the Saturnian System. Altogether, I see no end to the jobs. It's no good our depending on Earth for anything. Too expensive, too chancy. The Belt has to be made completely self-sufficient."

"With a nice rakeoff for Sword Enterprises," Gilbertson scoffed.

"Why, sure. Aren't we entitled to some return?"

"Yes. But not so out of proportion as the Belt companies seem to expect. They're only using natural resources that rightly belong to the people and the accumulated skills and wealth of an entire society."

"Huh! The people didn't do anything with the Sword. Jimmy and I and our boys did. No society was around here grubbing nickel-iron and riding out gravel storms; *we* were.

"Let's leave politics alone," Warburton snapped. But it was mostly Ellen's look of distress that shut Blades up.

To everybody's relief, they reached Central Control about then. It was a complex of domes and rooms, crammed with more equipment than Blades could put a name to. Computers were in Chung's line, not his. He wasn't able to answer all of Warburton's disconcertingly sharp questions.

But in a general way he could. Whirling through vacuum with a load of frail humans and intricate artifacts, the Sword must be at once machine, ecology, and unified organism. Everything had to mesh. A failure in the thermodynamic balance, a miscalculation in supply inventory, a few mirrors perturbed out of proper orbit, might spell Ragnarok. The chemical plant's purifications and syntheses were already a network too large for the human mind to grasp as a whole, and it was still growing. Even where men could have taken charge, automation was cheaper, more reliable, less risky of lives. The computer system housed in Central Control was not only the brain, but the nerves and heart of the Sword.

"Entirely cryotronic, eh?" Warburton commented. "That seems to be the usual practice at the stations. Why?"

"The least expensive type for us," Blades answered. "There's no problem in maintaining liquid helium here."

Warburton's gaze was peculiarly intense. "Cryotronic systems are vulnerable to magnetic and radiation disturbances."

"Uh-huh. That's one reason we don't have a nuclear power plant. This far from the sun, we don't get enough emission to worry about. The asteroid's mass screens out what little may arrive. I know the TIMM system is used on ships; but if nothing else, the initial cost is more than we want to pay."

"What's TIMM?" inquired the *Altair*'s chaplain.

"Thermally Integrated Micro-Miniaturized," Ellen said crisply. "Essentially, ultraminiaturized ceramic-to-metal-seal vacuum tubes running off thermionic generators. They're immune to gamma ray and magnetic pulses, easily shielded against particle radiation, and economical of power." She grinned. "Don't tell me there s nothing about them in Leviticus, Padre!"

"Very fine for a ship's autopilot," Blades agreed. "But as I said, we needn't worry about rad or mag units here, we don't mind sprawling a bit, and as for thermal efficiency, we *want* to waste some heat. It goes to maintain internal temperature.

"In other words, efficiency depends on what you need to effish," Ellen bantered. She grew grave once more and studied him for a while before she mused, "The same person who swung a pick, a couple of years ago, now deals with something as marvelous as this . . . ." He forgot about worrying.

But he remembered later, when the gig had left and Chung called him to his office. Avis came too, by request. As she entered, she asked why.

"You were visiting your folks Earthside last year," Chung said. "Nobody else in the station has been back as recently as that."

"What can I tell you?"

"I'm not sure. Background, perhaps. The feel of the place. We don't really know, out in the Belt, what's going on there. The beamcast news is hardly a trickle. Besides, you have more common sense in your left little toe than that big mick yonder has in his entire copper-plated head."

They seated themselves in the cobwebby low-gee chairs around Chung's desk. Blades took out his pipe and filled the bowl with his tobacco ration for the day, *Wouldn't it be great,* he thought dreamily, *if this old briar turned out to be an Aladdin's lamp, and the smoke condensed into a blonde she-Canadian——*

"Wake up, will you?" Chung barked.

"Huh?" Blades started. "Oh. Sure. What's the matter? You look like a fish on Friday."

"Maybe with reason. Did you notice anything unusual with that party you were escorting?"

"Yes, indeed."

"What?"

"About one hundred seventy-five centimeters tall, yellow hair, blue eyes, and some of the smoothest fourth-order curves I ever——"

"Mike, stop that!" Avis sounded appalled. "This is serious."

"I agree. She'll be leaving in a few more watches."

The girl bit her lip. "You're too old for that mooncalf rot and you know it."

"Agreed again. I feel more like a bull." Blades made pawing motions on the desktop.

"There's a lady present," Chung said.

Blades saw that Avis had gone quite pale. "I'm sorry," he blurted. "I never thought . . . I mean, you've always seemed like——"

"One of the boys," she finished for him in a brittle tone. "Sure. Forget it. What's the problem, Jimmy?"

Chung folded his hands and stared at them. "I can't quite define that," he answered, word by careful word. "Perhaps I've simply gone spacedizzy. But when we talked with Admiral Hulse, didn't you get the impression of, well, wariness? Didn't he seem to be watching and probing, every minute we were together?"

"I wouldn't call him a cheerful sort," Blades nodded. "Stiff as molasses on Pluto. But I suppose . . . supposed he's just naturally that way."

Chung shook his head. "It wasn't a normal standoffishness. You've heard me reminisce about the time I was on Vesta with the North American technical representative, when the Convention was negotiated."

"Yes, I've heard that story a few times," said Avis dryly.

"Remember, that was right after the Europa incident. We'd come close to a space war—undeclared, but it would have been nasty. We were still close. Every delegate went to that conference cocked and primed.

"Hulse had the same manner."

A silence fell. Blades said at length, "Well, come to think of it, he did ask some rather odd questions. He seemed to twist the conversation now and then, so he could find out things like our exact layout, emergency doctrine, and so forth. It didn't strike me as significant, though."

"Nor me," Chung admitted. "Taken in isolation, it meant nothing. But these visitors today— Sure, most of them obviously didn't suspect anything untoward. But that Liebknecht, now. Why was he so interested in Central Control? Nothing new or secret there. Yet he kept asking for details like the shielding factor of the walls."

"So did Commander Warburton," Blades remembered. "Also, he wanted to know exactly when the *Pallas* is due, how long she'll stay . . . hm-m-m, yes, whether we have any radio linkage with the outside, like to Ceres or even the nearest Commission base——"

"Did you tell him that we don't?" Avis asked sharply.

"Yes. Shouldn't I have?"

"It scarcely makes any difference," Chung said in a resigned voice. "As thoroughly as they went over the ground, they'd have seen what we do and do not have installed so far."

He leaned forward. "Why are they hanging around?" he asked. "I was handed some story about overhauling the missile system."

"Me, too," Blades said.

"But you don't consider a job complete till it's been tested. And you don't fire a test shot, even a dummy, this close to a station. Besides, what could have gone wrong? I can't see a ship departing Earth orbit for a long cruise without everything being in order. And they didn't mention any meteoroids, any kind of trouble, en route. Furthermore, why do the work here? The Navy yard's at Ceres. We can't spare them any decent amount of materials or tools or help."

Blades frowned. His own half-formulated doubts shouldered to the fore, which was doubly unpleasant after he'd been considering Ellen Ziska. "They tell me the international situation at home is okay," he offered.

Avis nodded. "What newsfaxes we get in the mail indicate as much," she said. "So why this hanky-panky?" After a moment, in a changed voice: "Jimmy, you begin to scare me a little."

"I scare myself," Chung said.

"Every morning when you debeard," Blades said; but his heart wasn't in it. He shook himself and protested: "Damnation, they're our own countrymen. We're engaged in a lawful business. Why should they do anything to us?"

"Maybe Avis can throw some light on that," Chung suggested.

The girl twisted her fingers together. "Not me," she said. "I'm no politician."

"But you were home not so long ago. You talked with people, read the news, watched the ThreeV. Can't you at least give an impression?"

"N-no—well, of course the preliminary guns of the election campaign were already being fired. The Social Justice party was talking a lot about . . . oh, it seemed so ridiculous that I didn't pay much attention."

"They talked about how the government had been pouring billions and billions of dollars into space, while overpopulation produced crying needs in America's back yard," Chung said. "We know that much, even in the Belt. We know the appropriations are due to be cut, now the Essjays are in. So what?"

"We don't need a subsidy any longer," Blades remarked. "It'd help a lot, but we can get along without if we have to, and personally, I prefer that. Less government money means less government control."

"Sure," Avis said. "There was more than that involved, however. The Essjays were complaining about the small return on the investment. Not enough minerals coming back to Earth."

"Well, for Jupiter's sake," Blades exclaimed, "what do they expect? We have to build up our capabilities first."

"They even said, some of them, that enough reward never would be gotten. That under existing financial policies, the Belt would go in for its own expansion, use nearly everything it produced for itself and export only a trickle to America. I had to explain to several of my parents' friends that I wasn't really a socially irresponsible capitalist.''

"Is that all the information you have?" Chung asked when she fell silent.

"I . . . I suppose so. Everything was so vague. No dramatic events. More of an atmosphere than a concrete thing.''

"Still, you confirm my own impression," Chung said. Blades jerked his undisciplined imagination back from the idea of a Thing, with bug eyes and tentacles, cast in reinforced concrete, and listened as his partner summed up:

"The popular feeling at home has turned against private enterprise. You can hardly call a corporate monster like Systemic Developments a private enterprise! The new President and Congress share that mood. We can expect to see it manifested in changed laws and regulations. But what has this got to do with a battleship parked a couple of hundred kilometers from us?''

"If the government doesn't want the asterites to develop much further—" Blades bit hard on his pipestem. "They must know we have a caviar mine here. We'll be the only city in this entire sector.''

"But we're still a baby," Avis said. "We won't be important for years to come. Who'd have it in for a baby?''

"Besides, we're Americans, too," Chung said. "If that were a foreign ship, the story might be different— Wait a minute! Could they be thinking of establishing a new base here?''

"The Convention wouldn't allow it," said Blades.

"Treaties can always be renegotiated, or even denounced. But first you have to investigate quietly, find out if it's worth your while.''

"Hoo hah, what lovely money that'd mean!''

"And lovely bureaucrats crawling out of every file cabinet," Chung said grimly. "No, thank you. We'll fight any such attempt to the last lawyer. We've got a good basis too, in our charter. If the suit is tried on Ceres, as I believe it has to be, we'll get a sympathetic court as well."

"Unless they ring in an Earthside judge," Avis warned.

"Yeah, that's possible. Also, they could spring proceedings on us without notice. We've got to find out in advance, so we can prepare. Any chance of pumping some of those officers?"

" 'Fraid not," Avis said. "The few who'd be in the know are safely back on shipboard."

"We could invite 'em here individually," said Blades. "As a matter of fact, I already have a date with Lieutenant Ziska."

"What?" Avis' mouth fell open.

"Yep," Blades said complacently. "End of the next watch, so she can observe the *Pallas* arriving. I'm to fetch her on a scooter." He blew a fat smoke ring. "Look. Jimmy, can you keep everybody off the porch for a while then? Starlight, privacy, soft music on the piccolo —who knows what I might find out?"

"You won't get anything from *her*," Avis spat. "No secrets or . . . or anything."

"Still, I look forward to making the attempt. C'mon, pal, pass the word. I'll do as much for you sometime."

"Times like that never seem to come for me," Chung groaned.

"Oh let him play around with his suicide blonde," Avis said furiously. "We others have work to do. I . . . I'll tell you what, Jimmy. Let's not eat in the mess tonight. I'll draw our rations and fix us something special in your cabin."

A scooter was not exactly the ideal steed for a knight to convey his lady. It amounted to little more than three saddles and a locker, set atop an accumulator-powered gyrogravitic engine, sufficient to lift you off an asteroid and run at low acceleration. There were no navigating instruments. You locked the autopilot's radar-gravitic sensors onto your target object and it took you there, avoiding any bits of débris that might pass near; but you must watch the distance indicator and press the deceleration switch in time. If the 'pilot was turned off, free maneuver became possible, but that was a dangerous thing to try before you were almost on top of your destination. Stereoscopic vision fails beyond six or seven meters, and the human organism isn't equipped to gauge cosmic momenta.

Nevertheless, Ellen was enchanted. "This is like a dream," her voice murmured in Blades's earplug. "The whole universe, on every side of us. I could almost reach out and pluck those stars.

"You must have trained in powered spacesuits at the Academy," he said for lack of a more poetic rejoinder.

"Yes, but that's not the same. We had to stay near Luna's night side, to be safe from solar particles, and it bit a great chunk out of the sky. And then everything was so—regulated, disciplined—we did what we were ordered to do, and that was that. Here I feel free. You can't imagine how free." Hastily: "Do you use this machine often?"

"Well, yes, we have about twenty scooters at the station. They're the most convenient way of flitting with a load; out to the mirrors to change accumulators, for instance, or across to one of the companion rocks where we're digging some ores that the Sword doesn't have. That kind of work." Blades would frankly rather have had her behind him on a motorskimmer hanging on as they careened through a springtime countryside. He was glad when they reached the main forward air lock and debarked.

He was still gladder when the suits were off. Lieutenant Ziska in dress uniform was stunning, but Ellen in civvies, a fluffy low-cut blouse and close-fitting slacks, was a hydrogen blast. He wanted to roll over and pant, but settled for saying, "Welcome back" and holding her hand rather longer than necessary.

With a shy smile, she gave him a package. "I drew this before leaving," she said. "I thought, well, your life is so austere——"

"A demi of Sandeman," he said reverently. "I won't tell you you shouldn't have, but I will tell you you're a sweet girl."

"No, really." She flushed. "After we've put you to so much trouble."

"Let's go crack this," he said. "The *Pallas* has called in, but she won't be visible for a while yet."

They made their way to the verandah, picking up a couple of glasses en route. Bless his envious heart. Jimmy had warned the other boys off as requested. *I hope Avis cooks him a Cordon Bleu dinner*, Blades thought. *Nice kid, Avis, if she'd quit trying to . . . what? . . . mother me?* He forgot about her, with Ellen to seat by the rail.

The Milky Way turned her hair frosty and glowed in her eyes. Blades poured the port with much ceremony and raised his glass. "Here's to your frequent return," he said.

Her pleasure dwindled a bit. "I don't know if I should drink to that. We aren't likely to be back, ever."

"Drink anyway. Gling, glang, gloria!" The rims tinkled together. "After all," said Blades, "this isn't the whole universe. We'll both be getting around. See you on Luna?"

"Maybe."

He wondered if he was pushing matters too hard. She didn't look at ease. "Oh, well," he said, "if nothing else, this has been a grand break in the monotony for us. I don't wish the Navy ill, but if trouble had to develop, I'm thankful it developed here."

"Yes. . . ."

"How's the repair work progressing? Slowly, I hope."

"I don't know."

"You should have some idea, being in QM."

"No supplies have been drawn."

Blades stiffened.

"What's the matter?" Ellen sounded alarmed.

"Huh?" *A fine conspirator I make, if she can see my emotions on me in neon capitals!* "Nothing. Nothing. It just seemed a little strange, you know. Not taking any replacement units."

"I understand the work is only a matter of making certain adjustments."

"Then they should've finished a lot quicker, shouldn't they?"

"Please," she said unhappily. "Let's not talk about it. I mean, there are such things as security regulations."

Blades gave up on that tack. But Chung's idea

might be worth probing a little. "Sure," he said. "I'm sorry, I didn't mean to pry." He took another sip as he hunted for suitable words. A beautiful girl, a golden wine ... and vice versa.... Why couldn't he simply relax and enjoy himself? Did he have to go fretting about what was probably a perfectly harmless conundrum? ... Yes. However, recreation might still combine with business.

"Permit me to daydream," he said, leaning close to her. "The Navy's going to establish a new base here, and the *Altair* will be assigned to it."

"Daydream indeed!" she laughed, relieved to get back to a mere flirtation. "Ever hear about the Convention of Vesta?"

"Treaties can be renegotiated," Blades plagiarized.

"What do we need an extra base for? Especially since the government plans to spend such large sums on social welfare. They certainly don't want to start an arms race besides."

Blades nodded. *Jimmy's notion did seem pretty thin*, he thought with a slight chill, *and now I guess it's completely whiffed*. Mostly to keep the conversation going, he shrugged and said, "My partner—and me, too, aside from the privilege of your company—wouldn't have wanted it, anyhow. Not that we're unpatriotic, but there are plenty of other potential bases, and we'd rather keep government agencies out of here."

"Can you, these days?"

"Pretty much. We're under a new type of charter, as a private partnership. The first such charter in the Belt, as far as I know, though there'll be more in the future. The Bank of Ceres financed us. We haven't taken a nickel of federal money."

"Is that possible?"

"Just barely. I'm no economist, but I can see how it works. Money represents goods and labor. Hitherto those have been in mighty short supply out here. Government subsidies made up the difference, enabling us to buy from Earth. But now the asterites have built up enough population and industry that they have some capital surplus of their own, to invest in projects like this."

"Even so, frankly, I'm surprised that two men by themselves could get such a loan. It must be huge. Wouldn't the bank rather have lent the money to some corporation?"

"To tell the truth, we have friends who pulled wires for us. Also, it was done partly on ideological grounds. A lot of asterites would like to see more strictly home-grown enterprises, not committed to anyone on Earth. That's the only way we can grow. Otherwise our profits—our net production, that is—will continue to be siphoned off for the mother country's benefit."

"Well," Ellen said with some indignation, "that was the whole reason for planting asteroid colonies. You can't expect us to set you up in business, at enormous cost to ourselves—things we might have done at home—and get nothing but 'Ta' in return."

"Never fear, we'll repay you with interest," Blades said. "But whatever we make from our own work, over and above that, ought to stay here with us."

She grew angrier. "Your kind of attitude is what provoked the voters to elect Social Justice candidates."

"Nice name, that," mused Blades. "Who can be against social justice? But you know, I think I'll go into politics myself. I'll organize the North American Motherhood party."

"You wouldn't be so flippant if you'd go see how people have to live back there."

"As bad as here? *Whew!*"

"Nonsense. You know that isn't true. But bad enough. And you aren't going to stick in these conditions. Only a few hours ago, you were bragging about the millions you intend to make."

"Millions *and* millions, if my strength holds out," leered Blades, thinking of the alley in Aresopolis. But he decided that that was then and Ellen was now, and what had started as a promising little party was turning into a dismal argument about politics.

"Let's not fight," he said. "We've got different orientations, and we'd only make each other mad. Let's discuss our next bottle instead . . . at the Coq d'Or in Paris, shall we say? Or Morraine's in New York."

She calmed down, but her look remained troubled. "You're right, we are different," she said low. "Isolated, living and working under conditions we can hardly imagine on Earth—and you can't really imagine our problems. . . . Yes, you're becoming another people. I hope it will never go so far that—No. I don't want to think about it." She drained her glass and held it out for a refill, smiling. "Very well, sir, when do you next plan to be in Paris?"

An exceedingly enjoyable while later, the time came to go watch the *Pallas Castle* maneuver in. In fact, it had somehow gotten past that time, and they were late; but they didn't hurry their walk aft. Blades took Ellen's hand, and she raised no objection. Schoolboyish, no doubt—however, he had reached the reluctant conclusion that for all his dishonorable intentions, this affair wasn't likely

to go beyond the schoolboy stage. Not that he
wouldn't keep trying.

As they glided through the refining and synthe-
sizing section, which filled the broad half of the
asteroid, the noise of pumps and regulators rose
until it throbbed in their bones. Ellen gestured at
one of the pipes that crossed the corridor overhead.
"Do you really handle that big a volume at a
time?" she asked above the racket.

"No," he said. "Didn't I explain before? The
pipe's thick because it's so heavily armored."

"I'm glad you don't use that dreadful word
'cladded.' But why the armor? High pressure?"

"Partly. Also, there's an inertrans lining. Jupiter
gas is hellishly reactive at room temperature. The
metallic complexes especially; but think what a
witch's brew the stuff is in every respect. Once it's
been refined, of course, we have less trouble. That
particular pipe is carrying it raw."

They left the noise behind and passed on to the
approach control dome at the receptor end. The
two men on duty glanced up and immediately
went back to their instruments. Radio voices were
staccato in the air. Blades led Ellen to an observation port.

She drew a sharp breath. Outside, the broken
ground fell away to space and stars. The ovoid
that was the ship hung against them, lit by the
hidden sun, a giant even at her distance but dwarfed
by the balloon she towed. As that bubble tried
ponderously to rotate, rainbow gleams ran across
it, hiding and then revealing the constellations.
Here, on the asteroid's axis, there was no weight,
and one moved with underwater smoothness, as if
disembodied. "Oh, a fairy tale," Ellen sighed.

Four sparks flashed out of the boat blisters along

the ship's hull. "Scoopships," Blades told her. "They haul the cargo in, being so much more maneuverable. Actually, though, the mother vessel is going to park her load in orbit, while those boys bring in another one—see, there it comes into sight. We still haven't got the capacity to keep up with our deliveries."

"How many are there? Scoopships, that is."

"Twenty, but you don't need more than four for this job. They've got terrific power. Have to, if they're to dive from orbit down into the Jovian atmosphere, ram themselves full of gas, and come back. There they go."

The *Pallas Castle* was wrestling the great sphere she had hauled from Jupiter into a stable path computed by Central Control. Meanwhile, the scoopships, small only by comparison with her, locked onto the other balloon as it drifted close. Energy poured into their drive fields. Spiraling downward, transparent globe and four laboring spacecraft vanished behind the horizon. The *Pallas* completed her own task, disengaged her towbars, and dropped from view, headed for the dock.

The second balloon rose again, like a huge glass moon on the opposite side of the Sword. Still it grew in Ellen's eyes, kilometer by kilometer of approach. So much mass wasn't easily handled, but the braking curve looked disdainfully smooth. Presently she could make out the scoopships in detail, elongated teardrops with the intake gates yawning in the blunt forward end, cockpit canopies raised very slightly above.

Instructions rattled from the men in the dome. The balloon veered clumsily toward the one free receptor. A derricklike structure released one end of a cable, which streamed skyward. Things that

Ellen couldn't quite follow in this tricky light were done by the four tugs, mechanisms of their own extended to make their tow fast to the cable.

They did not cast loose at once, but continued to drag a little, easing the impact of centrifugal force. Nonetheless, a slight shudder went through the dome as slack was taken up. Then the job was over. The scoopships let go and flitted off to join their mother vessel. The balloon was winched inward. Spacesuited men moved close, preparing to couple valves together.

"And eventually," Blades said into the abrupt quietness, "that cargo will become food, fabric, vitryl, plastiboard, reagents, fuels, a hundred different things. That's what we're here for."

"I've never seen anything so wonderful," Ellen said raptly. He laid an arm around her waist.

The intercom chose that precise moment to blare: "Attention! Emergency! All hands to emergency stations! Blades, get to Chung's office on the double! All hands to emergency stations!"

Blades was running before the siren had begun to howl.

Rear Admiral Barclay Hulse had come in person. He stood as if on parade, towering over Chung. The asterite was red with fury. Avis Page crouched in a corner, her eyes terrified.

Blades barreled through the doorway and stopped hardly short of a collision. "What's the matter?" he puffed.

"Plenty!" Chung snarled. "These incredible thumble-fumbed oafs—" His voice broke. *When he gets mad, it means something!*

Hulse nailed Blades with a glance. "Good day, sir," he clipped. "I have had to report a regrettable accident which will require you to evacuate the station. Temporarily, I hope."

"Huh?"

"As I told Mr. Chung and Miss Page, a nuclear missile has escaped us. If it explodes, the radiation will be lethal, even in the heart of the asteroid."

"What . . . what——" Blades could only gobble at him.

"Fortunately the *Pallas Castle* is here. She can take your whole complement aboard and move to a safe distance while we search for the object."

"How the *devil?*"

Hulse allowed himself a look of exasperation. "Evidently I'll have to repeat myself to you. Very well. You know we have had to make some adjustments on our launchers. What you did not know was the reason. Under the circumstances, I think it's permissible to tell you that several of them have a new, and secret, experimental control system. One of our missions on this cruise was to carry out field tests. Well, it turned out that the system is still full of . . . ah . . . bugs. Gunnery Command has had endless trouble with it, has had to keep tinkering the whole way from Earth.

"Half an hour ago, while Commander Warburton was completing a reassembly—lower ranks aren't allowed in the test turrets—something happened. I can't tell you my guess as to what, but if you want to imagine that a relay got stuck, that will do for practical purposes. A missile was released under power. Not a dummy—the real thing. And release automatically arms the warhead."

The news was like a hammerblow. Blades spoke an obscenity. Sweat sprang forth under his arms and trickled down his ribs.

"No such thing was expected," Hulse went on.

"It's an utter disaster, and the designers of the system aren't likely to get any more contracts. But as matters were, no radar fix was gotten on it, and it was soon too far away for gyrogravitic pulse detection. The thrust vector is unknown. It could be almost anywhere now.

"Well, naval missiles are programmed to reverse acceleration if they haven't made a target within a given time. This one should be back in less than six hours. If it first detects our ship, everything is all right. It has optical recognition circuits that identify any North American warcraft by type, disarm the warhead, and steer it home. But if it first comes within fifty kilometers of some other mass—like this asteroid or one of the companion rocks—it will detonate. We'll make every effort to intercept but space is big. You'll have to take your people to a safe distance. They can come back even after a blast, of course. There's no concussion in vacuum, and the fire-ball won't reach here. It's principally an antipersonnel weapon. But you must not be within the lethal radius of radiation."

"The hell we can come back!" Avis cried.

"I beg your pardon?" Hulse said.

"You imbecile! Don't you know Central Control here is cryotronic?"

Hulse did not flicker an eyelid. "So it is," he said expressionlessly. "I had forgotten."

Blades mastered his own shock enough to grate: "Well, we sure haven't. If that thing goes off, the gamma burst will kick up so many minority carriers in the transistors that the p-type crystals will act n-type, and the n-type act p-type, for a whole couple of microseconds. Every one of 'em will flip simultaneously! The computers' memory and program data systems will be scrambled beyond hope of reorganization."

"Magnetic pulse, too," Chung said. "The fireball plasma will be full of inhomogeneities moving at several percent of light speed. Their electromagnetic output, hitting our magnetic core units, will turn them from super to ordinary conduction. Same effect, total computer amnesia. We haven't got enough shielding against it. Your TIMM systems can take that kind of a beating. Ours can't!"

"Very regrettable," Hulse said. "You'd have to reprogram everything—"

"Reprogram what?" Avis retorted. Tears started forth in her eyes. "We've told you what sort of stuff our chemical plant is handling. We can't shut it down on that short notice. It'll run wild. There'll be sodium explosions, hydrogen and organic combustion, n-n-nothing left here but wreckage!"

Hulse didn't unbend a centimeter. "I offer my most sincere apologies. If actual harm does occur, I'm sure the government will indemnify you. And, of course, my command will furnish what supplies may be needed for the *Pallas Castle* to transport you to the nearest Commission base. At the moment, though, you can do nothing but evacuate and hope we will be able to intercept the missile."

Blades knotted his fists. A sudden comprehension rushed up in him and he bellowed, "There isn't going to be an interception! This wasn't an accident!"

Hulse backed a step and drew himself even straighter. "Don't get overwrought," he advised.

"You louse-bitten, egg-sucking, bloated faggot-porter! How stupid do you think we are? As stupid as your Essjay bosses? By heaven, we're staying!

Then see if you have the nerve to murder a hundred people!"

"Mike . . . Mike—" Avis caught his arm.

Hulse turned to Chung. "I'll overlook that unseemly outburst," he said. "But in light of my responsibilities and under the provisions of the Constitution, I am hereby putting this asteroid under martial law. You will have all personnel aboard the *Pallas Castle* and at a minimum distance of a thousand kilometers within four hours of this moment, or be subject to arrest and trial. Now I have to get back and commence operations. The *Altair* will maintain radio contact with you. Good day." He bowed curtly, spun on his heel, and clacked from the room.

Blades started to charge after him. Chung caught his free arm. Together he and Avis dragged him to a stop. He stood cursing the air ultraviolet until Ellen entered.

"I couldn't keep up with you," she panted. "What's happened, Mike?"

The strength drained from Blades. He slumped into a chair and covered his face.

Chung explained in a few harsh words. "Oh-h-h," Ellen gasped. She went to Blades and laid her hands on his shoulders. "My poor Mike!"

After a moment she looked at the others. "I should report back, of course," she said, "but I won't be able to before the ship accelerates. So I'll have to stay with you till afterward. Miss Page, we left about half a bottle of wine on the verandah. I think it would be a good idea if you went and got it."

Avis bridled. "And why not you?"

"This is no time for personalities," Chung said. "Go on, Avis. You can be thinking what records and other paper we should take, while you're on your way. I've got to organize the evacuation. As for Miss Ziska, well, Mike needs somebody to pull him out of his dive."

"Her?" Avis wailed, and fled.

Chung sat down and flipped his intercom to Phone Central. "Get me Captain Janichevski aboard the *Pallas*," he ordered. "Hello, Adam? About that general alarm . . ."

Blades raised a haggard countenance toward Ellen's. "You better clear out, along with the women and any men who don't want to stay," he said. "But I think most of them will take the chance. They're on a profit-sharing scheme, they stand to lose too much if the place is ruined."

"What do you mean?"

"It's a gamble, but I don't believe Hulse's sealed orders extend to murder. If enough of us stay put, he'll have to catch that thing. He jolly well knows its exact trajectory."

"You forget we're under martial law," Chung said, aside to him. "If we don't go freely, he'll land some PP's and march us off at gunpoint. There isn't any choice. We've had the course."

"I don't understand," Ellen said shakily.

Chung went back to his intercom. Blades fumbled out his pipe and rolled it empty between his hands. "That missile was shot off on purpose," he said.

"What? No, you must be sick, that's impossible!"

"I realize you didn't know about it. Only three or four officers have been told. The job had to be done very, very secretly, or there'd be a scandal, maybe an impeachment. But it's still sabotage."

She shrank from him. "You're not making sense."

"Their own story doesn't make sense. It's ridiculous. A new missile system wouldn't be sent on a field trial clear to the Belt before it'd had enough tests closer to home to get the worst bugs out. A warhead missile wouldn't be stashed anywhere near something so unreliable, let alone be put under its control. The testing ship wouldn't hang around a civilian station while her gunnery chief tinkered. And Hulse, Warburton, Liebknecht, they were asking in *such* detail about how radiation-proof we are."

"I can't believe it. Nobody will."

"Not back home. Communication with Earth is so sparse and garbled. The public will only know there was an accident; who'll give a hoot about the details? We couldn't even prove anything in an asteroid court. The Navy would say, 'Classified information!' and that'd stop the proceedings cold. Sure, there'll be a board of inquiry—composed of naval officers. Probably honorable men, too. But what are they going to believe, the sworn word of their Goddard House colleague, or the rantings of an asterite bum?"

"Mike, I know this is terrible for you, but you've let it go to your head." Ellen laid a hand over his. "Suppose the worst happens. You'll be compensated for your loss."

"Yeah. To the extent of our personal investment. The Bank of Ceres still has nearly all the money that was put in. We didn't figure to have them paid off for another ten years. They, or their insurance carrier, will get the indemnity. And after our fiasco, they won't make us a new loan. They were just barely talked into it the first time around. I daresay Systemic Developments will make them a nice juicy offer to take this job over."

Ellen colored. She stamped her foot. "You're

talking like a paranoiac. Do you really believe the government of North America would send a battleship clear out here to do you dirt?"

"Not the whole government. A few men in the right positions is all that's necessary. I don't know if Hulse was bribed or talked into this. But probably he agreed as a duty. He's the prim type."

"A duty—to destroy a North American business?"

Chung finished at the intercom in time to answer: "Not permanent physical destruction, Miss Ziska. As Mike suggested, some corporation will doubtless inherit the Sword and repair the damage. But a private, purely asterite business . . . yes, I'm afraid Mike's right. We are the target."

"In mercy's name, why?"

"From the highest motives, of course," Chung sneered bitterly. "You know what the Social Justice party thinks of private capitalism. What's more important, though, is that the Sword is the first Belt undertaking not tied to Mother Earth's apron strings. We have no commitments to anybody back there. We can sell our output wherever we like. It's notorious that the asterites are itching to build up their own self-sufficient industries. Quite apart from sentiment, we can make bigger profits in the Belt than back home, especially when you figure the cost of sending stuff in and out of Earth's gravitational well. So certainly we'd be doing most of our business out here.

"Our charter can't simply be revoked. First a good many laws would have to be revised, and that's politically impossible. There is still a lot of individualist sentiment in North America, as witness the fact that businesses do get launched and that the Essjays did have a hard campaign to get elected. What the new government wants is something like the eighteenth-century English policy toward America. Keep the colonies as a source of raw materials and as a market for manufactured goods, but don't let them develop a domestic industry. You can't come right out and say that, but you can let the situation develop naturally.

"Only . . . here the Sword is, obviously bound to grow rich and expand in every direction. If we're allowed to develop, to reinvest our profits, we'll become the nucleus of independent asterite enterprise. If, on the other hand, we're wiped out by an unfortunate accident, there's no nucleus; and a small change in the banking laws is all that's needed to prevent others from getting started. Q.E.D."

"I daresay Hulse does think he's doing his patriotic duty," said Blades. "He wants to guarantee North America our natural resources—in the long run, maybe, our allegiance. If he has to commit sabotage, too bad, but it won't cost him any sleep."

"No!" Ellen almost screamed.

Chung sagged in his chair. "We're very neatly trapped," he said like an old man. "I don't see any way out. Think you can get to work now, Mike? You can assign group leaders for the evacuation—"

Blades jumped erect. "I can fight!" he growled.

"With what? Can openers?"

"You mean you're going to lie down and let them break us?"

Avis came back. She thrust the bottle into Blades's hands as he paced the room. "Here you are," she said in a distant voice.

He held it out toward Ellen. "Have some," he invited.

"Not with you . . . you subversive!"

Avis brightened noticeably, took the bottle and

raised it. "Then here's to victory," she said, drank, and passed it to Blades.

He started to gulp; but the wine was too noble, and he found himself savoring its course down his throat, *Why*, he thought vaguely, *do people always speak with scorn about Dutch courage? The Dutch have real guts. They fought themselves free of Spain and free of the ocean itself; when the French or Germans came, they made the enemy sea their ally—*

The bottle fell from his grasp. In the weak acceleration, it hadn't hit the floor when Avis rescued it. "Gimme that, you big butterfingers," she exclaimed. Her free hand clasped his arm. "Whatever happens, Mike," she said to him, "we're not quitting."

Still Blades stared beyond her. His fists clenched and unclenched. The noise of his breathing filled the room. Chung looked around in bewilderment; Ellen watched with waxing horror; Avis' eyes kindled.

"Holy smoking seegars," Blades whispered at last. "I really think we can swing it."

Captain Janichevski recoiled. "You're out of your skull!"

"Probably," said Blades. "Fun, huh?"

"You can't do this."

"We can try."

"Do you know what you're talking about? Insurrection, that's what. Quite likely piracy. Even if your scheme worked, you'd spend the next ten years in Rehab —at least."

"Maybe, provided the matter ever came to trial. But it won't."

"That's what you think. You're asking me to compound the felony, and misappropriate the property of my owners to boot." Janichevski shook his head. "Sorry, Mike. I'm sorry as hell about this mess. But I won't be party to making it worse."

"In other words," Blades replied, "you'd rather be party to sabotage. I'm proposing an act of legitimate self-defense."

"*If* there actually is a conspiracy to destroy the station."

"Adam, you're a spaceman. You know how the Navy operates. Can you swallow that story about a missile getting loose by accident?"

Janichevski bit his lip. The sounds from outside filled the captain's cabin—voices, footfalls, whirr of machines and clash of doors—as the *Pallas Castle* readied for departure. Blades waited.

"You may be right," said Janichevski at length, wretchedly. "Though why Hulse should jeopardize his career——"

"He's not. There's a scapegoat groomed back home, you can be sure. Like some company that'll be debarred from military contracts for a while . . . and get nice fat orders in other fields. I've kicked around the System enough to know how that works."

"If you're wrong, though . . . if this is an honest blunder . . . then you risk committing treason."

"Yeah. I'll take the chance."

"Not I. No. I've got a family to support," Janichevski said.

Blades regarded him bleakly. "If the Essjays get away with this stunt, what kind of life will your family be leading ten years from now? It's not simply that we'll be high-class peons in the Belt. But tied hand and foot to a shortsighted government, how much progress will we be able to make? Other countries have colonies out here too, remember, and some of them are already giving their people a freer hand than we've got. Do you want the Asians, or the Russians, or even the Europeans, to take over the asteroids?''

"I can't make policy."

"In other words, mama knows best. Believe, obey, anything put out by some bureaucrat who never set foot beyond Luna. Is that your idea of citizenship?"

"You're putting a mighty fine gloss on bailing yourself out!" Janichevski flared.

"Sure, I'm no idealist. But neither am I a slave." Blades hesitated. "We've been friends too long, Adam, for me to try bribing you. But if worst comes to worst, we'll cover for you . . . somehow . . . and if contrariwise we win, then we'll soon be hiring captains for our own ships and you'll get the best offer any spaceman ever got."

"No. Scram. I've work to do."

Blades braced himself. "I didn't want to say this. But I've already informed a number of my men. They're as mad as I am. They're waiting in the terminal. A monkey wrench or a laser torch makes a pretty fair weapon. We can take over by force. That'll leave you legally in the clear. But with so many witnesses around, you'll have to prefer charges against us later on."

Janichevski began to sweat.

"We'll be sent up," said Blades. "But it will still have been worth it."

"Is it really that important to you?"

"Yes. I admit I'm no crusader. But this is a matter of principle."

Janichevski stared at the big redhaired man for a long while. Suddenly he stiffened. "Okay. On that account, and no other, I'll go along with you."

Blades wobbled on his feet, near collapse with relief. "Good man!" he croaked.

"But I will not have any of my officers or crew involved."

Blades rallied and answered briskly, "You needn't. Just issue orders that my boys are to have access to the scoopships. They can install the equipment, jockey the boats over to the full balloons, and even couple them on."

Janichevski's fears had vanished once he made his decision, but now a certain doubt registered. "That's a pretty skilled job."

"These are pretty skilled men. It isn't much of a maneuver, not like making a Jovian sky dive."

"Well, okay, I'll take your word for their ability. But suppose the *Altair* spots those boats moving around?"

"She's already several hundred kilometers off, and getting farther away, running a search curve which I'm betting my liberty—and my honor; I certainly don't want to hurt my own country's Navy—I'm betting that search curve is guaranteed not to find the missile in time. They'll spot the *Pallas* as you depart—oh, yes, our people will be aboard as per orders—but no finer detail will show in so casual an observation."

"Again I'll take your word. What else can I do to help?"

"Nothing you weren't doing before. Leave the piratics to us. I'd better get back." Blades extended his hand. "I haven't got the words to thank you, Adam."

Janichevski accepted the shake. "No reason for thanks. You dragooned me." A grin crossed his face. "I must confess, though, I'm not sorry you did."

*   *   *

Blades left. He found his gang in the terminal, two dozen engineers and rockjacks clumped tautly together.

"What's the word?" Carlos Odónoju shouted.

"Clear track," Blades said. "Go right aboard."

"Good. Fine. I always wanted to do something vicious and destructive," Odónoju laughed.

"The idea is to prevent destruction," Blades reminded him, and proceeded toward the office.

Avis met him in Corridor Four. Her freckled countenance was distorted by a scowl. "Hey, Mike, wait a minute," she said, low and hurriedly. "Have you seen La Ziska?"

"The leftenant? Why, no. I left her with you, remember, hoping you could calm her down."

"Uh-huh. She was incandescent mad. Called us a pack of bandits and—but then she started crying. Seemed to break down completely. I took her to your cabin and went back to help Jimmy. Only, when I checked there a minute ago, she was gone."

"What? Where?"

"How should I know? But that she-devil's capable of anything to wreck our chances."

"You're not being fair to her. She's got an oath to keep."

"All right," said Avis sweetly. "Far be it from me to prevent her fulfilling her obligations. Afterward she may even write you an occasional letter. I'm sure that'll brighten your Rehab cell no end."

"What can she do?" Blades argued, with an uneasy sense of whistling in the dark. "She can't get off the asteroid without a scooter, and I've already got Sam's gang working on all the scooters."

"Is there no other possibility? The radio shack?"

"With a man on duty there. That's out." Blades patted the girl's arm.

"Okay, I'll get back to work. But . . . I'll be so glad when this is over, Mike!"

Looking into the desperate brown eyes, Blades felt a sudden impulse to kiss their owner. But no, there was too much else to do. Later, perhaps. He cocked a thumb upward. "Carry on."

Too bad about Ellen, he thought as he continued toward his office. *What an awful waste, to make a permanent enemy of someone with her kind of looks. And personality—Come off that stick, you clabberhead! She's probably the marryin' type anyway.*

In her shoes, though, what would I do? Not much; they'd pinch my feet. But—damnation, Avis is right. She's not safe to have running around loose. The radio shack? Sparks is not one of the few who've been told the whole story and coopted into the plan. She could—

Blades cursed, whirled, and ran.

His way was clear. Most of the men were still in their dorms, preparing to leave. He traveled in huge lowgravity leaps.

The radio shack rose out of the surface near the verandah. Blades tried the door. It didn't budge. A chill went through him. He backed across the corridor and charged. The door was only plastiboard—

He hit with a thud and a grunt, and rebounded with a numbed shoulder. But it looked so easy for the cops on 3V!

No time to figure out the delicate art of forcible entry. He hurled himself against the panel, again and again, heedless of the pain that struck in flesh and bone. When the door finally, splinteringly gave way, he stumbled clear across the room beyond, fetched up against an instrument console, recovered his balance, and gaped.

The operator lay on the floor, swearing in a steady monotone. He had been efficiently bound with his own blouse and trousers, which revealed his predilection for maroon shorts with zebra stripes. There was a lump on the back of his head, and a hammer lay close by. Ellen must have stolen the tool and come in here with the thing behind her back. The operator would have had no reason to suspect her.

She had not left the sender's chair, not even while the door was under attack. Only a carrier beam connected the Sword with the *Altair*. She continued doggedly to fumble with dials and switches, trying to modulate it and raise the ship.

"Praises be . . . you haven't had advanced training . . . in radio," Blades choked. "That's . . . a long-range set . . . pretty special system—" He weaved toward her. "Come along, now."

She spat an unladylike refusal.

Theoretically, Blades should have enjoyed the tussle that followed. But he was in poor shape at the outset. And he was a good deal worse off by the time he got her pinioned.

"Okay," he wheezed. "Will you come quietly?"

She didn't deign to answer, unless you counted her butting him in the nose. He had to yell for help to frog-march her aboard ship.

"Pallas Castle calling NASS *Altair*. Come in, *Altair*."

The great ovoid swung clear in space, among a million cold stars. The asteroid had dwindled out of sight. A radio beam flickered across emptiness. Within the hull, the crew and a hundred refugees sat jammed together. The air was thick with their breath and sweat.

Blades and Chung, seated by the transmitter, felt another kind of thickness, the pull of the internal field. Earth-normal weight dragged down every movement; the enclosed cabin began to feel suffocatingly small. *We'd get used to it again pretty quickly*, Blades thought. *Our bodies would, that is. But our own selves, tied down to Earth forever—no.*

The vision screen jumped to life. "NASS *Altair* acknowledges *Pallas Castle*," said the uniformed figure within.

"Okay, Charlie, go outside and don't let anybody else enter," Chung told his own operator.

The spaceman gave him a quizzical glance, but obeyed. "I wish to report that evacuation of the Sword is now complete," Chung said formally.

"Very good, sir," the Navy face replied. "I'll inform my superiors."

"Wait, don't break off yet. We have to talk with your captain."

"Sir? I'll switch you over to——"

"None of your damned chains of command," Blades interrupted. "Get me Rear Admiral Hulse direct, toot sweet, or I'll eat out whatever fraction of you he leaves unchewed. This is an emergency. I've got to warn him of an immediate danger only he can deal with."

The other stared, first at Chung's obvious exhaustion, then at the black eye and assorted bruises, scratches, and bites that adorned Blades's visage. "I'll put the message through Channel Red at once, sir." The screen blanked.

"Well, here we go," Chung said. "I wonder how the food in Rehab is these days."

"Want me to do the talking?" Blades asked. Chung

wasn't built for times as hectic as the last few hours, and was worn to a nubbin. He himself felt immensely keyed up. He'd always liked a good fight.

"Sure." Chung pulled a crumpled cigarette from his pocket and began to fill the cabin with smoke. "You have a larger stock of rudeness than I."

Presently the screen showed Hulse, rigid at his post on the bridge. "Good day, gentlemen," he said. "What's the trouble?"

"Plenty," Blades answered. "Clear everybody else out of there; let your ship orbit free a while. And seal your circuit."

Hulse reddened. "Who do you think you are?"

"Well, my birth certificate says Michael Joseph Blades. I've got some news for you concerning that top-secret gadget you told us about. You wouldn't want unauthorized personnel listening in."

Hulse leaned forward till he seemed about to fall through the screen. "What's this about a hazard?"

"Fact. The *Altair* is in distinct danger of getting blown to bits."

"Have you gone crazy? Get me the captain of the *Pallas*."

"Very small bits."

Hulse compressed his lips. "All right, I'll listen to you for a short time. You had better make it worth my while."

He spoke orders. Blades scratched his back while he waited for the bridge to be emptied and wondered if there was any chance of a hot shower in the near future.

"Done," said Hulse. "Give me your report."

Blades glanced at the telltale. "You haven't sealed your circuit, Admiral."

Hulse said angry words, but complied. "Now will you talk?"

"Sure. This secrecy is for your own protection. You risk court-martial otherwise."

Hulse suppressed a retort.

"Okay, here's the word." Blades met the transmitted glare with an almost palpable crash of eyeballs. "We decided, Mr. Chung and I, that any missile rig as haywire as yours represents a menace to navigation and public safety. If you can't control your own nuclear weapons, you shouldn't be at large. Our charter gives us local authority as peace officers. By virtue thereof and so on and so forth, we ordered certain precautionary steps taken. As a result, if that warhead goes off, I'm sorry to say that NASS *Altair* will be destroyed."

"Are you . . . have you——" Hulse congealed. In spite of everything, he was a competent officer, Blades decided. "Please explain yourself," he said without tone.

"Sure," Blades obliged. "The station hasn't got any armament, but trust the human race to juryrig that. We commandeered the scoopships belonging to this vessel and loaded them with Jovian gas at maximum pressure. If your missile detonates, they'll dive on you."

Something like amusement tinged Hulse's shocked expression. "Do you seriously consider that a weapon?"

"I seriously do. Let me explain. The ships are orbiting free right now, scattered through quite a large volume of space. Nobody's aboard them. What is aboard each one, though, is an autopilot taken from a scooter, hooked into the drive controls. Each 'pilot has its sensors locked onto your ship. You can't maneuver fast enough to shake off radar beams and mass detectors. You're the target object, and there's nothing to tell those idiot computers to decelerate as they approach you.

"Of course, no approach is being made yet. A switch has been put in every scooter circuit, and left open. Only the meteorite evasion units are operative right now. That is, if anyone tried to lay alongside one of those scoopships, he'd be detected and the ship would skitter away. Remember, a scoopship hasn't much mass, and she does have engines designed for diving in and out of Jupe's gravitational well. She can out-accelerate either of our vessels, or any boat of yours, and out-dodge any of your missiles. You can't catch her."

Hulse snorted. "What's the significance of this farce?"

"I said the autopilots were switched off at the moment, as far as heading for the target is concerned. But each of those switches is coupled to two other units. One is simply the sensor box. If you withdraw beyond a certain distance, the switches will close. That is, the 'pilots will be turned on if you try to go beyond range of the beams now locked onto you. The other unit we've installed in every boat is an ordinary two-for-a-dollar radiation meter. If a nuclear weapon goes off anywhere within a couple of thousand kilometers the switches will also close. In either of these cases, the scoopships will dive on you.

"You might knock out a few with missiles, before they strike. Undoubtedly you can punch holes in them with laser guns. But that won't do any good, except when you're lucky enough to hit a vital part. Nobody's aboard to be killed. Not even much gas will be lost, in so short a time.

"So to summarize, chum, if that rogue missile

explodes, your ship will be struck by ten to twenty scoopships, each crammed full of concentrated Jovian air. They'll pierce that thin hull of yours, but since they're already pumped full beyond the margin of safety, the impact will split them open and the gas will whoosh out. Do you know what Jovian air does to substances like magnesium?

"You can probably save your crew, take to the boats and reach a Commission base. But your nice battleship will be *ganz kaput*. Is your game worth that candle?"

"You're totally insane! Releasing such a thing——"

"Oh, not permanently. There's one more switch on each boat, connected to the meteoroid evasion unit and controlled by a small battery. When those batteries run down, in about twenty hours, the 'pilots will be turned off completely. Then we can spot the scoopships by radar and pick 'em up. And you'll be free to leave."

"Do you think for one instant that your fantastic claim of acting legally will stand up in court?"

"No, probably not. But it won't have to. Obviously you can't make anybody swallow your yarn if a *second* missile gets loose. And as for the first one, since it's failed in its purpose, your bosses aren't going to want the matter publicized. It'd embarrass them no end, and serve no purpose except revenge on Jimmy and me—which there's no point in taking, since the Sword would still be privately owned. You check with Earth, Admiral, before shooting off your mouth. They'll tell you that both parties to this quarrel had better forget about legal action. Both would lose.

"So I'm afraid your only choice is to find that missile before it goes off."

"And yours? What are your alternatives?" Hulse

had gone gray in the face, but he still spoke stoutly.

Blades grinned at him. "None whatsoever. We've burned our bridges. We can't do anything about those scoopships now, so it's no use trying to scare us or arrest us or whatever else may occur to you. What we've done is establish an automatic deterrent."

"Against an, an attempt . . . at sabotage . . . that exists only in your imagination!"

Blades shrugged. "That argument isn't relevant any longer. I do believe the missile was released deliberately. We wouldn't have done what we did otherwise. But there's no longer any point in making charges and denials. You'd just better retrieve the thing."

Hulse squared his shoulders. "How do I know you're telling the truth?"

"Well, you can send a man to the station. He'll find the scooters lying gutted. Send another man over here to the *Pallas*. He'll find the scoopships gone. I also took a few photographs of the autopilots being installed and the ships being cast adrift. Go right ahead. However, may I remind you that the fewer people who have an inkling of this little intrigue, the better for all concerned."

Hulse opened his mouth, shut it again, stared from side to side, and finally slumped the barest bit. "Very well," he said, biting off the words syllable by syllable. "I can't risk a ship of the line. Of course, since the rogue is still farther away than your deterrent allows the *Altair* to go, we shall have to wait in space a while."

"I don't mind."

"I shall report the full story to my superiors at home . . . but unofficially."

"Good. I'd like them to know that we asterites have teeth."

"Signing off, then."

Chung stirred. "Wait a bit," he said. "We have one of your people aboard, Lieutenant Ziska. Can you send a gig for her?"

"She didn't collaborate with us," Blades added. "You can see the evidence of her loyalty, all over my mug."

"Good girl!" Hulse exclaimed savagely. "Yes, I'll send a boat. Signing off."

The screen blanked. Chung and Blades let out a long, ragged breath. They sat a while trembling before Chung muttered, "That skunk as good as admitted everything."

"Sure," said Blades. "But we won't have any more trouble from him."

Chung stubbed out his cigarette. Poise was returning to both men. "There could be other attempts, though, in the next few years." He scowled. "I think we should arm the station. A couple of laser guns, if nothing else. We can say it's for protection in case of war. But it'll make our own government handle us more carefully, too."

"Well, you can approach the Commission about it." Blades yawned and stretched, trying to loosen his muscles. "Better get a lot of other owners and supervisors to sign your petition, though." The next order of business came to his mind. He rose. "Why don't you go tell Adam the good news?"

"Where are you bound?"

"To let Ellen know the fight is over."

"Is it, as far as she's concerned?"

"That's what I'm about to find out. Hope I won't need an armored escort." Blades went from the cubicle, past the watchful radioman, and down the deserted passage-way beyond.

The cabin given her lay at the end, locked from outside. The key hung magnetically on the bulkhead. Blades unlocked the door and tapped it with his knuckles.

"Who's there?" she called.

"Me," he said. "May I come in?"

"If you must," she said freezingly.

He opened the door and stepped through. The overhead light shimmered off her hair and limned her figure with shadows. His heart bumped. "You, uh, you can come out now," he faltered. "Everything's okay."

She said nothing, only regarded him from glacier-blue eyes.

"No harm's been done, except to me and Sparks, and we're not mad," he groped. "Shall we forget the whole episode?"

"If you wish."

"Ellen," he pleaded, "I had to do what seemed right to me."

"So did I."

He couldn't find any more words.

"I assume that I'll be returned to my own ship," she said. He nodded. "Then, if you will excuse me, I had best make myself as presentable as I can. Good day, Mr. Blades."

"What's good about it?" he snarled, and slammed the door on his way out.

Avis stood outside the jampacked saloon. She saw him coming and ran to meet him. He made swab-0 with his fingers and joy blazed from her. "Mike," she cried. "I'm so happy!"

The only gentlemanly thing to do was hug her. His spirits lifted a bit as he did. She made a nice armful. Not bad-looking, either.

Interlude 2

"Well, says Amspaugh. "So that's the inside story. How very interesting. I never heard it before."

"No; obviously it never got into any official record," Missy replies. "The only announcement made was that there'd been a near accident, that the station tried to improvise countermissiles out of scoopships, but that the quick action of NASS *Altair* was what saved the situation. Her captain was commended. I don't believe he ever got a further promotion, though."

"Why didn't you publicize the facts afterwards?" Lindgren wonders. "When the revolution began, that is. It would've made good propaganda."

"Nonsense," Missy says. "Too much else had happened since then. Besides, neither Mike nor Jimmy nor I wanted to do any cheap emotion-fanning. We knew the asterites weren't little pink-bottomed angels, nor the people back sunward a crew of devils. There were rights and wrongs on both sides. We did what we could in the war, and hated every minute of it, and when it was over we broke out two cases of champagne and invited as many Earthlings as we could get to the party. They had a lot of love to carry home for us."

Again a stillness falls. She takes a long swallow from her glass and sits looking out at the stars.

"Yes," Lindgren says finally, "I guess that was the worst, fighting against our kin."

"Well, I was better off in that respect than some," Missy admits. "I'd made my commitment so long before the trouble that my ties were nearly all out in the Belt. Twenty years is time enough to grow new roots, which is what it took before the revolution happened."

"I suppose the ideal—the lost American ideal of personal freedom—needed that length of time to grow," Conchita says.

Missy starts, then laughs. "My dear," she replies, "I assure you the revolution was by and large not *for* anything grand; it was *against* excessive taxes and regulations. If transport hadn't improved and commerce expanded as it did, why, we might always have had too few bureaucrats and examiners and such-like nuisances to exasperate us till we rebelled." She draws pensively on her cigar. "Furthermore, I wish you'd stop thinking of my generation, the one that founded the Republic, as a set of glittering heroes. We weren't exclusively the rock rats Colin spoke of. But a lot of us were—oh, my, what I could tell you about some of my fellow fighters for liberation!—and the rest were all too human in their own fashions."

"You included?" Orloff jests.

"Why, certainly," she smiles. "My folks were aghast at my conduct. I only needed six months after the *Altair* incident to think things out, resign my commission, and catch the next Belt-bound ship. In their eyes, I was a brazen hussy, sacrificing a good and honorable career to boot—and you know, they were right. But you don't think I'd have let a man like Mike get away, do you?"

Say It with Flowers

Whiskey Johnny was eighteen hours out of Sam's when her radar registered another ship. There was no doubt about that. A natural object, a meteoroid or asteroid tumbling through the Belt, even a comet falling inward from near-infinity, could never have had such a vector as the computer printed out. And the vessel could hardly be anything but North American: hostile.

The pilot uttered expert obscenities. They bounced around his ears, in the tiny, thrumming cockpit where he sat. He punched for distance and velocity at closest approach, as if the keys under his fingers were noses in a barroom battle. The answer was unpleasantly small. However, that assumed he himself continued acceleration. If he went free . . . yes, better. The enemy craft—a big one, the radar said—was itself under power, so it would gain speed with respect to him. . . .

To reduce his detectability, he cut the Emetts and throttled his nuclear generator down to a minimum. The scoopship yielded to the pull of the sun, shrunken and brilliant to starboard. Her path did not curve much. She had already built up enough velocity to swing in a flat hyperbola that would take her out of the Solar System were it not modified. But she was, now, in free fall.

So was her pilot, since he had shut off the internal field generators. He floated in his seat harness, in a quiet so deep and sudden that he heard the blood beat through his own veins. A fan came on automatically, to keep fresh air moving past him, but that whirr only emphasized the silence. He peered out the inertrans canopy as if to see the patrolling warship from Earth. Of course he couldn't, at those distances. Stars crowded the blackness, unwinking and winter-cold; the Milky Way girdled the universe with diamond dust; Jupiter blazed enormous, not many astronomical units to port.

No asteroids were visible to the naked eye. Those clustered in the vicinity of Sam's lay far behind. Pallas, where *Whiskey Johnny* was bound, lay hours ahead, even at the high acceleration of which a scoopship was capable. As for the rest of the Belt—well, there are thousands of worldlets, millions of meteoroids, but space is huge and they spread thinly.

The pilot fished a cigar from his breast pocket. Presently the cockpit air was as thick as that of Venus, and nearly as poisonous. He didn't mind. He had spent half of his forty Earth-years digging and building on raw rocks where only the tough could hope to survive. His face was so craggy that the assorted scars looked natural. Half open, his frayed old zipskin revealed a chest like a barrel; through the hair showed an enormous tattoo in enormously bad taste, a comet which was also a flag. The naked woman who danced on his right biceps was probably in worse taste yet. His left forearm was shaven, which indicated that the design of roses and lilies inked into its skin was very recent. Some people never grow up.

He puffed hard. It was a strain, waiting. He

tried to think of matters more pleasant than the war. Like, say, that bender he went on back at Sam's, shortly before he started on this mission. Trouble was, the wingding had been too good. Several girls . . . yeah . . . and then afterward Billy Kirk showed up with a bottle in either fist . . . and then everything was blank, until he woke with volcanoes in his head and those silly posies on his arm. *Why* had he elected that design?

Well, there'd be a doctor at Pallas who could take it off for him. And plenty of booze and wild, wild women. The colonists had fleet enough to defend their capital and its supply lines. Otherwise they could only hold strong points like Sam's. But they were scattered through millions of kilometers, on hundreds of asteroids; their ships were manned with deadly skill; little by little, they wore down their one-time masters. Meanwhile, on Earth, their diplomats intrigued in various capitals. Other nations would bring pressure to bear on North America. Eventually the Republic would be free to shape its own destiny.

The pilot didn't think in any such high-flown terms. He'd just gotten sick and tired of being taxed to support a bureaucracy which seemed interested only in regulating his life for him.

The radio buzzed. A call on the universal band.

"Huh!" he growled. "I'm on to that stunt, buster. You broadcast, and I turn up my receiver, and you detect that." He went on to suggest, in some detail, what the American could do with his 'caster.

Although—wait! The signal was coming in much too strong. Either the warship had gotten close, or it was sending a maser beam. Sweat prickled forth on his skin. He got busy with his instruments.

Both cases were true. The ship had locked a

beam onto his vessel and it was coming about to make rendezvous.

So its sky-sweeping radars had picked him up after all, and never lost him again.

No choice, after that, but to answer. He flipped a switch. "Scoopship *Whiskey Johnny* receiving call," he said in a flat basso.

"NASS *Chicago* transmittin'. Prepare to match velocities."

"What the double blue hell is this? I'm minding my own business."

"I doubt that," drawled the Texan voice. "You're from Sam's for Pallas. Don't bother denyin' it. We got plenty good data on your path. So you're a courier."

"You're out of your ever-loving mind," said the asterite, in rather more pungent language.

"What else would you be, son, in a small fast boat like that? Listen, don't try to get rid of your dispatches. We're near enough to register anything you pitch out the air lock. As of this minute, you're a prisoner of war and subject to discipline."

Kirk warned me about narcoquizzes. And if I keep on claiming to be a civilian, I could be shot as a spy.

"Identify yourself," said the voice.

"Lieutenant Robert Flowers, Space Force of the Asteroid Republic," the pilot snapped.

Briefly, furiously, he considered making a run for it. He could out-accelerate a capital ship by several gees. Probably he could evade a missile. But no. The warhead needn't burst very close for radiation to kill him. Or a laser gun might track him and gnaw through to his engine. Flowers cursed some more and donned the battered officer's cap which put him legally in uniform.

"Well, you rebels call it a republic," said the

Texan. "Okay, punch these here instructions into your autopilot. And then you might as well relax. You'll be locked away for quite a spell, I reckon."

The cruiser was a great ovoid, dully agleam in the harsh spatial sunlight. Rifles poked dinosaurian from their turrets, missile launchers gaped like mouths. The scoopship edged inward, dwarfed.

"Cease drive," came the order. They weren't taking chances on a suicide plunge.

"Smelly," Flowers obeyed. He stuck a fresh cigar between his teeth and got up a good head of steam.

A geegee beam reeled him in. A boat hatch opened. He felt the slight shock and heard the clang as *Whiskey Johnny* entered a cradle. Now steel enclosed him. Air whistled back to the compartment. Four bluejackets appeared, and motioned him out. He slid back the canopy, which he had already unsealed, and jumped down. Smoke gushed from his mouth, into the nearest face. The man gasped and staggered.

"All right, funny boy," said the ensign in charge. "Give me that."

"Huh?" cried Flowers. "Can't a joe even have a smoke?"

"Not if I say he can't." The ensign yanked the cigar from the prisoner's lips, threw it to the deck and ground it under his heel. "Frisk him, Justus. Iwasaki, get his dispatches."

Flowers submitted. *I could take all these pups in a rough-and-tumble, and Judas, I'd love to,* he thought, *But their sidearms are a bit much.*

Iwasaki, in the cockpit, lifted a small steel tube. "Would this be it, sir?"

"I suppose so. Toss." The ensign caught it.

"Commander Ulstad will know. But search the whole craft and report anything unusual. You others come with me."

They went unspeaking down long, bleak corridors. The crewmen they passed stared at Flowers—for the most part, without the ensign's hostility. This had been a gentlemen's war, on the whole, and the asterite cause had its sympathizers in North America. After all, the colonists were American, too, and the rebellion was for the sake of that individual freedom to which lip service was still paid at home.

Probably the ensign was impatient to get back to his girl.

A murmur went through the metal, a slight shiver was added to the steady one *g* of the interior field. The ship was under weigh again, returning to its patrol orbit.

At the end of the walk, Flowers was urged through a door. He found himself in a small office. It was furnished with proper naval austerity, but a few scenic views of Earth were pasted on the bulkheads, and the desk bore pictures of wife and children. The man behind was lean, erect, gray at the temples, his long face reasonably kind.

However, onto this cabin there opened an interrogation lab.

The ensign saluted. "Reporting with prisoner, sir. He had this aboard his boat."

"Let me see." Commander Ulstad—must be him, and he must be Intelligence—reached for the tube. He unscrewed the cap and shook out a scroll of shiny plastic. Spreading it on his desk, he looked for a moment at the blank surface.

"Yes, evidently his dispatches," he murmured. "Magnetic, what else?" He rose and went into his laboratory. Flowers saw him thread the scroll into a scanner. The machine clicked to itself. A screen flickered with shifting dots, lines, curves.

Flowers knew, in a general way, how the system worked: analogously to an old-fashioned tape recording. The visual pattern of the message was encoded in a series of magnetic pulses which imposed a corresponding pattern on iron particles embedded in the plastic. Of course, for military purposes you first enciphered the message and then put a scrambler in the recording circuit. The result couldn't even be seen, let alone cleared, without a descrambler in the playback.

Ulstad frowned and made adjustments. Realization jarred through Flowers: *He expects to protect the thing. Blast and befoul! Somehow they've learned our scrambler patterns.*

The officer tried several other settings. Nonsensical images gibed at him. Flowers sank into a chair. A slow, happy grin spread across his mouth. So the Republic had gotten wise and adopted a new code, huh? Gr-r-reat!

"Well." Ulstad returned. Excitement barely tinged his voice. "We seem to have caught a rather big fish." He punched the intercom. "Commander Ulstad here. Get me Captain Thomas."

He sat down and held forth a pack of cigarettes. "Would you like a smoke, Lieutenant Flowers?" he invited.

The asterite leered at the ensign, who stood in the doorway with his guards. "How about that, chum?" he said, and accepted. "Thanks."

Ulstad turned on a recorder. "You understand I have to ask you some questions," he said. "Please state your correct name, rank, and serial number."

"Robert Henry Flowers, Space Force lieutenant,

number . . . uh, I never can remember the mucking thing." He read it off his ID bracelet. That was one more bit of junk he meant to throw into a sunbound orbit, when the war was over and he could be his own man again.

Ulstad smiled. "You don't look like anyone named Flowers," he remarked.

"Yeah, I know. That's how come I've got this busted nose and such. You should'a seen those other bums, though. I don't take being razzed."

"You won't be. I have every intention of treating you with the respect due a commissioned officer." The intercom buzzed. "Excuse me."

The cruiser's captain spoke out of it. "Yes, Commander, what do you want?"

"About this courier we just captured, sir," Ulstad told him. "I can't read his dispatches. That means the enemy has changed the scrambler code again, and no doubt the ciphers as well."

"So?"

"So in the first place, sir, the enemy probably realizes that we have cracked his last set of codes. He doesn't change them often or lightly, when word about new arrangements has to be sent over lines of communication as long as his. Therefore, our own GHQ has to know. Then second, this particular message must be delivered for analysis as fast as possible. I respectfully suggest that we shoot a speedster off to Luna Base at once."

"Um-m-m," grunted the captain. "Don't like that. Too many asterite frigates skulking around."

"Well, then, we'd better make rendezvous with a ship able to defend herself, and send the message by her."

"We've mighty few ships to spare, Commander." The captain paused. "But this is important. I'll contact CINCOBELT when our position allows, and they'll see what can be done."

"Thank you, sir." Ulstad turned off the intercom.

His gaze went to Flowers, who had gone rigid, and he nodded. "Yes," he said, "we have computers at Luna Base which can discover any scrambler pattern and then go on to break any cipher. Not too easily, I confess. You have some fiendishly clever people in your code section. But the machines can always grind out the answer, by sheer electronic patience."

Flowers recollected some remarks overheard when he reported for briefing. He hadn't paid much attention. But . . . yeah, asterite Intelligence must suspect the truth. There had been comings and goings of late, couriers bringing secret word from Pallas to Sam's as well as to other Republican centers. Only the higher-ups knew what that word amounted to. A warning?

His bemusement vanished in a puff of indignation. Space was too vast for the North Americans to blockade very effectively those places too well armed to capture. Most boats got through. Why did *his* have to be among the unlucky ones?

"I suppose you have no idea what message you were conveying," said Ulstad conversationally.

"Think I'd tell you if I did?" bristled Flowers.

"Yes, under drugs and brain stimulation," said Ulstad.

"Well, I don't know!"

"We'll find out."

"You rust-eaten mutant——"

"Please." Ulstad waved back one of the guards, who had taken a forward step with anger on his face. His own tone stayed mild. "The process doesn't hurt or do any damage. We're fighting this war by the Geneva convention, the same as you people are. But still, we consider it the suppression of an insurrection, which gives us the right to use police procedures. Your interrogators do likewise to our boys, without that legality."

Flowers finished his cigarette and flipped the butt into a disposal. "You can stuff those quibbles," he said. "Get on with your dirty work so I can get out of here."

"What's your hurry, Lieutenant? You'll be aboard the *Chicago* for a number of hours, till we can arrange your transfer to a supply ship. And it will only be going to Vesta, where you'll sit out the war in a prison camp. Dull place. We'll do our best to make you happy, on this ship. Cool your motors. Enjoy our hospitality. Would you like some coffee?"

Flowers swallowed his rage. Doubtless Ulstad was trying to disarm him, but the fellow seemed decent at heart. "Druther have booze," he said.

"Sorry. Me too, but regulations." Ulstad crossed his legs and leaned back in his chair. "Let's get acquainted. I'm always interested to meet a colonist. You weren't born out here, were you?"

Flowers had no wish to spill military information; not that he had much. But by gabbing a little while, he post-poned the humiliation of narco. Besides— "Brooklyn," he said. "Moved to space at eighteen. Uh, my parents are still alive. You wouldn't know about them, would you?"

" 'Fraid not. I'm from Wisconsin myself. Your folks must be all right, though. The government doesn't discriminate against anyone who happens to have rebel kinfolk, as long as they keep their own noses clean." Ulstad kindled another cigarette. "Really, we're not the monsters your more overheated propagandists claim. In fact, our society is a good deal more benevolent than yours."

"Yeah. So benevolent that I felt smothered, every visit I made back home."

"*De gustibus non disputandum est,* which personally I translate as 'There is no disputing that Gus is in the east.' You weren't a Jupiter diver in civilian life, I'm sure of that."

"No, a rockjack. Construction gang superintendent, if you must know. We only use scoopships for messenger boats because they're fast. Their regular pilots are too good for that kind of job. Do better at captaining warcraft."

"How well I realize that," Ulstad sighed. "I wonder, though, why you don't send more stuff directly by maser."

Flowers clammed up.

Ulstad grinned. "All right, I'll tell you," he said. "First, our side has too good a chance of intercepting a beam; and evidently your Intelligence suspects we can break your cryptograms. A courier flits away from the ecliptic plane and probably makes a safe trip. Second, if we really can use your own ciphers, and you relied too much on radio, we could send misleading messages to your commanders." He shrugged. "Of course, the courier system ties up boats that might be put to better use elsewhere. But then, it ties up a lot of our fleet on patrol duty, so honors are even."

"Not quite," Flowers snapped. "Especially after the last battle."

"The engagement near Sam's, you mean? I take it you were there?"

"I sure was, chum."

"In what capacity?" drawled Ulstad.

Flowers crammed on a deceleration vector. "Never mind. It's enough that you took a licking."

"We'd at least like to know what happened to those of our ships which never reported back. Were all of them utterly destroyed?"

"I suppose so."

Ulstad leaned across the desk. "Even if you weren't told officially, you may have heard something." His smile was wistful. "I'm interested for private reasons. A nephew on the *Vega*."

"Sorry. I can't help you, though."

"We'll find out about that."

"Go ahead!"

"Very well, Lieutenant." Ulstad rose. "If you please?"

Flowers tensed himself. His entire being rebelled. But he stole a glance behind, and saw that the ensign would be only too glad to use force. Like, say, a pistol barrel against the prisoner's head.

Flowers got to his feet. "Look me up after the war," he invited. "I know some back alleys where the cops won't interfere."

"I might at that," said the ensign.

"Control yourself, young man," said Ulstad. He led the way into the lab. "If you will lie down on this couch. Lieutenant. . . ."

The anesthetic shot took rapid hold and Flowers spiraled into a darkness full of voices.

Afterward he lay with closed eyes, letting will and strength creep back. He must be recovering faster than was usual, because he heard Ulstad say, as if across a black gulf:

"Nothing to speak of. He's what he claims to be, a big dumb rockjack who ordinarily commands an engineer group. I suppose they dispatched him precisely because he doesn't have any worthwhile information. And I hope the poor devil doesn't go stir crazy in prison camp, with so few inner resources."

"What'll we do with him now, sir?"

"Oh, lock him in a spare cabin. How long will he be on your hands?"

"I checked that, sir. We'll make contact with the transport in five hours."

"He'll only need one meal from us, then. Inform the cook. Regular mess time is okay, three hours hence." Ulstad chuckled. "Maybe I do him an injustice, calling him an ignorant boor. His cussing under dope was sheer poetry!"

Save for a bunk, the cabin was bare. Tiny, comfortless, atremble with the energies of the ship, it surrounded Flowers like a robot womb. That was his first thought as again he struggled back to consciousness.

Then, through the racking stutter of a pulse run wild, he knew that hands lifted his head off the deck. He gasped for breath. Sweat drenched his zipskin, chill and stinking. Fear reflexes turned the universe into horror. Through blurred vision, he looked up at the bluejacket who squatted to cradle his head.

"Flip that intercom, Pete!" the North American was saying. "Get hold of the doc. Fast!"

Flowers tried to speak, but could only rattle past the soreness in his throat.

The other guard, invisible to him, reported: "The prisoner, sir. We heard him call out and then fall. He was unconscious when we opened the door. Came to in a couple of minutes, but he's cold to touch and got a heartbeat like to bust his ribs."

"Possibly cardiac," said the intercom. "Carry him to sickbay. I'll be there."

Flowers tried to relax in the arms of the young men and bring his too-rapid breathing under control. That wasn't easy. When they laid him on an examination bench, amidst goblin-eyed instruments, he must force his spine to unarch.

The medical officer was a chubby man who poked him with deft fingers while reeling off, "Chest pains? Shortness of breath? Ever had any seizures before?" He signaled an orderly to attach electrodes.

"No. No. I ache all over, but——"

"Cardiogram normal, aside from the tachycardia," the doctor read off the printouts. "Encephalogram . . . hm-m-m, hard to tell, not epileptiform, probably just extreme agitation. Neurogram shows low-level pain activity. Take a blood sample, Collins." He ran his palms more thoroughly over abdomen, chest, and throat. "My God," he muttered, "where did you get those tattoos?" His gaze sharpened. "Redness here, under the chin. Sore?"

"Uh-huh," whispered Flowers.

"What happened to you?"

"I dunno. Started feeling bad. Blacked out."

A chemical analyzer burped and extruded a strip of paper. The orderly ripped it off. "Blood pH quite low, sir," he read. "Everything else negative."

"Well—" the doctor rubbed his chin. "We can't do more except take an X-ray. A warcraft isn't equipped like a clinic." He nodded at Flowers. "Don't worry. You'll transfer to the other ship in half an hour or so, and I understand she's going almost directly to Vesta. The camp there has adequate facilities. Though you look a little better already."

"What . . . might this . . . 'a been?" Flowers managed to ask.

"My guess," said the doctor, "is an allergic reaction to something you ate. That can overstimulate the vagus nerve and produce these other symptoms. You asterites never see a good many terrestrial foods, and this navy prides itself on its menus. I'll find out what went into your dinner, including seasonings, and give you a list. Avoid those things, till the culprit has been identified, and you may have no more trouble."

Flowers lay back while they X-rayed him. That was negative, too. The doctor said he could stay where he was, under guard, till transfer time. He stared at the overhead and concentrated on getting well.

The *Chicago* slid into orbit and halted her Emetts. The doctor came back with his list. "You appear to be in much better shape," he said. "Got some color, and your breath and pulse are nearly normal. Think you can walk?"

"I'll try." Flowers sat up. Slowly he swung his legs off the bench, put feet to deck, and raised himself. He staggered. Leaning on the bench, head hung low, he mumbled, "I get dizzy."

"Okay, we'll take you on a stretcher," said one of his guards. "Captain's orders are to get you out fast so this ship can proceed to where she belongs."

Flowers would have enjoyed the ride had there not been such a tension gathering in him.

At the air lock where they went, two sidearmed men from the transport waited. "What the hell?" exclaimed the right-hand man.

A bearer related the situation. The newcomer made a spitting noise. "You're mighty tender with a rebel," he said.

"Oh, ease off, Joe," said his companion. "They're not bad fellows. Hell, after we've beaten some sense into their thick heads, I've half a mind to quit the service and come live in the Belt myself."

Joe spoke a bad word, but took his end of the stretcher. They passed through a jointube, into the boat. As Flowers had expected, this was merely a gig, with a single cabin where the pilot sat in the forward end. You don't bring full-size ships together if you can avoid it; too chancy an operation. The freighter lay several kilometers off; he glimpsed its bulky shape through a port, among the constellations.

His new guards put his stretcher down in the aisle between the seats, dogged the air lock, and retracted the jointube. The pilot tickled his controls and the boat slid smoothly away from the *Chicago*. The bluejackets returned to sit on either side of their prisoner.

"How you feel?" asked the man who had sympathized.

"Like a court-martialed kitten," Flowers whispered.

The man laughed. His companion still looked sour.

"I'd like to try sitting, though, if you'll help me," Flowers went on.

"Sure you ought to?"

"Well, I might be able to board your ship under my own power, but I'd better practice first."

"Okay. Gimme a hand, Joe."

Both guards bent close to the lying man. Flowers laid an arm across either pair of shoulders. They raised him.

His hands slid to the backs of their necks. His gorilla arms cracked the two skulls together.

They lurched, stunned, blood running from their scalps. Flowers snatched the nearest pistol from its holster and sprang into the aisle.

"Hands up or I shoot," he rapped. To the pilot: "Cut the drive. Now. Get out o' that chair."

Oaths ionized the atmosphere. He grinned. "I'm a desperate man," he said. "As soon kill you as look at you. Maybe rather. Git!"

The pilot got. Flowers approached him in the aisle. His hands were aloft, his belly exposed. Flowers' unoccupied fist rocketed forward to the solar plexus. As the pilot doubled, Flowers hooked him in the jaw. He fell.

The man called Joe reached for his gun. He was slow about it, and Flowers clopped him. With some regret, the asterite gave the same treatment to the other man, who had been nice to him. Before consciousness could return, he trussed all three with their belts and shirts and harnessed them in chairs.

The radio buzzer sounded hysterical. Flowers vaulted to the pilot board and clicked the receiver switch. "What's going on there?" bawled a voice.

"Listen," Flowers said. "This is the asterite. I've got your men prisoners. They're not hurt to speak of. But I'm bound home. You can stop me, sure—by destroying this boat. That'll cost you three North American lives, because I'm not issuing any spacesuits. It don't seem like much of a bargain. Better just say good riddance to me."

Words squawked. Flowers used the time to swing the gig around and apply a vector in the general direction of Pallas. Later he would calculate an exact path; right now he wanted nothing more intensely than distance between himself and the guns of the *Chicago*.

His victims awoke. He made them speak, to prove

to their buddies they were alive. Cruiser and
freighter dwindled beyond naked-eye vision. Stars
blazed everywhere about.

Ulstad's tones leaped over the kilometers, cool
and almost amused. "I'm not sure we ought to let
a man of your capabilities escape, Lieutenant. My
fault. I took you for a stupid laborer. I should have
remembered, stupid people don't survive in space."

Flowers gulped. "I'm no prize, Commander. But
you got three good men here. I'm sorry I had to be
rough with them, and I'll treat them as decent as I
can."

"How did you manage this caper?"

"Tell you after the war."

Ulstad actually laughed. "Very well," he said.
"Seeing that we have no alternative except to fire
on our own men, Captain Thomas has decided to
let you go. After all, we have your dispatch, which
is the important thing. I'm unmilitary to say this,
but . . . good luck."

"Same to you," Flowers husked.

He broke the beam and concentrated on driving
the boat.

The revolutionaries were so short of manpower
that quite a few women held high rank. Colonel
Adler of Intelligence was among them. In uniform,
her hair cut short, she didn't much suggest the
opera star who had once dazzled the capitals of
Earth. But her tunic couldn't flatten out every
curve, and Flowers was in some respects a very
suggestible man.

He leaned back in the swivel chair, flourished
his cigar, and tried to be modest. "Faking sickness
was easy," he said. "I counted time till I knew the
transfer boat 'ud be along pretty soon."

"How did you count?" she asked.

"Oh, I sang songs in my head. I'd timed that years ago. Often useful to know how long, say 'The Ballad of Eskimo Nell' takes—well, never mind that, ma'm. Anyhow, then I started hyperventilating. Do that a while and you get the doggonedest symptoms. When my body chemistry was way off kilter, I let out a yell, then pressed my carotid arteries till I passed out."

"That took courage," she murmured, "when fear is part of the syndrome."

"You said it, I didn't. Of course, I couldn't be sure I'd get away with anything. The doc could've spotted the cause. However, since they took me for an ignorant nank, he never thought I could be faking it. Naturally, I recovered my strength fast, and didn't let on. I kind of hoped I'd have a chance to do something, because they'd be off guard with a sick man. But, sure, I had luck with me."

Colonel Adler drummed fingers on her desk and glanced out the viewplate. Pallas Town bustled under a dark, starry sky. The geegee fields gave Earth weight and held atmosphere, but it was a thin atmosphere and space glittered through, cold and huge. She turned back to Flowers. "Why did you proceed here?" she asked. "Sam's was closer."

"Uh, well, I figured GHQ should know as soon as possible about those code-busting machines of the enemy's."

"GHQ already did, as your interrogator believed. In any event, the information could have been sent from Sam's, along with a duplicate of your original dispatch."

Flowers reddened. He had expected to be treated like a hero. "So I made a mistake. I'm no professional."

She smiled. "Perhaps you did not err after all, Lieutenant. But come, let's get the quizzing over with. Then I'll authorize some furlough time for you. You've earned it."

Flowers nearly swallowed his cigar. "Quiz? You mean narco?"

She nodded. "An examination in depth."

"Whatever *for?*"

"SOP in cases like this. If nothing else, we have to be sure the enemy hasn't begun on that dirty trick of implanting posthypnotic suggestions. I'll handle the job myself, and anything personal which might come out will never get past me."

"You? Huh? I mean . . . look, I'll go along with this if I've got to, but not with a lady!"

The colonel chuckled. "I'm older and I've seen more of the universe than you might think. You won't outrage any propriety of mine. Now come with me. That's an order."

When he woke, he found her regarding him most thoughtfully. Her cheeks were a bit flushed.

"Whuzzamattuh?" he mumbled.

"I made a discovery," she said. "I can be shocked."

Anger whipped him to full consciousness. He sat up and growled, "My private life's my own. Isn't that one of the ideas we're supposed to be fighting for? Now with your permission, ma'm, I'll get out of here."

"Please." She fluttered hands at him. Also eyelashes. "I didn't think I could be shocked any more. It was a delightful surprise. You mentioned some fascinating—well, Smelly, I mean to say, I get off at eighteen-hundred hours and I do have some civilian clothes and if you'd like to meet me somewhere. . . ."

*   *   *

Trade boomed after independence was won, and Pallas boomed loudest. Each time he visited the place—which was often, since his construction business required him to see people there—Flowers thought it had doubled in population and noisiness. But one little bar near the space docks remained unchanged. You could sit in a booth, under a stereo mural of Saturn, and have an honest beer and an uninterrupted talk.

"I see you changed tattoos," Ulstad remarked.

Flowers glanced at his left forearm, bare in an incandescent sports shirt, and grunted. "Yeah. That one. Very soon after I escaped from you, in fact. A dame I was going with for a while said she didn't like the design. I didn't either, so I had it removed. I, uh, this is a kind of sentimental thing to say, but I had reasons for substituting this eagle. Symbol of friendship with the mother country and all that sort of engine spew, huh?"

"Yes. I'm glad you feel that way." Ulstad took a swallow of Tuborg. "Glad I could finally get hold of you, too, and learn how you did get away from us. What a yarn!"

Flowers grinned. "I didn't know the whole story till after the war."

Ulstad pricked up his ears. "Go on."

"This is no secret any longer, or I wouldn't've been told yet. But the message I was carrying—you never did decipher it, did you?"

"No. We finally decided it was a blind, wasting much too much valuable computer time."

"Kee-rect. A pure random pattern. Quite a few of our couriers carried similar ones for a while. It was a safe bet that at least one man would get captured and so confuse you. I happened to be the man."

Ulstad frowned. "Seems like poor strategy. You couldn't spare that many ships for a single trick."

"Oh, no.'Course not. But you see, messages were being sent anyway."

"What? How in the name of——"

Flowers drained his beer and bellowed for another. While he waited, he produced a cigar. "That tattoo on my arm," he said. "I only knew I'd gotten blind drunk. Figured I must've ordered the damn thing put on and never remembered afterward. Actually, my booze had been mickeyed.

"The message was important. They did capture the *Vega* in the battle off Sam's, you know. And maybe by now you also know they locked onto her code books. Pallas had to be told what your ciphers were, but we couldn't risk a maser beam being intercepted."

"Certainly not." Ulstad grimaced. "It took several disasters before we realized what must have happened."

"That code was in my tattoo," Flowers said. "There're thousands of punctures in any such picture. For some of 'em you can use a needle with a special dye—standard color, nothing different except for a few iron atoms—to write anything you please. Put the arm under a scanner while I'm anesthetized and can't blab, and there you are."

The beer arrived and he drained half the tankard. "I really needn't have bothered escaping, I suppose," he mused. "Our high command would've gotten me included in the next prisoner exchange. Still, I did get the information to HQ faster, and saved myself a bad time."

Ulstad whistled. After a while, with a touch of malice, he said: "Remember I told you I had a nephew on the *Vega*? Not true. I was only trying to soften you up a bit."

Flowers started. Then he guffawed and raising his draught, he said, "You know, I could use a man like you in my business."

"Might be fun at that," said Ulstad. The tankards touched.

Interlude 3

"Ahem." Amspaugh clears his throat. "I suppose we should resume our business meeting. The majority opinion seems to be that it's both harmless and desirable for our schools to represent our ancestors as—ah—ordinary fallible human beings."

"Including a hefty share of crooks, toughs, and bums," McVeagh nods.

"No," Amspaugh says, "I do believe you lean too far backward, Colin. We can admit history has a seamy side without claiming it's the only side, or that the good part doesn't matter most. The Founding Fathers were honorable men, and statesmen; the Constitution of the Asteroid Republic is one of the noblest documents ever written."

"Why not?" McVeagh drawls. "It's mainly plagiarized from the original United States Constitution."

"And what's wrong with using the best model around?" Lindgren responds. "Besides, they adapted creatively. And the adaptation was to more than the physical, social, technological, or economic differences between Earth and the Belt. They drew lessons from history, and made sure the daughter Republic won't get crusted over with the kind of unfreedom that the mother country did."

"Don't worry," McVeagh says, "future generations will find new ways to bollix things up."

"I would not claim, nor wish to teach, that the Constitution is perfect." Orloff lifts a thin hand. "Please! Let me finish. Don't forget, I was not born in the American asteroids, I was not caught up in their revolution, I came afterward, from the Soviet colonies. I chose my nationality. But that does not mean I cannot offer loving criticism. No work of man is flawless. It seems to me, the extreme libertarianism of the Republic has tended to produce individuals who are too selfish, too materialistic, too little concerned for their society as a whole. Can we not do better here on *Astra*?"

"I don't imagine we have room aboard for unregulated capitalism," Lindgren says. "But I'd hate to see an outright socialism evolve. Not simply because it's stifling. I think it'd discourage the creativity this ship will need for long-range survival. Only consider what advances, how fast and dazzling, the asterites made once they were free. Invention, exploration, construction. . . . And it's got to be because they'd been liberated as individuals. The members of the Belt that remained under Earth governments didn't do nearly as well."

"In part," Missy answers dryly, "that was because we, the ungrateful and rebellious children, stopped sending very much of our wealth back to America. This in turn lured the ablest—and greediest—colonials elsewhere into joining us."

Conchita sounds impatient: "However that may be, you can't deny that our forefathers *were* able, and had won ample scope for their abilities. Those that became wealthy deserved to, because they'd produced that wealth by their personal efforts."

"We-e-e-ell," Missy murmurs, "I remember various real estate speculators, loan sharks, bucket shop operators, vice barons, and assorted con men who ended rich." Soberly: "I also remember damn good men who died broke, or who never got the chance to get rich because they died young."

"I spoke statistically, of course."

"Yes, I realize that. But a statistic can mislead you pretty badly if you don't know everything that's behind it. On the whole, true, the Republic saw a brilliant era. Nevertheless, I doubt if everything—I wonder exactly how much of anything—was due to cool economic calculation, any more than it was due to the altruism we agree was in short supply. I've seen, myself, how many things just happened, as a result of blind stumbling. Nobody was more astounded at the outcomes than the people who'd been most directly concerned."

"Like the development of the geegee?" asks hitherto silent Echevaray.

"I wanted more to emphasize that being a free entrepreneur does not automatically make you a prophetic genius or put you in control of events," Missy says. "For instance, do you know about the Odysseus affair? I chanced to get a first-hand account not long after. Can you stand to have me tell another story? In a way, this was the cause of our being starbound today. And yet at the same time . . ." In her extreme age, she keeps the sweet laughter of a young woman.

Ramble with a Gamblin' Man

Avis' youngest boy, Tommy, came headlong down the garden. Its paths wound between blossoming hedges. In his haste he sprang over them, aiming himself straight at Lake Circe. Those were substantial jumps, even though the geegee field made weight on the Odyssean surface equal to the mere three-quarter terrestrial that Earthside tourists enjoyed. But he was active at his age, which was less than one year. (That was a local year, of course. With orbital periods as variable as they were among the asteroids, colonists had no choice but to keep the old calendar. Not that Tommy's parents would have denied him in any case the ten birthdays and Christmases he had known.) "Mom!" he shouted. "The ship's coming!"

She was about to remind him that she detested any such corruption of the good old word "Mother." But he came so fast and happily among the flowers; his hair was flying in a light breeze; every day he looked more like his father. "What ship?" she asked when he panted to a halt before her. "We're beginning to get quite a few, after all, now the war's over."

"The, the, the Northa Merican ship. Gover'ment people. They jus' masered in. Dad told me to go find you. He wants you to help meet them. I fig-

ured you'd be here." Tommy straightened himself
with such an air of masculine responsibility that
she wanted to kneel and hug him.

But he'd never forgive her that—when Jack
Herbert, superintendent of the construction gang
and its great machines, stood burly in his coveralls and watched. Therefore Avis said gravely,
"Thank you. I'll come right away."

"What's this about, Mrs. Bell?" Herbert asked,
with a bare touch of truculence. Like most of his
men, he was a resident of the local group and thus
still a North American national. But such folk were
not unanimously pleased with a peace treaty that
had left the mother country in possession of the
leading Trojan asteroids.

"A commission," Avis explained. "That is, not
just another set of inspectors from the vice governor's
office——"

"Hector inspectors," Tommy chortled.

Avis shook her head at him. Hector was in fact
the seat of regional colonial government, but she
wished her son had not overheard the scurrilous
limerick her husband had composed on that basis.
"Not even from Vesta," she went on, referring to
the worldlet which was the capital of all remain-
ing North American territories in the Belt. "Washington. A special mission, I understand."

Herbert scowled and tugged his blond beard.
"What for?"

Avis let her glance stray from his. The weather
felt suddenly less warm and she noticed too clearly
how dark the sky was.

That duskiness always prevailed. Trapped by
geegee fields, the artificial atmosphere of a terraformed asteroid could be as dense at the bottom as
Earth's; but it could not extend nearly as high, nor

scatter light nearly as much. And then the sun was remote: in the case of a Trojan body, more than five times as distant, shrunken to a spark of brilliance which gave less than 4 percent the illumination Earth receives. The human eye is sufficiently adaptable that this did not seem murky. But heaven on Odysseus was a deep blue-black wherein the brighter stars were visible by day.

The scene about her felt as if that endless surrounding night had touched it. *I've been a coward*, she reproached herself. *I knew Don was worried, but he never lets on, so I told myself this will only be a standard official visit, and hid in the pleasure of landscaping.*

That joy was a high one, after the despair of the war years. Isolated, at their immense distance, from any but the rarest callers, the Trojan settlers had been concerned with little except survival. Donald Bell's sympathies inclined toward the Republic, though basically he was apolitical. He might have tried to run supplies, if not actually to fight. But there were no spaceships to bring him to the scene: only a few patched-together scooters and flitboats, in which a few reckless men hauled essentials from one to another of the half-dozen leading asteroids. Bell turned his parks and gardens into miniature farms, let his shops, theaters, restaurants, and half-built new facilities molder, and settled down to help keep as many folk fed as possible. (Well, he did maintain a distillery, which gave him brandy as a byproduct of his vineyards; but confound it, that had rescued the local sanity!)

Now that traffic was resuming, the waterworks again in business and expanding fast, fresh immigration as well as returned veterans coming in to ransack the natural wealth of the group, Dingdong

Enterprises had gone back to its original undertakings. Reconstruction and new growth went apace. Around Avis leaves rustled, flowerbeds stood bright against the green of lawns, fountains splashed, fragrance filled the air. Above a weeping willow she could see the hotel, a literal skyscraper, its rooftop dome high enough in this shallow atmosphere to provide a fantastic view for dancers. Across the small, glittering lake, where several canoes floated lazily past the zoo island Aeaea, sounded noises of building; the casino was nearing completion.

We worked so hard for this, Avis thought. *Now we could lose it.*

Realizing with a start that Herbert was waiting for an answer, she said, "Oh. Why should a special delegation come here? Well, we're making a good profit once again. Tax assessment or something——"

"Might be more than that, ma'm," the superintendent said. "If your husband keeps on buying into the water-works at the rate I hear he is, he could end up owning this whole planetoid, pretty near. The government mightn't like that. You know, Earthside they don't think any man ought to become a lot bigger than any other."

"Maybe," Avis said. *If only it's no worse! We don't need more money than we're earning. It'd be nice, certainly—and not just for Don and the kids and me; we could do so much, out here where so much needs doing. But that isn't vital to us, I suppose. Let them forbid us to make further investments in industry. We can stand that. If, though, they take away this thing we built together—*

"I'd better go," she went on with forced brightness. "We'll talk further about the Hall of Alkinous idea when I can get free, Jack. Meanwhile——"

"Sure, I'll find plenty of jobs for the boys." Herbert watched her stride off. She must be pushing fifty standard years, he thought, but antisenescence treatment had taken well on her; she remained petite, bounciness in her gait, hair flowing dark to her shoulders, maybe no stun-blast beauty in the face but sure okay to look at, especially when one of her frequent enthusiasms lit her up from within. . . .

"Where you going, Mr. Herbert? Can I come too?"

The superintendent looked down at his employer's son. School was out for "summer." He smiled. "Well, I guess we might go check on the 'dozer crew."

They walked along the shore. Wavelets chuckled and glittered on white sand.

"Mr. Herbert?"

"Yes?"

"Why is water so, uh, important?"

The man gave the boy a surprised glance. "You drink it. You wash in it. You get most of your oxygen from it when you're terraforming. You couldn't run any industry without it."

"I know," Tommy said. "And I know 'bout the container effect. You can't carry hydrogen gas by itself so well, under pressure. It either leaks out b'tween the atoms of the tank, or you need a lot of cry—cryogenic stuff to keep it liquid. But you got to have hydrogen for fusion power. So you bring the water where you want it, and crack the molecules, and use the oxygen for something else."

"Now that we're through reciting elementary science at each other," Herbert suggested, "suppose you tell me why water shouldn't be important."

Tommy flushed. "'Course it is! I mean the water here. The ice they mine, that Daddy keeps buying shares of. We're a far ways from anyplace else, and they can't use sunjammers here. Why don't they get the water from closer-in asteroids? Or maybe cook it right out of rocks?"

"I see." Herbert's respect for his small companion went up. The question was actually shrewd, revealing an intuitive grasp of economics. "You mean, you wonder how it can pay to dig ice out of Odysseus and ship the water all over the Belt. We are at the end of a long haul, in an orbit that's particularly hard for carriers to maneuver out of. Well, the answer is that it does pay. They haven't found many bodies like this one, with an ice core and rich lodes of the stuff. It's cheaper to work these deposits and meet extra shipping costs than it is to grub around on the average sunward asteroid or spend energy and use expensive equipment to extract water from minerals."

"Why not go to Jupiter? It's no farther from the sun than we are. My planetology teacher says it's got ice in its air and on the big moons."

"Uh-huh. However, the skydivers into Jupiter's atmosphere are after still more valuable materials. And as for the moons, they're in a deeper gravitational well than we are, and besides, they're too big to terraform, which means you'd have to buy fancy life support gear and pay premium wages. No, we're sitting pretty here." Again Herbert tugged his beard. "Too pretty, perhaps. We've attracted Washington's attention, and some men are greedy for other things than money." He shrugged. "Well, I can always emigrate."

On this small and highly irregular spheroid— maximum diameter 230 kilometers—no one bothered with private ground vehicles. A person might travel around it on a scooter, but normally he would use the autorail. There was a station near Lake Circe. Like the rest of the buildings in the Dingdong area, it was in vaguely classical style and surrounded by a garden. Like most architecture on most of the planetoids that had been made habitable, it was flimsy, with large doors and windows. Little protection was needed against the mild weather generated in thin gaseous cloaks far from the sun; no protection was needed against temperatures which, between greenhouse effect and waste heat from nuclear powerplants, were always balmy. In the unlikely event that a large meteroid struck or a spaceship crashed out of control, computer-linked radars would give ample warning to the endangered section.

A car drew into sight one minute after Avis arrived. She waved it to a halt. A signal ran back and forth along the rails; other cars elsewhere adjusted their speeds. She boarded the ovoid and sat down, not bothering to close its canopy, and punched *Space terminal* on the board. The car started, with a smooth acceleration that soon had wind whistling by the forward screen.

Avis leaned back and watched the recreational park give way to a residential district. Though neat, it was somewhat gaudy. The settlers in the leading Trojan cluster were quite as individualistic as those in the trailing group, which had gone to the Republic.

A few kilometers beyond, the car plunged into night. Avis paid scant attention at first, because lamps made artificial day for the industrial quarter through which she was passing. Colonists usually ignored the rapid rotations of their tiny worlds and stuck by a twenty-four-hour clock. But then the car reached a switchpoint and headed north across an as yet undeveloped territory. The land humped aloft in barren, pitted hills and grotesque crags. Mostly they were hidden by darkness. But without man's works in the way, each time she crossed a ridge Avis could see the horizon, black and topplingly near, and stars swinging out of it, up and over her. They blazed with a keenness she remembered from Earth's northern winters—how very long ago!

She made no attempt to pick out Hector, Achilles. Nestor, Agamemnon, or Ajax, the largest of Odysseus' cluster mates. Their oscillations seldom brought them close enough to be naked-eye objects. She did seek Jupiter and found it, but only because she knew where to look. The king planet was not the brightest gleam in this heaven; it was twice as far away as it ever got from Earth.

And yet, she recalled, with an awe that somehow never had faded in her . . . and yet that spark, together with the dwarfed sun, reached across to grip this orb on which she dwelt and lock it fast for eternity.

Well, maybe not. That'd be a long time. Over millions or billions of years, the slow slight perturbations of Saturn might cause a Trojan asteroid or two to wander away. Or maybe that actually was impossible. Lagrange had proved in the eighteenth century that this was a stable situation: a giant body like Sol, a lesser giant like Jupiter circling it, and a midget in that same orbit but leading or lagging by sixty degrees. The tug of another planet, as it reached its still enormous minimum distance, was too variable, too soon dwindling, to change the configuration much. The midget might start to sneak off, but then the outside influence would diminish again and the vectors of Sol and Jupiter would haul the truant back.

Six major asteroids leading, five trailing, together with assorted meteroids—cosmic débris drifting age by age into the Lagrangean trap—and, for a flicker in time, some bits of organic matter rooting about, re-creating the accidentally determined conditions of the remote globe that had brought them forth, dreaming about homes here and even, some of them, about those scornful stars. . . .

Avis shook herself out of her reverie. *I'm past the romantic phase of life. Am I not?*

Lights glowed ahead, Odysseus spaceport. A water tanker was in, looming huge on the ferrocrete, men and machines scurrying to pump her full. Avis hardly noticed. Her pulse beat in her ears.

The car stopped at the terminal building. She got out and hastened inside. Several men and women stood waiting: the mayor, his council, executives of various Odyssean companies, their wives. Donald Bell waved at Avis. "You're right on the mark, darlin'!" he boomed across the chamber. The screen above him declared that the official passenger transport *Walter Schirra* would make groundfall in three minutes.

She noticed the semiformal clothes on everybody else and remembered her own blouse and slacks. "I should have changed," she said.

"No, that's okay," her husband answered. "We may not want to look too prosperous. Besides, you're beautiful in anything." He bent close. His lips tickled her hair. "Or nothin'," he whispered.

She squeezed his hand and thought how lucky she was. *Oh, yes,* she recognized for an instant, *I was on the rebound, hurt, embittered, come to Flora in search of a new job, and I don't know which of us seduced the other, but I know how we quarrelled the first few years. His flamboyance, his recklessness, his almost compulsive gambling, his repeated failures to hold down steady work, agaist my . . . well, my unconfessed memories of someone else, which made me prim, overcautious, often shrill with him, much too often concerned with the children at his expense. . . .* The admission was unremorseful. Avis Page had long since become a stranger, as had that early Avis Bell. After Don had gradually accepted some domestication, and she some liberation . . .

Thought faded to nothing before the reality of him. He was big, dark, trim, usually smiling, always gracious, with a lingering trace of New Orleans accent to evoke girlhood days within her. In the elegance of black tunic and trousers, white lace, discreet gold arabesques, diamond rings, silver shoecaps—none of which he imagined might look "prosperous"—he was too handsome to be true.

"Pardon the interruption, Dave," he said, not breaking the light contact of his fingers with hers. "Please go on."

"Well, I really have little to tell," Mayor Pirelli answered. His tone was not glad. "My office has received nothing since that short-notice message." Bitterness tinged his quoting: " 'The President has dispatched a commission, now en route, for the purpose of investigating conditions in the Trojan colony and making recommendations as to desirable changes—' Not so much as their names. It's a flat-out insult."

"Suggests they've already made up their minds what to do about us," growled Pete Xenopoulos, who owned a fruit ranch, "and they don't give a curse how we feel."

"Ladies, gentlemen," Bell said. "Let's not borrow trouble. The interest rate is so high. Let's begin, at least, with speakin' softly, and listenin' more than we speak, and instead of arguin', just pointin' out how matters look to us. Now what occurs to me along that orbit is, we'll put them up in the hotel as planned, but we'll invite them to our homes, individually, and give them the grand tour individually. Can't hurt none, and it might win our side some friends."

"Hm-m . . . maybe," said Roth, proprietor of the community's largest machine shop. "We can try. But in that case, Don, Avis, you two better take charge of the leader. You put on a fancier spread than anybody else can, and . . . uh——"

"And he's likely to be the most obnoxious of the lot, and we're the most used to handlin' difficult customers, eh?" Bell stroked his mustache. "Yes, reckon so."

The speakers woke with announcement and the transport ship, which had crossed space in days but was awkward near soil, lumbered down out of the sky.

The Bell house stood atop Mount Ida, where the air was too thin to breathe. You took a liftshaft straight up through the rock and emerged in a sealed complex of rooms, pools, conservatories riotous with color. Most spectacular was surely the living room. Besides its spaciousness, its furnishings, its imported hardwood floor, its central hearth of copper where a genuine fire burned synthetic but realistic logs, it had a vitryl dome for the roof that began at waist height. Thus you could look from the peak in one direction to see the gaiety and frail beauty of Dingdong; in another direction for a glimpse of an ice mine, machines, buildings, unending energy; and elsewhere down a sheer cliff to a country still raw and dark and empty of life. When the sun happened to be away, as it was at the moment, every spot overhead was diademmed with stars, nebulae, Milky Way and sister galaxies.

The butler set coffee and liqueur on a table carved from a single great quartz crystal. The three diners took their places in armchairs around it, and he left them on cat feet. Music lilted forth, not loud, meant for a pleasing background to conversation—something by Haydn, Avis seemed to recall, though she lacked Donald Bell's ear and memory.

"Cigar?" The host offered a silver humidor.

"No, thank you," James Harker said. His voice was not really stiff, nor was his seated posture, but they gave that impression. "Do smoke yourselves if you wish."

"Thank you, I will. I hope you enjoyed your dinner?"

"Why . . . yes, of course. I'm sorry, Mrs. Bell. I should have expressed my pleasure earlier. Frankly, I never expected a gourmet meal in these regions. You're a superb cook."

Avis overcame her dislike of her guest sufficiently well to smile. "Actually," she said, "my cook is."

"You seem to have quite a large personal staff," Harker remarked.

Bell shrugged. "About a dozen. Place this size; and then we do a lot of entertainin'." He lounged back and streamed a blue cloud out between appreciative lips.

"Live servants are scarcely to be had anywhere

at home," Harker said. "Scarcely anywhere on Earth, I believe."

"In spite of mass unemployment?" Avis asked.

Harker frowned. He did not look like a stereotypical puritan. His garments, while modest in hue and cut, were of good material, and his middle-aged features were blobby and undistinguished till you noticed the big chin and the hard eyes. He had been polite, in a noncommittal fashion, when the Bells escorted him around. But it was not possible for the head of the Presidential Investigating Commission to hide altogether his disapproval of unabashed luxury.

"Americans traditionally consider that kind of work degrading," he said.

"Well, we've developed a different tradition in space," Bell drawled. "That was necessary, back in the days when people used their hands because they hadn't any machine to substitute, maybe no machine'd been designed for a particular job yet . . . except man himself, the all-purpose gadget. And then, well, look at it this way. The pioneers had to be self-reliant, or they died. But they also had to be mutually helpful, or they died. So they evolved, more or less unconsciously, the notion that anyone who did well was morally obliged to find jobs for the less fortunate; and that there was no disgrace in takin' those jobs, because every erg of work contributed to improvement. The disgrace would lie in freeloadin'."

"You have *no* unemployables?" Harker sounded sarcastic.

"Oh, some, sure," Bell said. "A few extremely handicapped—though in this day of prosthetics and regrowth, those're mostly mental cases. Otherwise our philosophy of public assistance is the same as our independent neighbors'. Give the deservin' person a leg up, no more. Like, say, a widow with young children to look after and no close relatives to help her. But cases like that are rare, most families bein' large and close-knit." He took a sip of Drambuie. "I don't imply we're saints, Mr. Harker. We're everything but. In the usual blind, blunderin' human style, we've developed institutions that serve our needs. Nothin' fancier'n that."

"If you will forgive my outspokenness," the man from Washington said, "I am not convinced they do serve your needs, at least not any longer. And they certainly are counterproductive for the country as a whole." From the way in which he raised his coffee cup to his mouth. Avis could see how tense he was becoming.

"M-m-m, yes, now the Social Justice party is back in power. . . ."

The dilute acid in Bell's voice did not escape Harker. "Sir," he replied, "—and madame, of course—you're both intelligent, well-informed people. You may have voted for the opposition, but you must know that the Essjays won by better expressing the popular will."

"Reaction to defeat," Avis said. "Let's be honest. In spite of every face-saving formula, the asterites beat the Americans."

"If you wish to put it that way," Harker said testily. "I'm inclined to credit their diplomats more than their naval men. Asians, Russians, even Europeans didn't mind at all if North America lost its best spatial possessions. They weren't hard to talk into putting on pressure, giving clandestine aid. . . . They'll be sorry when the example gets imitated. . . . But besides that, the game stopped being worth the candle. Too much that was too expensive was too badly overdue at home. And that's what Social Justice is all about. Rebuilding the country, first internally, afterward in its foreign relations; regaining our position as a first-class power."

A silence followed.

"More coffee?" Avis lifted the pot.

"Yes, thank you," Harker said. "It's good."

"Kona," Avis told him. "From one of our experimental plantations."

"You've been generous to me," Harker said. "I would almost feel guilty if—" He paused. "I would, if each of us didn't already bear a greater guilt: that we are glutted while others are poor."

"If they'd bred a little less eagerly, they wouldn't be so hard up today," Bell said. His tone stayed mild.

"Perhaps," Harker answered. "But we're confronted with a fact, not a might-have-been."

"I didn't think anybody in North America was starvin'."

"No, they aren't. However, when a person's grown accustomed to an ever-mounting standard of living, and suddenly it not only stops rising, it takes a sharp downturn—that's a hardship and a cause for grievance. You may have seen 3V replays of the marches and riots, but believe me, they're quite different from the real thing. Then we must also take account of more conventional political forces. The discontented command a majority of votes."

Bell puffed for a moment before asking almost lightly, "What do you aim to do?"

"The war was costly," Harker replied. "The loss of most of our asteroids, with their resources and tax revenues, is proving costlier still. We've got to

work together, mobilize what we have left, organize our efforts, in space as well as on Earth."

"No doubt. I was just wonderin' what you,
specifically, have in mind. Maybe we locals could
offer you an idea or two."

"That's one of the reasons for my commission."
Fervor bloomed in Harker. "You realize, my group
has a strictly fact-finding assignment. Our report
will be one element among many in reaching a
decision and writing new legislation. But we do
want to learn the wishes of you residents."

M-m-m . . . a million or so American asterites,
three hundred and fifty million Americans at
home. . . . I doubt if our wishes will butter many
parsnips. And I do think—considerin' the distances
involved—your recommendations will count mighty
heavily." Bell drew breath. "Now I'm aware you
haven't yet seen everything or interviewed everybody you'd like to on Odysseus, let alone the rest
of the cluster. Please don't think I'm askin' you to
commit yourself right off. On the other hand, y'all
must've studied a lot of material about us before
leavin'. And livin' in the middle of things, y'all
must have a lot better feelin' for what policy's
likely to be, than we can have at this far end of
yonder." Bell refilled his liqueur glass. "I'd appreciate gettin' some notion of what to expect."

"Yes. Quite." Harker stared at his own knees.
"Well, it's a hard thing to say, after you've been so
hospitable."

"I understand you don't make policy by yourself.
I'm only askin' for your prognosis."

"Well, then." Harker straightened and met his
host's glance squarely. *He has manhood*, Avis admitted to herself. Her hands tightened against each
other till the fingertips hurt. "I'm afraid you won't

like what you're about to hear. Let me begin by underlining that no one wants to ruin you. The President and Congress agree that reward should be proportionate to public service, within decent limits, of course."

And who decides what those limits are? Avis thought.

"You've proved, Mr. Bell, that you're potentially capable of rendering valuable service. It's simply a question of finding a socially useful place for your talents."

"Thanks for the compliment," Bell smiled.

Put more at ease, Harker continued: "In better times, you could carry on what you are doing. I don't deny your, ah, entertainment industry has brightened lives, though I must say, ah"—he pinched his lips into a line—"gambling and certain other things—but let that go for now. The point is, at this time of crisis . . ."

. . . when the home country is starting to run short of 3V sets, Avis thought, and air conditioners, and machinery to do the jobs that everybody on the public assistance rolls finds are too degrading . . .

". . . we can't afford frivolity, not to speak of vice. I make no accusations, Mr. Bell. But that's how your enterprise looks from across four or five astronomical units. And, frankly, in my personal opinion . . . well, for a fraction of the labor and resources used in your park, we could put taped entertainment—the same shows, the same number of choices that they enjoy on Earth—into every home in this cluster. Do you follow me?"

Avis smothered a curse and half rose to her feet. Bell waved her back, caught her eye and shook his head slightly. Turning to Harker he said, unruffled, "In other words, you feel Dingdong Enterprises ought to be closed down. You'll recommend that in your report, and the recommendation is sure to be taken."

"You'd not be required to liquidate overnight," Harker said, "except perhaps for, ah, those certain operations I mentioned. You'd be given time to dispose of your holdings. I suggest you use the proceeds to invest further in the waterworks. Of course, it appears likely that Congress will put a legal ceiling on personal incomes and fortunes. But for you, enough comes under 'business expenses' that you'd remain comfortable."

"No doubt." Bell stroked his mustache. "You'd better talk to some plain, everyday workin' people, though. The Trojans are kind of harsh—which means you can barely survive—except for here. I'd say recreation, pressure-ventin', 'vice and frivolity' if you like, I'd say those're just about necessities of life hereabouts."

"I spoke of wholesome taped entertainment."

"I wonder. If a man, or a woman, has the blood to come to these parts and buck for a better future, will 'wholesome taped entertainment,' from an Earth that's hardly relevant any more, will that fill leisure time? I can foresee a lot of trouble."

"I don't set policy," Harker repeated.

Avis could hold herself back no longer. "At least you can listen!" she exclaimed. "You can go home and tell them the truth. What about our ecological research, for instance, if we must show some humorless public service? Is it worth nothing?"

"Pardon me?" Harker asked.

Avis was breathing too hard to speak further, in this moment when she saw her universe crumbling. *What will become of Don? He can't sit in an office playing with stupid numbers, no matter what sums of money they stand for. He's a warhorse, not a plowhorse. What saved our marriage—what saved him, which is more—was that we did start making real and firm-foundationed the glamour, the merriment, the make-believe he's always needed around him. O God Who plays dice with the world, help us!*

Her husband remained as cool as if he sat in a table stakes game with a busted flush: "A sideline, but interestin'. I meant to show it to you tomorrow. Some while back, a couple of scientists talked me into it, and I'm glad they did. Idea is, we theorize about self-maintainin' ecologies like Earth's; but Earth is a mighty big piece of real estate. We can recycle air and so forth, in spaceships, in dome bases; we can grow food usin' biological wastes for nutrients; but all material doesn't get back into circulation. Trace products like acetone pile up, slow but steady. And things like, oh, fingernail clippin's, skin sheddin's, woody parts of plants—do you track me? Earth's an entire planet. It can absorb those wastes and take its time, maybe centuries, about breakin' them down. A ship can't. Nor can a terraformed asteroid thus far. The cleanup job has to be completed artificially."

"So?"

"So, long's I'm buildin' these gardens and plantations and such, the scientists might as well experiment. What is the minimum size for a wholly balanced biosystem? Could be useful to Earth itself, like in ocean bottom colonies, if we find an answer."

Harker shook his head. "I'm sorry, but I can tell you at once, Mr. Bell, that argument won't work. If the problem in question becomes urgent, the government can do the R and D on it. We need our spatial resources *now*. And the ice of Odysseus will be a huge help in developing them. We must maximize production."

"Do you mean," Avis whispered, "everything else has to go? Every blade of grass, every flower, every forest we'd planned, where you might stroll off to be alone in greenness—we're not to have anything except ugly industrial buildings?"

"You overstate."

"I don't. I come from Earth myself, and I've been back on visits. You've gone far toward that kind of hell. Must you drag us along with you?"

"Our guest—" Bell tried to interrupt.

She couldn't help herself, it burst from her: "Why didn't the asterites take us into their Republic?"

"Both sides settled for what they could get," Bell reminded her.

"Just Odysseus. They could have traded something else, some lump with nothing but minerals, for Odysseus. All parties would have been happier."

"Excuse my wife," Bell said to Harker. "She's a tad overwrought."

Surprisingly, he smiled. "I understand. No apologies needed. As a matter of fact, I happen to know that that very proposal was made at the peace conference."

"What?" The Bells spoke together.

"Briefly and informally," Harker said. "I was there in a secretarial capacity. It never got to the floor because—actually, a Republican delegate pointed it out—serious difficulties would have been caused."

Avis settled back with her despair. Bell, anxious to clear the atmosphere by a discussion of something impersonal, said, "Do go on. I'm intrigued. As I remember the law of sovereignty that the Convention of Vesta established, long before the

war . . . uh . . . possession of a body depends on the
nationality of whoever first lands and files a claim
with Space Control Central, unless other arrangements are made like purchase."

"True," Harker said. "But how is an asteroid,
one among countless thousands, to be identified
except by its orbit? Which the law does. And the
members of a Trojan group have essentially the
same orbit. Or so it was agreed, for legal purposes,
in order to avoid pettifogging debate. Either side
wanted a positive end to hostilities more than it
wanted an enclave in the other fellow's space. So
everything in a particular Trojan position is considered part of a single body." Again he made his
stiff smile. "I hope we North Americans can be
that sensible in our family squabbles."

Like hell we can! Avis wanted to shout. *Not when
one branch of the family insists on taking everything!*

A few days afterward, when the commission had
proceeded elsewhere, another meeting took place
in the house on Mount Ida. Being larger, it was
held in a gold-paneled conference room; being composed of friends, it drank beer in huge quantities;
being likewise made up of the magnates, those
whose work and risk had made Odysseus come
alive, it growled its business forth in angry words.
Occasionally an oath broke loose—but a mild one,
for a few women were present and asteroid colonists preserved the archaic concept "lady."

Also, Avis thought, seated by her husband, *they
keep the outmoded notion of democracy. Oh, they
use that word back in the States, use it till the last
meaning has been rubbed off; but in the end, collectivism, under whatever name, is elitist. Somebody
makes a career of knowing what is good for you*

better than you're supposed to know it yourself. In his heart, and ever oftener in his behavior, how can he respect you?

Whereas Jack Herbert sat at the long table as proudly as Reuben Roth or David Pirelli. They might have more money than he did, Pirelli might be mayor as well as principal stockholder in the H₂Odysseus Corporation, but they couldn't do without the kind of skills he owned, and each man concerned knew that. Herbert was no more a spokesman for "labor" than engineer Richard Buytenstuyl for "the technologists" or farmer Pete Xenopoulos for "agriculture." Bell had asked them to sound out their colleagues, but his basic reason for inviting them here was that he thought highly of their judgment.

"This conference has no official standing, of course," Pirelli declared. "In fact, I believe we'd be wise to keep our proceedings confidential and merely say we've had a party."

"A wake, rather," Herbert retorted.

"Perhaps not." Pirelli turned to Bell. "Don, will you take over?" He sat down.

Bell rose. "The idea," he said, "is to compare notes on our various encounters with the Feds, and what we reckon the outcome of this thing is likely to be, and how people feel about it, and what we might do. I got kind of sociable with the chief, James Harker—don't look shocked, Pete. He's not an evil man, only a man doin' his duty as he sees it, and maybe he's right from the standpoint of the mother country. Problem is, obviously, our mother country is this asteroid, not a continent which some of us have never seen.

"Anyhow, he warned me repeatedly that a shakeup here is unavoidable. The new government has to make a good showin' fast, and it'll help to exploit Odysseus to the limit. They need our water to expedite their projects elsewhere in space—minin', mostly, no development, no conservation, just grub out and get out. What water they can't use themselves they'll sell for foreign exchange. Plain to see, our little world will revert to rock. Only the abundance of water has made it possible to create and keep the lushness we've got.

"I'm not sayin' this is necessarily bad. We're North Americans too, with citizenship obligations. My pet business will have to go, and at a loss, but that won't break me. The waterworks will boom for years. Most Odysseans can expect fat pay or profit.

"Harker urged me, and through me all of us, to start plannin' the changeover right away and carry it out voluntarily. It'll take about a year to pass legislation and set up administrative machinery. If we fought the case clear to the Supreme Court, and dragged our feet after we lost, we might stall matters for another five years or so. But in the end we'd be forced to go along—by condemnation proceedin's if need be—and we'd be called unpatriotic reactionaries who'd rate no sympathy or concessions, and many would have to sell out for a dime on the dollar. Contrariwise, if we cooperate, if we take the initiative, we can gain. For instance, if I don't have to hurry, I might get a fair price in the Republic for the stock in trade of Dingdong. I could sell my land to the waterworks and buy shares. I'm sure each of you can see applications to his particular case."

Beside him, Avis cried, "No! You can't! Or is a man really able to rape himself?"

"Darlin', please," Bell whispered. Jack Herbert blushed.

"Well, actually, I wouldn't," Bell informed them. "I'd sell, yes, but then I'd move over to the Republic. I may be kind of old to start fresh, but I'm not so old I have to sit and take whatever they choose to shovel onto me. However, that's strictly personal. I've said my say. Let's hear from somebody else." He resumed his chair.

Talk rumbled and spat for more than an hour. The indignation was unanimous. Pirelli, who stood to profit most, stated: "If I want to become filthy rich, and I do, I'll diversify. There're plenty of airless rocks to find metals on. Odysseus is my home. Be damned if I'll turn it first into an industrial slum, last into a dry-sucked corpse."

Herbert: "You should've heard us, a hundred of us, yellin' ourselves hoarse at that Earthlubber who spoke to us in Agate Hall. He blatted about jobs, paychecks . . . and when we asked what we'd spend the paychecks on, he blatted about consumer goods. Judas on a jet, doesn't he *know* what it's like in space? This is a pretty little world, we tried to tell him; but has he been anywhere else in the group where they haven't yet got the money to terraform? Can he imagine never being anywhere but in a ship, a suit, a dome, always, death just a centimeter outside, darkness, naked stone—? Well, he quacked about gambling and other vices, and somebody asked him what a fellow come in from months in the black is supposed to do, and when he said, 'Healthful sports and clean entertainment' we booed him off the platform." Swallowing: "Sorry. I got carried away. But you can't leave, Mr. Bell, you and your fun and greenery and, and—if you go, I'm going too, and I know a lot of boys who'll come along."

"I may be prejudiced," Bell said, "but I agree, this action could kill the aurovarian goose. It's not as if we were in the Belt proper, with plenty of good places in easy reach. Without Dingdong or somethin' like it, maybe no labor can be gotten in the American Trojans except at prohibitive wages." He sighed. "What can we do, though?"

"Tell them," Xenopoulos urged. "Send men to Washington. Organize a lobby."

"Not that simple, I'm afraid." Bell started a cigarette and signaled his butler for more beer. "People don't believe facts, they believe what they want to believe, till the facts finally lose patience and club them with some catastrophe. I don't have my finger on the pulse of the States, but I've been back there from time to time, I have friends there, we correspond, I read a lot. The tide of puritanical collectivism is runnin' stronger each year. If we don't go along, we'll be unpatriotic wastrels who ought to be punished."

"Unpatriotic, hell!" Buytenstuyl exploded. "I did my hitch in the war, but a country that won't give me any rights isn't my country any longer."

"Essentially," said Roth in his scholarly manner, "deterritorialized technicians and politicians, managing a society of mobile, interchangeable, practically indistinguishable human units, cannot comprehend that when a man has a real home, that's where his real loyalty lies."

"What hope have we got?" Xenopoulos pleaded.

"I'll tell you what." Buytenstuyl leaned across the table edge. "They talk about democracy till I'm sick of the word. Okay, let's give them democracy. Let's hold a plebiscite. I'll lay you ten to one, at least three-quarters of the Odysseans will want to join the Republic, once they learn what's planned for them in Washington."

Pirelli took the negative. "No use, Dick. I'd guess the percentage higher, but a hundred percent would be too little." He raised a hand. "Don't say it. Secession would mean useless bloodshed. A single naval unit could end it. The Republic would not help. Odysseus is valuable, yes, but the treaty makes it American and it isn't valuable enough for anyone to go to war about."

Avis said, half in tears: "Haven't you ever wished we, the ordinary people, who only want to cultivate our gardens in peace ... haven't you ever w-w-wished we could steal away, *with* our gardens, all of us, one night, and hide where the politicians and generals and officials and crowds and mobs couldn't find us? Then what would they do, with nobody else's lives to run?"

"You'd never escape the need for government, defense, civil service, everything you hoped to leave behind," Pirelli said gently. "That's how humans are."

Bell clasped his wife's hand. "She has got a point, however," he declared. "I used to gamble every spare minute, and I'd still hate to swear off entirely. But when a game got too much for me— not a bad streak of luck, I hope I've more sportin' instinct than that, but when the stakes got absurdly high or I suspected cheatin'—I'd get out and find me another game, takin' my money with me. Our trouble today is we could leave individually, but we've got so big an investment in Odysseus, emotional more than financial, it's hard to see how we could——"

And the cigarette dropped from his fingers, and

he stared into a vision for a minute that became very silent in the room, until he breathed, *"Or could we?"*

Hundreds of persons cannot conspire together. Statistical variation guarantees that somebody out of such a number will be a fink or a blabbermouth. In the time that followed, Avis was haunted at first by the dread that one among the score or so whom Bell and his associates sounded out would betray them. It grew ever harder to continue in everyday life. After a while she was swallowing more tranquilizers than she dared count.

Bell remained insouciant as befitted a gambling man. "We needn't fret about bein' discovered," he assured her. "There's hardly anything to discover. That's the whole idea."

"Our group has had secret conversations, not only with Americans but with agents of the Republic—a foreign power," she said.

"Well, privacy's not illegal yet."

She clenched her fists. "I've checked the law, Don. Conspiracy is a felony, even if it's only conspiracy to commit a misdemeanor. And you—no, we—let's be honest, we're planning treason."

"Are we? A nice point." Bell chuckled. "I've discussed it with a high-powered lawyer in our cabal. He thinks we may not have anything whatsoever unlawful in mind. Treason? We're not about to levy war on the United States of North America, and it bein' at peace with the Republic, we won't be givin' aid and comfort to an enemy. Theft? No one's property is to be taken away from him. Recollectin' that the Convention of Vesta, as a treaty, is part of the supreme law of the land, you could make a pretty good case for each of our

actions bein' entirely legal." He patted her shoulder.
"Not that I expect the affair'll go to criminal court.
An international tribunal, sure—and won't that be
a hooraw's nest!"

"But if they find out our intentions——"

Bell shrugged. "Be hard to prove we had any
intentions other than what we've announced. If
somebody does notice the possibilities in our project,
and takes action, well, then we'll've lost our bet."

Lost everything, Avis thought.

She drew herself erect. *My job*, she told herself,
is to be my man's partner, not his burden. She smiled,
reached up and stroked his cheek. "Sure, sweet-
heart," she told him. "I'm simply a worrywart.
What would you like for dinner?"

Afterward she took another tranquilizer.

But ordinariness wears down more than youth
and daydreams; it also erodes fear. You can't endlessly be on edge when you must see to your
children, run your household, budget, entertain,
prepare lists of off-planet needs, wrestle with
accounts, stand watches on civic betterment com-
mittees and as hostess of your bridge club, fight a
mutant weed that is playing Attila in the flowerbeds,
worry about your older daughter's slightly wild
boy friend, integrate color schemes, watch shows,
read, eat, drink, make love, sleep . . . and nothing
else happens.

The magnates of Odysseus agreed on the plan
and signed the petition. The vice governor on Hector okayed it and sent it on to Earth with his
positive recommendation. (He was among those
who knew the real objective. He accepted it largely
because he was worried about the fate of his other
asteroids if their recreations were abolished.) After
commissions had sat and assorted paperwork had

been done, Washington approved the proposal.
James Harker wrote an open letter to the Odysseans,
saying how pleased he was by their constructive
attitude.

As a matter of fact, the average Odyssean com-
plained furiously, and a certain amount of emigra-
tion took place. But you couldn't let him into the
secret.

You could merely announce:

"It is vital for us to develop our ice mines to
their full potential. The government has plans that
call for vast amounts of water. Our duty is to
cooperate with whatever the government has decided is best. Now one major factor holding back
exploitation of our mines has been our Trojan
position. Because it is dynamically stable, space-
ships require extra power to leave this region. The
new sunjammer cargo vessels can't do it; and they,
fuelless, are the coming thing in transport of nonperishable goods. The imaginative answer to our
dilemma is to move Odysseus itself.

"True, a considerable amount of native hydrogen must be consumed in getting the fusion energy
for this large a project. But cost analysis shows
that, in the long run, the saving in freight charges
will more than compensate; and meanwhile we
will have an eager market for the oxygen and other
byproducts.

"Yes, the planned orbit will cause Odysseus to
leave the cluster. But that won't happen soon. This
much mass cannot be accelerated fast. Calculation
shows that more than a year, terrestrial, will be
required simply to maneuver out of the Trojan
area. After that, further maneuvers will gradually
ease the asteroid back into the same orbit as Jupiter,

but leading by about seventy instead of sixty degrees. This will not be too far from its ancient companions for easy visiting in powered spacecraft. Nor will the new orbit be grossly unstable. Thousands of years will be required for perturbation to deform it significantly.

"We will have gained the capability of using free solar energy to move our water to our markets. Society will have gained the part of that water which would otherwise have gone to fuel tankers.

"In view of this far-sighted cooperation with the government, and of the fact that we shall have to engage many outside workers, the authorities have agreed that the recreational complex may continue operations for the years it will take to complete the project."

That reconciled a number of Trojanites, at least temporarily.

And the ordinariness went on. Nothing happened in a hurry. Besides the usual human reasons for this, there was the size of the undertaking. It was common practice to put a geegee engine on a meteoroid and ride it off to where facilities existed for getting at its ores. But Odysseus was bigger by several orders of magnitude, so big that man's puny terraforming would never even circulate enough heat through that mass to thaw the interior ice. The drive system must be designed and tested virtually from a cold start. That alone took a year. The time would have been longer except for modern computers and scale-up methods. But in the course of it Avis decided that anyone who could put a finger on the real objective would have done so by then.

Slowly she stopped being frightened. A growing

influx of tourists, eager to see the spectacular construction going on, helped by keeping her busy in Dingdong. She herself was fascinated by watching the drive units rise, and thought them beautiful when finished.

By coincidence, their activation took place on the exact fourth anniversary (terrestrial) of that furious meeting in her home. The persons who had been there were, on this day, among the dignitaries who crowded a flag-draped grandstand. They looked as excited and happy as anyone. Avis felt the same upsurge, squeezed her husband's hand and waited impatiently for the speeches and ceremonies to end. She wanted the governor to pull the master switch.

Finally he did.

Staring across the parade ground, Avis saw its grassland drop sharply away till it met the plum-dark sky. On her left rose a grove of trees—she had helped plant them once—whose leaves rustled in a slight cool breeze and caught the tiny sun in shivers of light and shadow. On her right a jagged jaw of primeval rock thrust over the horizon. She gazed straight ahead. The buildings, the control tower, the pumping stations and storage tanks, were not hideous like those ramshackle works which were all that the mines required; these had the clean lines of an aircraft or scoopship, where every contour was necessary. By themselves, they might have looked smug in their sleekness. But they culminated in what they surrounded, the breathtaking upward leap of a giant Emett, whose drive cone was invisible to her because its supporting tower soared above the air.

A rumble awoke, soft but bone-deep. Outpouring forces, which could not be altogether shielded from atmosphere, laid hold upon it and started a gentle cyclonic motion. Humans perceived this only as a ripple and whisper through leaves, an occasional swirl of dust devils, a wind in their hair and on their faces which seemed to chant, *Outward bound!*

The cheer they raised, though lusty, was dwarfed by that quiet, resistless music of power. Well it might be. Deep-buried fusion generators were turning almost a kilogram of matter into energy every second. This did not require the breakdown of a ton of water in the same time—proton-metal reactions were used, less efficient but more sparing of the asteroid's prime resource—but the fuelling machinery alone was among the most ambitious enterprises men had carried out thus far in history. And nevertheless Odysseus, little Odysseus, was so massive that no instrument would have registered any change in its path across the stars.

Not yet. But the thrust of gyrogravitic force would go on, and on, and on. Cunningly blended with the tug of sun and planets, in an Earth year it would have pushed the asteroid free of the Trojan well. Thereafter maneuvering would be easier. It would still take some years to reach the target orbit—but the job would be done, and men would have done it.

Suddenly Avis thought: *No matter if our private scheme doesn't assay out. Something bigger than us was born today.*

Before long, the sounds and drafts faded. Rotation had caused the drive unit to point too far off the desired line. It shut down automatically. Another one, elsewhere on the equator, took up the work.

The spectators began to disperse. Avis drew Donald Bell aside. They walked off, still hand in hand, feeling young again, until they stood in the grove. Cool shadowy greenness, smelling and whispering of life, hid them.

"Why, you're cryin'," he said and drew her close to him. "Is anything wrong?"

"No. Except, except—" She buried her face against his breast. A part of her noticed afresh, with sensuous delight, how thick and rubbery those muscles remained. "I'm so happy."

"Me, too." He held her with one arm, ruffled her hair with the other hand. "Looks like we're really goin' to pull it off."

"M-maybe. I hope we will. For you, darling. But don't you see—it came to me in a flash—today we launched the first starship."

"Hm?" He thought for a while. "Y-y-yes, reckon you're right," he said, largely to himself. "We know, now, Odysseus is bigger'n needful for a balanced ecology. And, of course, a giant ship wouldn't have near this much mass; it'd mostly be hollow. If we can move a good-sized asteroid, livin' on it meanwhile, traffic movin' in and out as usual, we can do a lot better with a ship. . . ." The sun was sinking. More stars burned forth each minute. He glanced past the leaves, toward heaven. "Our grandchildren may get to go."

"And you first thought of it, Don."

"Me?" His laughter vibrated through her. "Sorry. You know damn well I'd no such exalted purpose in mind. My real project isn't finished yet."

It was, when Odysseus had definitely left the Trojan territory. One prearranged day, a ship from the Asteroid Republic landed. Others took orbit, and they were warcraft. Meanwhile a representative on Earth filed claim.

Diplomats were standing by in all countries. Notes had been prepared for them to deliver, speeches for them to make, logrolling bargains for them to propose. A stunned North America hesitated and was lost. Had it seriously threatened war, the asterites would have withdrawn. Instead, they trumpeted that they would defend themselves against "aggression" but were willing to have the case judged by the World Court.

There they maintained, entirely truthfully, (a) that sovereignty over an asteroid was determined by first landing and claim; (b) that asteroids were legally defined by their orbital elements; (c) that members of a Trojan group were lumped together for purposes of this definition; (d) that Odysseus no longer had a Trojan orbit; (e) that no North American had staked a fresh claim. Lest this seem casuistry (though that word does not necessarily mean dishonest reasoning), the asterite spokesmen pointed to the result of a neutral-supervised plebiscite. It showed an overwhelming majority of Odysseans in favor of joining the Republic.

The wrangling, and subsequent bargaining, lasted three years. Meanwhile the Republic was in possession. Social changes took place. They were not readily reversible. In off stage conversations, that were more amicable than public ones, asterite negotiators suggested that their American counterparts reflect on the history of regions "temporarily" occupied in the past—say, by Communists or Israelis in the twentieth century, or for that matter by British or Americans in the nineteenth. Would it not be better all around to accept a *fait accompli* and, perhaps, certain advantageous trade agreements?

In the end, the asterites won their point. Naturally,

their free-and-easy government was delighted to let Dingdong Enterprises continue its merry way.

A stately banquet on Odysseus followed the signing of the treaty. After the food, the toasts, the interminable speeches, various participants repaired to the house on Mount Ida for a real celebration. At one point the President of the Republic drew Donald Bell aside. "Would you tell me something?" he requested.

"Maybe." Bell's gaze above the rim of his champagne goblet was friendly but alert.

"I'm newly elected, you know. Whole new government. How could you, planning over a decade, how could you be sure we'd follow through on your secret agreement with our predecessors?"

"The probabilities favored it, sir. The character of asterites makes it likely that any bunch of them, regardless of their faction, will be quick and bold about seizin' an advantage—which sovereignty over Odysseus definitely is." Bell grinned. "There were risks, sure, but my friends and I were playin' the odds. In the old country they discourage greed, so the bet was fairly good that they wouldn't be as alert to the chance of a double play as people are out here. I wouldn't have tried any such stunt on the Republic."

"I should hope not!" The other man frowned. "Still . . . I can't say I really like that philosophy. I mean, well, surely man has more important drives than . . . than cupidity, damn it!"

"I wouldn't argue about that myself, sir, one way or the other. Now if you'll excuse me . . ." Bell disengaged from the President and made his way through the guests. The orchestra was striking up a dance tune, and he wanted to find Avis.

Interlude 4

"Well well" says Lindgren. "I always suspected collusion between our government and the top Odysseans, but this is the first I've heard that anybody ever admitted it."

"Why shouldn't they have?" I wonder. "At least, after they were safely citizens of the Republic."

"Might make it a touch difficult for them to visit North American territories, or even do business at long range," McVeagh points out.

"Besides," Dworczyk adds, "regimes never admit to rascality. A revolutionary government might, perhaps, accuse the one it overthrew of terrible things. But one which has legitimately succeeded, as by election, can't do the same. If it did, it'd either have to confess it was enjoying the fruits of misconduct, or else give up those fruits."

"Not that I know of any revolutionaries who voluntarily disgorged anything," McVeagh responds. "In fact, they're apt to grab fresh chunks of other people's property."

"Would you say that of the Asteroid Republic?" Conchita disputes.

"Why, certainly, at least in its young and bumptious days. As witness the case of Odysseus."

Conchita has no reply except a slightly indignant sniff. Echevaray speaks aside to Missy. "Will you permit me to inquire who has told you this story?"

"Oh, Avis Bell," she answers. At his look of surprise, she laughs. "We met again soon afterward, when the Sword expanded its operations to her world. It didn't take our two families long to become the best of friends." For a moment she goes away from us, elsewhere into time. Because I have keen ears, I hear her whisper: "She was a dear . . . like our men, Avis . . ." and wish I hadn't.

It is a relief when Amspaugh clears his throat and says, "We'd better get back once more to business. I don't think we should put your account into our official histories, Missy."

She returns. "No, no."

"Why not?" McVeagh gibes. "Afraid it'd corrupt the morals of the young?"

"Yes, but not in the way you're imagining, Colin," Lindgren tells him. "It's hearsay. No documentation. We've got to uphold standards of scholarship, if only because it's a foundation stone of science and technology."

I venture to interject, "A foundation stone with standards—banners—flying?" The chuckles tickle me.

"We seem to be converging on some areas of agreement," Orloff says. "No hypocrisy in our textbooks; only the plain truth, insofar as we can ascertain and describe it. We are still wondering how much of the whole truth should be included."

"Excuse me," Conchita breaks in. "I don't hold with pious frauds, of course. However, the truth is more than covetousness and bungling and the law of least effort. It's also hopes, dreams, aspirations, adventures." She waves her hand in an arc that encompasses the constellations toward which we drive. Her eyes match the starshine. "It's us, here, now, alive—eventually, it's the human race—headed into the universe!"

"If any of us denied that," Orloff replies calmly, "he would not have signed on. But it isn't what I am talking about. I am talking about the essential preliminaries to a new stage of evolution, and the requirement of recognizing what they were and how they continue to affect later events. Man is not less man because he is descended from simians, ultimately from some bit of pre-Cambrian slime. But he cannot understand himself unless he acknowledges that ancestry. Nor can he use the laws of nature until he has discovered them and admits that he too is bound by them."

"What has that to do with the subject?" asks Conchita.

"Why, this, my dear young lady. The laws of historical development are also natural laws. No one seriously considered space travel until the nineteenth century, when the possibility became evident. And nothing could actually be done before the essential technology and wealth existed. When they did, the will to use the technology and spend the wealth to reach the planets appeared. But the possibility had to come first. I think we should make it clear in the children's minds that society creates, as well as realizes, its ambitions step by patient step."

"I can't quite agree," Amspaugh declares. "Granted, the Foundation—in effect, the Republic—couldn't commence on a project as vast as this starship before it was able to. That's a tautology. But what made it able to? What improved the technology and expanded the wealth? Where did the work, the research, the development come from? No visionaries did it, nor any vague, apotheosized society. It was the result of individual persons, usually quite unremarkable persons who faced the stark necessities of their daily lives and made those lives fit to live. In the process of that, they couldn't help making the Republic great."

Lindgren stirs in his seat. "Uh, friends," he says, "it seems to me you're all unable to see the trees for the forest. Conchita thinks civilizations get from here to there because a few bold, inspired leaders have exalted goals. Ivan, I suppose due to his Russian background, Ivan thinks the goals will occur to us more or less automatically as we build up our capabilities. And our revered president"—he nods in jesting wise at Amspaugh—"no doubt because of his capitalistic background, thinks the capabilities and the goals alike are the result of letting individuals fearlessly work out their private destinies. You might call it the market theory of progress."

"Well, what's your view, then?" McVeagh demands.

Lindgren shakes his head. "I don't have a theoretical turn of mind. I'm just an old rockjack who went into business. Maybe I'm only reading my limited life's experience into what I've studied of history. But it seems to me that things simply happen. I can't find any general rules. That goes for you too, Colin. Damn it, there've been important events, there've been whole periods, when ideals counted for more than greed or fear; and the idealists weren't always misguided."

He gusts out a breath. "As for the great developmental era in space," he continues, "I saw no romance in it at the time—excitement aplenty, sure, but no bright romance—and neither do I see anything automatic, looking back, nor any master plans. We were a wildly diverse lot of people, going in a lot of separate directions, mostly unforeseen ones. If we'd happened to be different people, the vector sum of all our goings would've been different from what it turned out to be. Very few, if any, even had as simple a goal as to get rich. They were only after their bread and butter and, they hoped, a swipe of jam on it. Whatever they acquired beyond that would be largely a matter of luck. Oh, and as for 'facing the stark necessities of life'—surely, Joe, you don't imagine they wanted to! They weren't given any choice, that's all."

Que Donn'rez Vous?

K-B2.

Q-K7. "Check," said Roy Pearson.

Captain Elias ben Judah did not swear, because it was against his principles. But his comment was violent enough. "Second blinking check in a row," he added, moving the black kings to refuge at Kt3.

"*And* the third," said his operations manager with a parched chuckle. The white queen jumped in his artificial hand to Q8.

"Do you mean that?" asked ben Judah, astonished. He was a medium-sized man, fifty Earth-years old, his hair gray, his eyes brown and gentle in a face that sagged a little with weariness. The blue uniform of the Jupiter Company sat neatly on him; insignia of rank and service, ribbons of past achievement, glowed beneath the fluorescent overhead of his cabin. It was more homelike than most, that cabin. Besides the usual pictures of wife and children, he had a shelf of books, not microspools but old-style volumes, for the pleasure of binding and typography. In a corner stood a little workbench where he had half completed a clipper ship model. Above was a flowerbox bright with poppies and violets.

Pearson's ruined features twisted into a grimace. "I do," he snapped. "Want to resign?" He was small and hunched, five years younger than the captain, but looked ten years older—not entirely because a goodly fraction of him was prosthetic.

"Certainly not." R X Q.

"I expected that, you know," said Pearson. His bishop scuttled across the board and captured the black queen. "Check . . . and mate."

Ben Judah studied the board for a moment before he sighed. "Right. Good game."

"You could have had me a while back," Pearson said, "when——"

"Never mind." Ben Judah got up and moved across the deck, heavily under the ship's internal gyrogravitic field, to his dresser. He began to load an old pipe. "I'm afraid I can't concentrate on chess. I keep thinking about the pilots."

Pearson observed him narrowly. "Don't," he said.

"I must. I'm the captain."

"Not in their case. I am."

"*Nu?*" Ben Judah swung about, indignant. This was his first Jupiter-diving cruise, and he admitted there was much he didn't yet know. But——

"You are the captain of the mother ship," Pearson said. "However, we're in orbit now. Only the scoopships are under weigh. And I direct their operations. Under the laws of the Republic, they're my responsibility. You'll find working for the Jupiter Company is a lot different from an inner-planet merchant run."

Ben Judah relaxed. "You needn't tell me," he said with a rather wan laugh. "Everything in the Belt is different. I don't envy you, trying to keep those wildcats of yours under control." He sobered. "But what disturbs me—now that I'm here with the actuality, not a textbook abstraction; now that I *feel* what is involved—what makes me wonder if

I should have come at all, is the business of send-ing men out time after time, ordering them to possible death, while we sit safely here."

"They aren't ordered," Pearson reminded him. "Any pilot may refuse any flit. Of course, if he does it repeatedly, he'll be fired. We can't afford to ship deadheads."

"I know, I know. And yet, well, you asterites are obsessed with economics." The captain lifted a hand to forestall the manager's retort. "I am quite aware of how closely you must figure costs. But there's a . . . a callousness in your attitude. You often seem to think a machine is worth more than a human life."

"It is, if several other human lives depend on it." Pearson gave him a quizzical look. Himself an introvert, he had not yet gotten to know the new skipper very well. "Why did you come to the Belt, anyhow?"

Ben Judah shrugged. "I was approaching com-pulsory retirement age. Earth's too crowded for my liking. Beside, spacing is my trade, the thing I want most to do. JupeCo offered me good pay for as long as I'm able to stay in harness. Also a downright luxurious homeship for my family. I've no personal complaints. But sometimes I can't help wondering, meaning no offense, if I want my chil-dren to grow up as asterites."

He flipped a switch on his viewscreen. The panel darkened into a simulacrum of the outside, uncount-ably many frost-cold stars, the curdled ice of the galaxy, and Jupiter. The planet hung monstrous in its nearness, amber with multitudinous colored bands, blotted by storms that could have gulped all Earth, the Red Spot a glowing ember. One moon was coming into sight around that terrible horizon. Its face was tinted saffron by reflection.

"Live men, diving into yonder kettle of hell," ben Judah said low. The susurrus of the ventilators made an undercurrent to his words, as if the ship tried to tell him something. "And it isn't necessary. You could automate the operation."

"Doubling the capital investment in every scoopship," Pearson said. "Also increasing the rate of loss by an estimated twenty-five percent. Too many unforeseeable things can go wrong down there. An autopilot can act only within the limits of its programming. A man can do more. Sometimes, when he runs into trouble, he can bring his ship back."

"Sometimes." Ben Judah's hands returned blindly to his pipe. He finished stuffing it, touched an igniter to the tobacco, and blew nervous puffs.

"We get more applications than we can find qualified men to accept," Pearson said. "Pay, prestige. And most of the boys actually enjoy the work."

"Maybe that's why I'm scared," ben Judah said. A corner of his mind observed that his English, hitherto Oxford with an Israeli accent, was slipping into the Belt dialect. The citizens of the young Asteroid Republic had every national origin, but North Americans predominated and put their stamp on language and folkways. "When my sons are grown, they might put in for those berths . . . and get them."

Master Pilot Thomas Hashimoto eased his craft away from the mother ship with a deftness born less of experience in this job—though he had plenty—than of several years of Earthside test piloting. His motions at the control board were nearly unconscious. Most of his attention was on the view before him.

His heart knocked. *I'm not afraid*, he assured himself. *I can't be. At least I'd better not be. This isn't any more dangerous than what I did back home.*

The thing is, though, I was doing those things there.

"Clear track," said the dispatcher's radio voice. Static buzzed around the words. No tricks of modulation could entirely screen out the interference of Jovian electrical storms. "Good gathering, Tom."

"Roger," said Hashimoto, mechanical response to a ritual farewell, "thanks, and out." His eyes focused on instrument needles, his fingers jumped over switches. The computer clicked and muttered. Otherwise the cockpit was silent, making the beat of blood loud in his ears. He grew conscious of the spacesuit enclosing him, a thick rubbery grip. Its helmet was left off, like its gloves, until such time as an emergency arose. So his nostrils drank smells of machine oil and the ozone tinge that recycled air always has in close quarters. For the minute or two that he traveled in free fall he felt weightlessness: scoopships didn't waste mass on internal field generators. But there was no dreamlike ease to the sensation, such as he had known in other days. The seat harness held him too tightly.

The computer gave him his vectors and he applied power. The nuclear reactor aft was noiseless, but the Emetts of the gyrogravitic generators whirred loudly enough to be heard through the radiation bulkhead which sealed off the engine compartment. Field drive clutched at that fabric of relationships that men call space. Acceleration shoved Hashimoto back into his seat. *Mary Girl* leaped Jupiterward.

He had a while, then, to sit and think. This interval of approach under autopilot was the worst time. Later the battle with the atmosphere would occupy all of him, and still later there would be the camaraderie of shipboard. But now he could only watch Jupiter grow until it filled the sky. Until it became the sky.

The trouble is, he realized, *I'm so near the end of my hitch. I didn't count the days and the separate missions at first, when I began this job. But now that there's only a few more months to go. . . .*

Three years!

He hadn't needed to stay in the Belt that long, as far as his wife was concerned. She wanted desperately to have children, yes, and her frail body would miscarry again and again unless she spent each pregnancy under next-to-zero weight, and obstetrical facilities for that kind of condition existed nowhere but in the Asteroid Republic. (No country on Earth would spend money to establish a geegee-equipped maternity hospital, or an orbital one; anything that increased population, however minutely, was too unpopular these days.) Hashimoto had been more than glad to land a contract with JupeCo that enabled them to move out here. But two healthy children were plenty. Now they wanted to return home.

However, JupeCo insisted on a minimum of three years' service, and the bonus he would lose by quitting before the term was over amounted to half his total pay. He couldn't afford it. No contract that harsh would have been allowable in North America. But once they concluded their war of independence, the asterites had gone their own way.

It was not Hashimoto's. He remembered too well

how sunset touched the mists of San Francisco Bay and made it a bowl of gold, how gardens lay vivid and trees stood rustling about his house in the Marin County hills, how men moved and spoke and exchanged friendship according to rules worn gentle with long usage. The asterites were as raw and stark as their own flying mountains.

He did not fear Jupiter because it could kill him. Any untried spaceflitter might do that at home. But it would be horrible to die without having slept once more in the house that had been his grandfather's, without having walked Earth's living soil and felt Earth's wind on his face again.

Or without seeing his and Mary's children grow into the heritage that was theirs.

Throttle down, Hashimoto told his mind. *You've got work to do.*

The scoopship thrummed around him. Through the low, thick inertrans canopy he looked forward along the flaring nose. By twisting his neck he could have looked aft to the tapered stern. The metal shimmered blue in the light that poured from Jupiter. He could not see that open mouth which was the bow, gaping upon emptiness, but he could well visualize it. He had watched the service crew often enough, to make sure that their periodic inspections of every accessible part were thorough. *Mary Girl* was getting along in years, as divers went—which wasn't very far. (She had been *Star Pup* when passed on to him, but every pilot had the right to name his own craft.) Hashimoto didn't trust his life to someone else's estimate of her soundness. Most of his fellows did; but then, most scoopship pilots played a hell-for-leather role that he secretly considered rather childish.

They were good joes, though, he thought. He

must admit he would miss that gang. Often on Earth he would remember escapades and shared laughter.

And by the Lord Harry, it was something to steal from Jupiter himself and come back to brag about it!

The ship drove onward.

Eventually the planet filled his entire vision. But then it was no more a planet, hanging in heaven; it had become the world. It was not ahead but below. Cloudfields stretched limitless underneath him, layered, seething, golden-hued but streaked with the reds and browns, greens and blues of free radicals. To port he saw a continent-sized blot of darkness that was a storm, and shifted course. Deceleration tugged angrily at him, and the planet's own pull, nearly three times Earth's. His muscles fought back. The first thin keening of cloven air penetrated to him. The ship quivered.

He switched off the autopilot and plunged downward on manual. The noise grew until it was thunder, booming and banging, rattling his teeth in the jaws and his brain in the skull. Winds did not buffet this craft traveling at many times supersonic speed, but gigantic air pockets did, back and forth, up and down, till metal groaned. Darkness overwhelmed him as he passed through a cloud bank. He emerged below it, looked up and saw the masses towering kilometer upon kilometer overhead, mountainous, lightning leaping across blue-black cavern mouths and down the faces of roiling slaty cliffs, against a distant sky that was hell-red. Briefly an ammonia storm pelted him, the hull drummed with the blows of gigantic poisonous hailstones. Then he was past, still screaming downward.

Presently he was too deep for sunlight to touch

his eyes. He flew through a darkness that howled. He ceased to be Tom Hashimoto, husband, father, North American citizen, registered Conservative, tennis player, beer drinker, cigarette smoker, detective-story fan, any human identity. He and the ship were one, robbing a world that hit back.

The instruments, lanterns in utter murk, told him he was at sufficient depth. He leveled off and snapped the intake gate switch. The atmosphere ceased to whistle through the open tube of the hull—for now the tube was closed at the rear. A shock of impact strained him against his harness. The ship bucked and snarled. He reduced the drive to let the atmosphere brake him.

That air was mostly hydrogen and helium, but rich in methane, ammonia, carbon dioxide, water vapor; less full of ethylene, benzene, formaldehyde, and a dozen other organics, but nonetheless offering them in abundance. This far down, none of them were frozen out. The greenhouse effect operated. Jupiter's surface was warm enough to have oceans like Earth's. No man had seen them. The weight of atmosphere would have crumpled any hull like tinfoil. Even at this altitude, *Mary Girl* sped through an air pressure several times that of sea-level Earth.

Rammed into her open bow by sheer speed, the gases poured through a narrower throat. The wind of their passage operated an ionizer and a magnetic separator. Most of the hydrogen and helium were channeled off into a release duct and thrown away aft. Some of the other gases were too, of course, but there was more where they came from. An enriched mixture flowed—hurtled—through rugged check valves into the after tanks.

The process did not take long. This was actually

not the time of maximum hazard—though ships had been known to break up when the stress proved too much for some flaw in their metal. The dive downward from orbit had killed most of those who had perished, and the climb back was not always completed. Gales, lightning, hailstorms, supersonics, chemical corrosives, and less well understood traps could be sprung. If the pilot was simply knocked unconscious, or lost control for a couple of minutes, Jupiter ate him.

A needle crossed the Full mark. The intake gate opened again and the tank valves shut. Hashimoto swung the ship's nose toward the hidden sky and poured power into the field drive.

He was once more out in sunlight, a storm-yellow dusk that showed him nothing but a cloud wrack tattered by wind, when his engine began to fail.

Master Pilot Charles de Gaulle d'Andilly approached the mother ship with a song. What a dive that last one had been! He was still ashiver from it, tumbling end over end in a doomsday blackness until he found an updraft that he rode toward safety. Within the spacesuit, his zipskin sopped sweat. He wanted a drink in the worst way. There were only two kinds of occasion when every cell of a man's body was absolutely alive, and Jupiter expeditions didn't take women along.

He'd compensate himself for that when he got back to Ceres. Few girls could resist a scoopman's uniform and reputation. Especially when Charles de Gaulle d'Andilly wore them.

> . . . *Dans le jardin d'mon père*
> *Les lilas sont fleuris.*
> *Tous les oiseaux du monde*

Y viennent fair' leur nid.
Auprès de ma blonde
Qu'il fait bon, fait bon, fait bon. . . .

The radio receiver buzzed. He flipped the switch. "*Vesta Castle* calling ship detected at . . ." The dispatcher's voice gave coordinates which indicated him. "Come in, please."

"*Mignonne* responding to *Vesta Castle*," said d'Andilly. "Everything okay."

"Hi, Chuck. How was the trip?"

"Rough. Later I shall elaborate my experiences for you at some length. But being me, I had no unconquerable problems. So give me a guide beam to discharge, please."

"Roger." Cartesian axes flickered to life within the globe of a signal 'scope. D'Andilly aligned the dot that represented his own craft and rode on in. Approach must be under his personal control, with Jupiter's radio interference potentially so great. Nevertheless, he needed to devote little of his mind to it. After a dive, the matching of vectors in space was nothing but relaxation.

Auprès de ma blonde
Qu'il fait bon dormir!

His thoughts drifted back to that certain blonde who was responsible for his having left the United European Space Corps a few years ago. He didn't blame her. He should have known better than to play games with the daughter of his commanding officer. But she was so very tempting. He might try to find her again, when at last he must retire; Jupiter-diving was not for men past thirty-five or so. No, she was doubtless married by now. Well, there would be many others. And it would be good to stroll along the Seine, nurse an apértif in a café on the Champs-Elysées, dine on civilized food before proceeding to the opera. He had no intention of staying in the Belt forever. With his accumulated pay he could buy into a good small business on Earth and live like a gentleman.

Not that he regretted his time out here. It had been glorious fun, mostly.

The *Vesta Castle* grew before his eyes, a great metal egg with softly glowing ports, the smooth curve broken by turrets, air locks, and boat blisters. Her orbit had carried her near the Jovian terminator line, so that the shrunken sun glared hard by the vast hazy crescent of the planet, but there was still ample light. Shadows lay sharp across the hull. Large though it was, it was dwarfed by the balloon harnessed to the stern. And the latter would double its present radius before it was considered full.

D'Andilly edged close to the gas bag. He could see stars through it. The plastifilm had to be thin, to save mass. He didn't worry about ripping it in case of collision. That elastomer was quite incredibly tough, could even bounce back small meteoroids. But one could all too easily start the whole awkward ship-and-balloon system twisting around three simultaneous axes, and have the devil's own job getting rid of that angular momentum.

On such a whisper of drive that he felt no weight worth mentioning, he matched velocities. A radar at the balloon's main valve locked onto him. He followed the beam to within meters of target. A hose snaked out from *Mignonne*'s stern, its nozzle driven by a miniature geegee and homing on the valve. They coupled. Between them, the pilots of the two ships killed what slight rotation was induced.

Pumps throbbed, forcing the scoopship's cargo of Jovian gas into the balloon. The sphere did not expand much; a single load was a small fraction of its total capacity. D'Andilly continued working to balance forces and hold the entire system steady in orbit.

At the end, he directed the hose to uncouple and retract. Then he slipped smoothly toward his assigned blister on the mother ship. This far spaceward there was seldom need to operate hydromagnetic screens against solar particle radiation, so approach and contact were simple. While he got out of his harness and suit, the final adjustments of angular momentum were made. The balloon waited quietly for the next arrival.

Who would not be d'Andilly. He had twenty hours off till he dove again.

Whistling he climbed through joined air locks into the *Vesta Castle*. Two maintenance men waited in the companionway to clean his gear. Afterward the ship would be inspected. That was no concern of d'Andilly's. He gave the tech monkeys a greeting less condescending than compassionate— imagine so dreary a job!—and sauntered to pilot's country; a short, stocky man, brown hair carefully waved and mustache carefully trimmed, blue eyes snapping in a hook-nosed square face.

Ulrich von Raaben, tall, blond, and angular, was emerging from the showers as d'Andilly entered. "Whoof!" he exclaimed. "You smell like an uncleaned brewer's vat." He saw the condition of the undersuit that the Frenchman began to strip off, and paused. "Bad down there?"

"I hit an unobserved storm," d'Andilly said, as casually as he could manage.

Von Raaben stiffened. "We shall have a word with the weather staff about that."

"Oh, I will report the matter, of course. But they cannot be blamed. It must have risen from the depths faster than normal. Our meteorologists can only observe so far down."

"A cyclonic disturbance does not rise for no reason. Surrounding conditions ought to give a clue, at least to the probability of such a thing happening. If they tell us a given region looks calm, and it proves not to be, by heaven, they will have some explanations to make!"

D'Andilly cocked his head at the other. "You are too Prussian to believe. Where were you born . . . Milwaukee?" Von Raaben reddened. D'Andilly slapped his back and laughed. "No matter, *mon vieux*. For a filthy Boche you are quite a good fellow."

He ducked under the shower and wallowed in an extravagance of hot water. That was one of numerous special privileges enjoyed by the scoopship pilots. Others included private cabins, an exclusive recreation room, seats at the officers' mess with wine if desired, high pay, and a dashing uniform that one was free to modify according to taste. In exchange they made a certain number of dives per Earth-year, into Jupiter.

One must be young and heedless to strike such a bargain. Sensible men, even among the asterites, preferred a better chance of reaching old age. No wonder that scoopship pilots off duty tended to act like ill-disciplined sophomores. *Including me, no doubt.*

There are exceptions, to be sure. Like poor Tom

Hashimoto. I should take him out with me when we reach Ceres and show him the proper way to valve off accumulated pressure. But no, he is much too married.

In his own quarters d'Andilly put on lounging pajamas. From there he proceeded to the rec room. He found von Raaben, battered and eagle-decorated military cap shoved back on his head, playing rummy with Bill Wisner. The latter, who affected loud clothes and foul stories, was one of the few native-born asterites aboard. Immigration was still ahead of birth in expanding the population of the Republic.

"Hi," Wisner said. "I hear you hit some weather."

"Yes. I'd best report it before someone else dives into that region." D'Andilly observed the glasses on the table and headed for the liquor cabinet himself. "Are we the only ones here?"

"The only divers, yes," von Raaben said in his meticulous way. "None others are due for several hours, I believe." The scoopships operated on a staggered but loose schedule, and no one liked to discharge by starlight alone. Those who had completed a flit would assume parking orbits and rendezvous when the *Vesta Castle* was back in the sunshine.

"Well, the more for us, then." D'Andilly poured a stiff drink, tossed it off, and sipped appreciatively at a second. "Ah! Praise be that the cognac is holding out. When we are reduced to asterite booze, then it is time to head for Ceres, and never mind whether the balloon is full or not."

"Oh, Comet Blood isn't that bad," said Wisner defensively.

"It is for any man whose palate was not burned out by it in infancy. Your liquor is one excellent reason I shall not remain in the Belt after they shelve me as a diver."

"You ought to, though, Chuck," Wisner said with characteristic patriotism. "The life's rough and risky, sure. But with any luck at all, you stand to make a fortune. And no bureaucrat's going to tax most of it away and tell you how you can spend the rest, either."

"True. I admire the pioneer spirit, in an abstract fashion. But do you see, I am not interested enough, myself, in wealth or fame or power. There are so many other things to do."

"If one lives that long. Well"—von Raaben raised his own glass—*"prosit."*

"May we love all the women we please," Wisner toasted, "and please all the women we love."

D'Andilly was about to propose something equally traditional when the emergency summons cut loose.

The wardroom was also used for briefings and conferences. Captain ben Judah stood looking down the green length of the table. Roy Pearson sat on his right, the chief engineer on his left, other officers not on watch beyond them. But the three scoopship pilots, clustered at the foot, were those whose eyes he must meet.

He felt sick. The words dragged from his throat:

"Gentlemen, we have received a call. Hashimoto is down."

There could be no adding to the silence that followed. But Wisner lost color and von Raaben slowly took off his cap.

"Not exactly down, yet," ben Judah went on. "His engine quit on him. But not too suddenly. When it first began misbehaving, he got as high as he could and threw himself into orbit. That's how

we were able to receive his 'cast. He was above the
sources of atmospheric interference, though it was
still bad enough.''

D'Andilly half rose. *"Pardieu!* Why do we sit
here? I can go fetch him myself.''

If he were in clear space, yes,'' ben Judah said.
"But he didn't get that far. There's still a trace of
gas where he is. Frictional resistance—he's spiraling inward.''

"How fast?'' von Raaben barked.

"That can only be estimated. We know his approximate altitude, from the orbital velocity as
given by Doppler shift of his signal. That is thirty-
one-point-five kilometers per second, in the same
sense as our own path. On the basis of the average
density-altitude relationship in the Jovian atmosphere, the weathermen figure he should . . . should
start burning in five or six hours.''

"No chance that Stuart or Dykstra or any of the
others can give a hand?'' asked Wisner.

"We've tried to raise them,'' said ben Judah.
"No luck, as expected.'' Only a tight beam could
drive a recognizable message from the *Vesta Castle*
to a scoopship deep in the radio chaos of Jupiter's
air. And the exact position of such a ship was
never known—constantly and unpredictably changing, anyway. A broadcast could be received by a
man in clear space, over considerable distances.
But the parking orbits of those who had taken on
full loads and were waiting to rendezvous on dayside were eccentric ellipses, crossing the mother
ship's circle at the space-time point of the meeting.
Now Jupiter lay between, a wall to block off any
cry. Unless some man still in its neighborhood
should find some reason to call, and come around
the edge of the radio shadow for that purpose,

there was no measurable probability of getting in touch.

"'We could accelerate toward dayside ourselves, couldn't we, till we can get a 'cast through?" asked the engineer.

"Don't be ridiculous," Pearson snorted. "We could, sure. But they'd all be far out, farther out than we are now. It would only waste time."

"So the problem's ours," Wisner said. "Well, I don't see why you're looking so down in the nose about it. What the hell, even at one *g* a scoopship gets from here to the atmospheric fringes inside of two hours. Let's see . . . if you got his call a few minutes ago, he must still be on our side of Jupe, and his period just about three hours. You don't gain much by flitting a high-acceleration curve over such a short distance, seeing that you also have to brake, but you do gain a little. Yes, I think I can meet him in something like two hours. Three at the most, to allow for matching speeds and so forth. . . . Sure, we can do it. Assume I start out half an hour from this moment at five *g*'s, and have a curve computed for me. It'll take me that long to get ready. Got to dope up with stim and gravanol——"

"No, I shall go," said d'Andilly, and "*Nein, ich*," von Raaben. They began to rise.

"Sit down!" rapped Pearson.

Men's gazes focused on him, the ship's officers' with incomprehension, the pilots' with flaring resentment. The manager clamped his lips together for a space before he asked, "Precisely what do you propose to do?"

"Equalize velocities, couple air locks, and take him aboard," said d'Andilly. *"Voilà!"*

"Easy in space," Pearson said. "But do you realize that he's in atmosphere?"

"Very thin atmosphere thus far," the engineer said. "Nearly a vacuum."

"He'll be down where it's thicker by the time another ship can arrive," Pearson said.

"If he has five hours to go before he hits such a density that metal volatilizes," d'Andilly said, "it will not be too thick three hours from now for a scoopship hull to stand orbital speeds."

"No. You can't do it, I tell you."

D'Andilly reddened. "Well, perhaps not. But we must try, or stop claiming to be men."

"Very dramatic," Pearson scoffed. "Too bad the laws of physics don't sympathize."

"What do you mean?"

"Look, I admit the air friction is slight where he is now. If only we could contact one of the men now diving, rescue would not be hard. But by the time you can reach him, he'll be down to a level where it's considerably worse. Oh, the air will still be tenuous, upper stratosphere density or less. Aerodynamic forces will tend to keep the hull aloft, preventing an extremely quick plunge to destruction.

"But . . . at thirty-odd KPS, that thin air is equivalent to an Earthside wind of more than hurricane force. It doesn't much resist the smooth, streamlined shape of a hull with an open gate; they're designed that way. But how does your screw engine open an air lock against such pressure? How can a tube be extended and secured? You'd accomplish nothing except to generate so much turbulence that your own craft would spin out of control."

D'Andilly sank back in his chair.

"Grapple onto his hull, then, and bring home ship and everything," von Raaben said.

"You can't do that either, for the same reason. The grapnel field doesn't seize hold till it's within a centimeter or so of metal. Otherwise the thing would be unmanageable in space. In such a wind, you'd never be able to swing it into contact."

"Are you certain of that?" Wisner asked.

"Certain enough," Pearson said.

"That means you aren't one hundred percent sure. Who could be, with so many unknowns in the equation? Okay, we'll see. Personally, I think that we three between us might well be able to slap a claw or two on him."

"No. You'll only get tossed against each other in the attempt. I don't consider suicide heroic."

"You just can't understand, can you?" Wisner said in a soft voice. "Tom Hashimoto is one of ours."

"He isn't, really. He's not planning to renew his contract."

"So what? I've drunk his beer too often. His wife's a hell of a sweet girl. You think I can go back to Ceres and tell her we didn't even try to rescue her husband?"

"If it will make you feel better," Pearson said coldly, "I'll turn that into an order. You stay put."

"Tu chameau pouilleux," d'Andilly whispered. He climbed erect, with a loud suggestion for the manager's private recreation. "Let us get started, friends."

"Sit down!" Pearson shouted. A vein pulsed in his temple, above the plastic that replaced his right cheek. "Or do you want to face charges of mutiny?"

"Monsieur le capitaine." D'Andilly turned to ben Judah. "I appeal to you."

"I . . . no, I am not a diver," the Israeli croaked.

Sweat glittered on his forehead. "I can't go against a man who knows the subject better than I do."

D'Andilly spat on the deck. "He's no diver himself."

Von Raaben tugged at his companion's sleeve. "Sit. Charles. Contain yourself. This does nothing." He dragged d'Andilly back into his chair, then looked squarely at Pearson and said:

"Perhaps you do not know what morale means. I have heard a story about the British in one of their wars with my ancestors. Their army was beaten on the Continent and had to evacuate or be captured. The men were taken onto ships off Dunkirk. Afterward the naval commander whose warships had given what help they could was reproached for taking so great a risk. If we had brought up our own battleships and heavy artillery to the narrows, or if a storm had arisen, he would have lost his entire fleet. Let me tell you what he replied. 'We could build another fleet in four or five years. But it would have taken us three hundred years to build another tradition.' "

Pearson's eyes dropped. He stared for a space at his artificial hand, inert on the table. Finally he said, "But I do know. I was a space pilot once myself. Not scoopships, no, but prospecting, which is pretty dangerous, too, in a rock cluster. Some good friends of mine died in the same collision that shelved me. I managed to get into an intact compartment, alone. But I'd soon have died too, if the survivors hadn't risked their necks to search the débris for casualties.

"But . . . that was sound doctrine. The ship was a total loss. Nothing more was being hazarded except men, who'd die in any event if they couldn't pool their efforts to jury-rig sufficient shelter until help came. This case is different. You have to multiply values to be gained or lost by the probability of success or failure. Exposing three ships and three men to a very high chance of destruction, for the sake of one ship and one man whom there's only the smallest likelihood of saving . . . no, that's much too bad economics."

"Economics?" d'Andilly exploded.

"That's what I said," Pearson answered. Steel underlay his tone. "The dollar cost of building and outfitting a ship, of training and equipping a man. It's the only basis we've got.

"Wisner, you're an asterite born, and von Raaben has been one for a number of years. But I guess I'll have to spell the facts out for you, Pilot d'Andilly. You're kept like a fighting cock, because that's the only way to attract men to your job. So you aren't aware, I suppose, how thin a margin we asterites live on. Can you imagine what it means to carve a living from airless rocks? Sure, they're rich in metal; atomic power is cheap and solar power is free; but what is there otherwise? Why raid Jupiter at such enormous effort, if we didn't have to have those gases to form the basis of chemical synthesis, of our whole chemical industry, which equals our survival?

"Okay. It's barely possible that three ships working together could grapple onto Hashimoto's and haul him into clear space. I don't believe they could, but I'll grant a slight possibility. So if you did pull off that stunt, every boy on every asteroid would cheer himself hoarse for you, and every girl would fall into your arms, and every *man* would curse you for a pack of dangerous idiots. Because any operation which consistently gambled at those

odds would soon go broke—and we've got to have
the operation or the whole Republic dies.

"Now do you understand?"

D'Andilly's look traveled wildly from one pilot
to the other. Von Raaben's face had congealed,
Wisner's fingers twisted together like snakes. But
each of them nodded.

After a time when no one spoke, Pearson turned
his head toward ben Judah. The captain stood
unmoving, backed against the bulkhead. "Are we
still in contact with Hashimoto?" the manager
asked.

"I believe so," ben Judah said dully.

"Then I suggest you return to the radio room
and offer him what consolation you can. If he has
a coreligionist aboard—" Pearson had raised his
prosthetic hand a little. He let it fall. The clatter
was so loud that he jerked in his seat.

"I wonder what happened to conk out Tom's
engine?" Wisner muttered.

"We'll never know," the chief engineer said. "That
compartment's sealed off behind a rad shield,
remember. It's only cracked for direct inspection
at refueling time, every five years or so—why am I
telling what everybody knows?"

"I'll have nightmares thinking it might happen
any time, to me or . . . or anyone."

"Me, I shall have nightmares about Tom,"
d'Andilly said. "Whirling so utterly helpless, yes,
the helplessness is the real horror."

"He did not stop to think we could not get him
out of orbit," von Raaben said, "or he might not
have bothered."

"Well, we could, if he'd gotten into clear space,"
Wisner said. "Or, of course, if Jupe's mass didn't
produce that kind of orbital speed." His chuckle

was without humor. "But then, if Jupe were a minor planet, it wouldn't have an atmosphere worth exploiting, and this would never have happened in the first place."

"If we could slow him somehow," von Raaben floundered. "By aerodynamic braking? No, he has no control surfaces, and with his engine dead——"

D'Andilly sprang to his feet. His chair fell over backwards. *"Mon Dieu!"* he shouted.

"Huh? What?" Startlement ran around the table.

"Control surfaces!" d'Andilly chattered. He waved his arms and forgot to put his torrent of words in English.

"Climb down from the mast, you nut," Wisner exclaimed. "Do you have an idea?"

"Oui . . . yes, yes . . . the balloon, *n'est-ce pas?* Dump the gas out, make a drogue. Ha, quick, draw some plans, *Monsieur l'ingénieur,* time is a-wasteful!"

"You're crazy!" Pearson snapped. He, too, leaped up.

"No, wait," ben Judah said. Hope kindled in his face. "I do know something about this. The first experimental spacecraft were retrieved in some such way. It might work. And it doesn't look too risky to the men."

"You'd abort this whole cruise," Pearson said. "Not to mention the whopping cost of the balloon. Even getting Hashimoto's vessel back, we'd stick the company for a terrific net loss."

"Economics can only go so far," ben Judah said.

"But don't you see?" Pearson's voice turned pleading. "It's not that I'm inhumane. Dollars and cents are nothing but shorthand for resources and human effort. And the Republic has only so much of either to go around. To us, an unprofitable operation is a socially evil one. We've got to operate under economic doctrine!"

"Not every time." Ben Judah's eyes were no longer mild. "If these pilots are willing to go, they shall."

Pearson bit his lip. "All right," he said. "Somebody has to take the blame of all the emotional morons. It may as well be me. I haven't any family to ostracize. So I directly forbid any attempt."

"As captain, I overrule you."

"You can't. This isn't in your province."

"Isn't it?" ben Judah murmured. His officers, who had crowded close, moved nearer Pearson. The second mate laid a hand on the manager's thin shoulder. "You heard the captain," he said.

Pearson shook himself loose, stumbled back to his chair and buried his face in his hands.

Presently the gang went aft to begin work. Pearson raised his head. The cabin had grown very still again. Only ben Judah remained, puffing his pipe at the opposite side of the table.

"I'm sorry, Roy," the skipper said.

"I'm sorrier," Pearson told him. "When we reach Ceres, I'm going to prefer charges against you."

"Really?"

"Yes. I don't want to. How I don't want to! But we can't keep sentimentalists on the payroll, and we need an object lesson. It's my duty to get you fired." Pearson rubbed his live hand over his plastic jaw. His voice was empty. "What have I got to live for, except my duty?"

The atmosphere of a high-gravity planet has a correspondingly high density gradient. Streaking downward, the scoopships hit perceptibly thick air—still thin even by Martian standards, but thick

enough to matter at this speed—almost before the
pilots realized they were about to do so. Then it
was all their drug-stimulated bodies could do to
maintain formation.

There ought to be an art to this, d'Andilly thought
amid thunder. Given time, an art could be developed, a whole profession of . . . droguedragging?
His teeth gleamed behind his faceplate, a taut and
short-lived grin. God grant this was the last as
well as the first occasion the thing was tried!

Mignonne reared like a whipped horse. The cable had pulled on her. D'Andilly applied sidewise
field thrust. Give that line some slack or it'll yank
the guts out of her! But not too much slack, or
you'll lose control of the whole crazy package.
Then you and your comrades may tumble into
Jupiter ready wrapped in a plastic shroud. Death
as a shooting star sounds romantic, but any man
of sense prefers to die in bed, at the end of a long
and misspent life.

"Whoa, there!" Wisner's voice came to d'Andilly's
earphones, barely audible over the interference,
the wind, and the cry of tormented metal. "You're
pulling on me now."

The Frenchman cast a glance outside. They were
still so high that heaven was clear. Stars glittered
inhumanly serene and a moon rode in an ice-crystal
halo, turning the cloud layers far below into snow
mountains. That Jovian horizon stretched farther
than a man could see; it did not lose itself in
curvature but in mists and blacknesses. He saw
his companion ships above him, *Sky Thief* to starboard and *Seeadler* to port—himself at the lowest
point of an equilateral triangle—as shimmering
curves where the light struck them, occulting shadows elsewhere.

The cables trailing aft of the three vessels were harder to see. They'd been smeared with luminous paint; but in this howling, shuddering chaos, one's head slapped back and forth in the helmet—yes, there. Wisner's line was too taut, von Raaben's too slack. More by feel than brain, d'Andilly decided how he should adjust his own place in the formation.

Mignonne groaned and lurched when he touched the controls. Her Emetts whined, nearly as loudly as the air she split at orbital speed, feeding energy into the drive field. Any change of course under these conditions was like slugging through a brick wall. Sweat stung the pilot's eyes, half blinding him. His tongue was a block of wood and his nose full of his own stink. Vibration quivered his bones. Wind shrieked and hooted. Now and again there came a great flat smack of noise.

But . . . so! He'd completed the shift. The dive proceeded more smoothly.

The balloon snakedanced at the end of the cables. Deflated, slashed open, rolled in a sausage shape and stuffed into a long metal tube, the thing had not been hard to manage in space. But now when they slanted through atmosphere—D'Andilly hoped the plastic wouldn't be damaged. But no, that stuff was intended for spatial conditions. The engineers had needed a laser torch to cut it.

"Tom," he said into his radio, for the dozenth time. "Tom, are you there? Do you read us?"

We should *be heard to intercept him, according to the last fix the mother ship relayed us. But anything can have happened.* "Tom! Rescue party from *Vesta Castle* calling *Mary Girl*. Come in!"

"He may have passed out," said von Raaben's tiny drowned voice in the earphones. "He may be dead."

"We'll never find him without some kind of signal to home on," Wisner predicted, through teeth clenched against shock waves. "Too big a search field, not enough light to see by."

Everything would have been easier on dayside and at a greater altitude, d'Andilly thought. His mind was buffeted into stupidity, able only to repeat the obvious, over and over. Where the air was thinner than here, less unpredictable variation of windage and density, adequate light, Tom would have been more readily seen as well as rescued. But preparing the drogue had been a maddeningly slow task, when one must stop and plan out every step. The rescuers had arrived very late. Perhaps too late, *Mary Girl* might already have taken the final plunge.

If she wasn't found within the next few minutes, the attempt must be abandoned. They were too near the burnup point. The instrument panel showed outside temperature rapidly rising. Soon the intake scoops would be redly glowing dragon mouths. And soon after that——

"*Hei! Dort!*" von Raaben bellowed. "Eleven o'clock low, see him? There, I say!"

"Jumping Judas, yes," Wisner exclaimed. "I was wrong. We really and truly located him with our own bare eyeballs." Crispness entered his tone. "Okay, Chuck, you still want to be squadron leader?"

"*Mais oui.* Who is better qualified?" D'Andilly had now spotted the distant shape himself. With a pilot's sense of dynamic relationships he gauged how to intercept, and issued his instructions. He knew that he was in fact not superior to his associates. But a single command was essential to coordinated effort.

And they would have to do one all-time job of coordination!

The three ships slewed about, fighting for every degree of turn, and dove on *Mary Girl*. Relative velocities were not great, and they established position quickly. There they flew not far ahead of the wreck, which they surrounded by the tow lines. For a moment, then, a kind of stability prevailed.

"Tom, can you hear me? Come in, Tom," Wisner called.

"Stow the conversation," d'Andilly said. "Are you ready? Let's brake a little . . . back, back, easy does it . . . not so fast, Krauthead . . . raise a bit, Bill . . . ah, we're snagging him."

About halfway between ships and balloon, the three cables were linked by three connecting strands, which in turn supported a flexible metal net. *Mary Girl* was just behind that net. Inchmeal, struggling with a turbulence that threatened to tangle their lines and dash them together, the rescuers allowed the net to move more slowly than the wreck. The scoop nose entered; the mesh snugged close around; the fish was caught.

"Everything seems okay, true?" d'Andilly said. *Bien*, let her go."

The hastily adapted hose mechanisms in *Mignonne*. *Sky Thief*, and *Seeadler* cast loose. The tow lines whipped backward. A radio instruction went to a small package in the balloon's container. It detonated. The metal peeled away. As the furious thrust of air entered its folds, the parachute opened.

D'Andilly brought his staggering ship under control, glanced back, and forgot all else in his awe. High over the stormclouds that looked like white mountains, a transparent hemisphere with a ghostly moon-shimmer across its surface began to bloom. Ever wider it swelled, until d'Andilly thought surely the fabric must rip across and release the shooting star.

But the fabric held. Expanding that elastomer took a great deal of energy, which *Mary Girl* supplied from her velocity. She started to fall more steeply, but at a fast-diminishing rate. Decelerating under power to keep pace, d'Andilly found himself under almost three gravities, besides Jupiter's own pull. Well, that shouldn't be too hard on Tom's body for the short time it must continue. *His live body, one hopes.* "Tom, are you there? Do you read us?"

The four ships fled on eastward. They crossed the sunrise line and saw long light, the color of roses, across endless vapor fields. The dwarfed sun climbed higher for them. They descended toward the clouds, until they saw lightning lick its chops.

But by that time nearly their whole speed had been lost. The wreck was parachuting quite gently. It was downright anticlimactic when they closed in on *Mary Girl* and grappled fast. A second radio command ignited thermite cartridges on the cables and burned them loose from the net.

Engines strained skyward. Looking aft, d'Andilly saw the parachute seized by a wind and sent fluttering in the direction of a thunderhead a thousand kilometers tall. *Jupiter wants revenge,* he thought weirdly. *Well, to hell with him. We'll be back.*

After a while, stars crowded a clear darkness. A great silence opened up. The planet seemed no more than some painted backdrop. D'Andilly shook himself gingerly, as if afraid that the bruised flesh would drop off. But no permanent harm seemed done. "Let's go into orbit," he said. His voice sounded odd to him, heard through ears that still tolled. "I want to board and see how Tom is."

He dreaded what he might find.

"Shucks," said Wisner, with a shaken catch of laughter, "I can tell you that. I can see into his cockpit from here. He's waving and shaking hands with himself like a lunatic. Nothing wrong with him."

Joy jumped in d'Andilly.

"It must just be that his radio went out," von Raaben said. "With a dead engine he was depending on the emergency accumulators for everything, and I think they must be drained. Come on, let us take a sight and lay a course and get back as fast as possible. I want some beer."

"Beer you shall have," d'Andilly warbled, "all the beer you wish, you foam-at-the-mouth Boche, beer in Jupiter-sized steins until it cataracts from your ears. Provided, of course, that I get as much cognac."

He adjusted thrust vectors according to navigational directions. The three ships and their load moved toward rendezvous. D'Andilly could almost taste the liquor now. He filled his cockpit with hoarsened song.

> . . . 'Que donn'rez vous, la belle,
> Pour le voir revenir?
> "Auprès de ma blonde
> Qi'il fait bon, fait bon, fait bon,
> Auprès de ma blonde
> Qu'il fait bon dormir!

The *Vesta Castle* throbbed with energy, accelerating homeward.

Captain ben Judah wreathed his head in smoke

and squinted at a tiny spar. With much care he brought it to the clipper foremast and held it in place a moment until the glue began to set. His inner eye visualized this *Witch of the Waves* as a real thing, soon to be commissioned, to raise her cloud of sails and ride the wind across the world. Gulls wheeled above, no whiter than the wake she cut through infinitely blue water . . . .He sighed. One might as well face facts. Romance had long died out of the universe.

There was a diffident knock. He laid down his tweezers and said, "Come in."

Roy Pearson shuffled through. Ben Judah was shocked at the man's drawn appearance. "Hello, there! What the blazes have you had afoot?" he asked, as heartily as he was able. "Taking your meals in your cabin like that, the past half dozen watches. If I hadn't been so busy getting us under weigh, I'd have come to see what ailed you."

"Oh, save it." Pearson lowered himself to the edge of the bunk and stared between his knees at the deck. His voice was hardly audible. "You know why I kept out of sight."

"Come, now. Nobody's angry at you for giving advice that turned out to be mistaken. You should know your pilots better than that. They might crow a little, as they well deserve to, but nobody that extroverted can nurse a grudge. Even Tom Hashimoto remarked at mess, when he'd heard the story, that in your place he'd have done exactly as you did."

"It isn't that." The voice grew louder, saw-edged. "It's you. I thought I could be smug about filing my complaint. But it's no use, I can't be." Pearson achieved an upward glance. "But I'm still going to do so," he said. "I've got to. If we don't stand by doctrine, how many other young men will die or be crippled?"

"Well, for everything's sake!" Ben Judah broke into laughter. "Is that what was eating you? Roy, Roy, we need you for comic relief. Haven't you heard the C.E.'s report on the salvaged vessel?"

"N-no. What—" Pearson tried to rise, but his legs wouldn't obey.

"He made a cursory inspection, and found immediately what had caused the trouble. In the engine, of course. Sulfuric acid fumes had corroded the cross-linkages between reactor and geegee generator."

"Where in confusion did it come from?"

"That's clear, too. There have been similar incidents in the past, Mac tells me, involving other kinds of machinery. You see, steel is usually pickled in sulfuric acid, and some of the acid seeps in, gets right in between the crystals. Then, in a sealed environment like that engine compartment, and under the encouragement of nuclear radiation and stray field-drive impulses the acid leaks out again. Very, very slowly, but it does. Precautions had been taken against that type of thing, but evidently they weren't thorough enough. You recall *Mary Girl* is one of the oldest scoopships in service. She'd had a long time for the effects to accumulate."

"But this means—" Pearson's brain began to click in accustomed patterns. "Yes, it shouldn't be hard to deal with. Install pH meters, or something of the sort, to give warning."

"I thought of that, too," ben Judah said. "Hindsight is always so much sharper than foresight, isn't it? Okay. Suppose I had not countermanded your orders and we had not gotten that ship back.

How many more would have been lost before the cause was found?"

Pearson stared at him. "That's right."

"Therefore my decision resulted in a net profit for the company, or at least in avoiding a serious net loss. So your duty is to give me the highest commendation and nominate me for a raise in pay."

Pearson sprang clumsily to his feet and extended a hand that quivered. Tears touched his eyelids. "You can bet I'll do that, Elias!"

"Now, now," rumbled ben Judah, embarrassed. "No need to make a fuss. Relax. Have a drink."

Before long, Pearson had recovered enough self-possession to suggest a game of chess.

Interlude 5

Again we sit quiet a while. The music romps around us. My whisky-and-water wets my tongue with faint smokiness, complement to the odors from Missy's cigar and Amspaugh's pipe. Lindgren raises his big frame and moves toward the bar.

"We seem to be wandering over a whole small universe of discourse," Amspaugh remarks at last. "But I suppose that's inevitable in a philosophical discussion, which this has obviously turned into."

Dworczyk glances at his watch and I remember he wants to get back to an experiment. "Do we have to go that deep?" he asks. "We're not scheduled to write the text ourselves, and I don't hold with straitjacketing their authors. We simply want to propose some guidelines."

"But what are the guidelines to be?" Echevaray replies softly. "That is the whole question before us.

"Well, I don't think they have to be as complicated as some of you are claiming. Look, you realize just a fraction of the kids will remember much of what they learned in elementary history; and just a fraction of those will want to dig deeper. Let's give 'em the basic dates—1492, 1776, 1969, 2002, the usual ones—and the basic information about what happened. A factual skeleton, in other words. Those who get interested can flesh it out later, maybe articulate it in an entirely different way, but that's not our concern here and now."

"It is, though, Tom," says Missy. "If nothing else, a bare-bones account would be so dull that every pupil would forget it the minute exams were over. None would feel like further study. You might as well not bother."

"Oh, sure, I realize that," Dworczyk agrees. "Do let the authors throw in picturesque stuff. Romance, adventure, fine! Whatever you may say, Colin, Conchita's right: the story of the conquest of space is full of the wildest episodes. And, uh, the most inspiring too, once in a while."

The young woman surprises me by replying soberly: "Good, but not sufficient. We want to, we must give the next generation examples of courage and self-sacrifice. But we have to show how these work in a larger context. Otherwise I can easily imagine a future emergency where someone's loyalty to his immediate friends is stronger than his loyalty to the ship. And that could destroy the entire crew.

"Besides, without getting too prosy, we'd better bring home the fact that the interesting virtues like heroism aren't the only essential ones. We need to cultivate the dull ones also."

"We might convey the lesson subtly," Orloff suggests, "as by choosing an episode which illustrates all these points . . . .Heh!" He snaps his fingers. "What about the herdship *Merlin*?"

"The what?" I ask.

The older people look intrigued. Clearly they were alive when the happening was a *cause célèbre*. Conchita, Echevaray, and I exchange blank glances.

"Excellent," Amspaugh says. "In fact, you could

point out more, as embodied in the story. Cooperation, for instance. After all, the economic expansion of the Republic, of the entire Belt, benefitted Earth likewise; and the asterites, in turn, had a great deal to gain from close relationships with the mother planet. The children might get some idea of the unity of mankind—if their teachers refrain from droning on and on about it."

"And the sunjammer that was involved," Lindgren chimes in from the bar. "I'm no poet, but I'd assume any writer could make a symbol of the sunjammer fleet—you know, driven by the same light that keeps life itself going; weaving the worlds together the way the sun holds them together; that sort of thing. Where's the brandy gotten to?"

McVeagh snorts. "Come off that, people! You know as well as I do, no individual worked to improve the lot of any part of mankind except Number One. And you know the improvement that did happen never led to any immediate brotherhood. I got interested in the *Merlin* case once and read several books about it, so I'm not vaguely remembering old 3V 'casts. If you ask me, it beautifully illustrates my own point. Commercial as well as political relationships went right on in squabbling, scrambling, bungling, friction, prevarication, and general inefficiency. In short, business as usual."

"Pardon me," Echevaray says, "but what are you talking about?"

"You don't know, Luis?" Missy lifts her brows. "It did happen before you were born, but I thought you, raised on Earth—and the affair was so crucial to Earth——"

"I fear it was forgotten, at least in my little Pyrenees village."

McVeagh laughs. "So much for a hero's undying fame."

"We remember, Colin," Missy reproves him. "And the books do."

"But Miss Montalvo and I don't, either," I interpose.

"Why not tell 'em, then?" Lindgren says. He has found the brandy bottle and I hear a vigorous gurgle into a glass. "We can argue the best way of telling it to kids as we go along, and even the historico-philosophico-economico-politico-tally-ho implications if you insist."

Thus we hear the tale in a rather fragmented form, and have to re-create it in our own minds.

Sunjammer

Ol' Jonah was a transporteer, he was, he was.
Ol Jonah was a transporteer, he was, he was.
  A storm at sea was getting mean,
  So he invented the submarine.
Bravo, bravo, hurrah for the transporteers!

Lazing along a cometary orbit, two million-odd
kilometers from Earth the herdship *Merlin* resem-
bled nothing so much as a small, bright spider
which had decided to catch an elephant and had
spun its web accordingly. The comparison was not
too farfetched. Sometimes a crew on the Beltline
found they had gotten hold of a very large beast,
indeed.

Stars crowded the blackness in the control cabin
viewports, unwinking wintry points of brilliance;
the Milky Way cataracted around the sky, the
Andromeda galaxy shimmered mysterious across
a million and a half light-years. The sunward port
had automatically closed off, refusing so gross an
overload for itself and its men. But Earth was
visible in the adjacent frame, a cabochon of clear
and lovely blue, with Luna a tarnished pearl beyond.

Sam Storrs, who was on watch, didn't sit day-
dreaming over the scene as Edward West would
probably have done. He admitted there were few

better sights in the System, but he'd seen it before and that wasn't his planet yonder. He was a third-generation asterite, a gaunt, crease-cheeked, prematurely balding man who remembered too well the brother he had lost in the revolution.

Since there was no work for him at the moment, he was trying to read Levinsohn's *Principles of Modern Political Economy*. It took concentration, and the whanging of a guitar from the saloon didn't help. He scowled as Andy Golescu's voice continued to butcher the melody.

King Solomon was a transporteer, he was, he was.
King Solomon was a transporteer, he was, he was.
He shipped his wood on a boat for hire,
'Cuz a wheel's no good without a Tyre.
Bravo, bravo, hurrah for the transporteers!

"Ye gods," Storrs muttered, "how sophomoric is an adult allowed to get?"

He reached for the intercom switch, with the idea of asking Golescu to stop. But his hand withdrew. Better not. It'd be a long time yet before their orbit brought them back to Pallas and the end of their patrol, even though the run would be finished under power. Crew solidarity was as important to survival as the nuclear generator.

And Andy's okay, Storrs argued to himself. *He just happens to be from Ceres. What do you expect of anyone growing up in that kind of hedonistic boom town atmosphere? It was different for me, out on the trailing Trojans.* His mouth bent wryly upward. *There puritanism still has survival value.*

No doubt the company psychomeds had known what they were doing when they picked Storrs, West, and Golescu to operate *Merlin*. You needed a balance of personality types . . . .Storrs wondered about asking for a transfer when they returned to base.

Ulysses was a transporteer, he was, he was . . . .

The long-range radio receiver buzzed and flashed a red light. Storrs jerked in his seat. What the hell? That was no distress signal from a sunjammer. A wide-beam call on the common band— He sucked in a breath and snapped the Accept switch.

*. . . He stopped at Calypso's isle for beers,
And didn't proceed for ten more years . . . .*

The speaker seethed with cosmic static. A voice cut through. "International Space Control Central calling Beltline Transportation Company maintenance ship number eleven, computed to be in Sector Charlie. Come in, number eleven . . . .International Space Control——"

"Here we are." Storrs recollected his dignity. No Earthling was going to say that a citizen of the Asteroid Republic didn't know the rituals. "Maintenance ship eleven, *Merlin*, out of Pallas, Storrs on duty, acknowledging call from International Space Control Central," he intoned. "My precise position and orbit are . . ." He read the figures off the autonavigator screen.

There was no need for him to adjust the transceiver web outside the hull. Its detector antenna had already fixed the direction of the incoming beam, and now the maser swung itself about to face squarely that way. The ship counterrotated a trifle. Storrs touched the controls. The generator purred; power ran into the Emetts; the field dissipated angular momentum into the general mass-energy background of the universe.

> *Columbus was a transporteer, he was, he was.*
> *Columbus was a transporteer, he was, he was.*
>   *They put the royal crown in pawn*
>   *To shut him up and move him on.*
> *Bravo—*

Golescu must have noticed the motion all at once, to judge from how his singing cut off. Storrs flipped the intercom open. "Got a call from Earth," he said hurriedly. "I don't know why, but assume condition red."

Feet clattered on the decks. Storrs's skin began to prickle. What the blazes was going on? Earth's SCC knew approximately where *Merlin* was, of course. Every herdship's orbit went on file in every traffic monitoring station throughout the System. If an orbit was changed, that news was also beamcast between the planets. But it was strictly an in-case precaution. The messages which drew a herdship off her path had always been automatic: beeps from a sailship whose interior sensors had registered trouble.

Always—until now?

His signal had leaped forth. Half a dozen seconds later it had reached the relay stations orbiting Earth. The operator stopped chanting, heard Storrs out, and began to talk back.

"International Space Control Central acknowledging reply from maintenance ship eleven. Stand by, please. I'm going to switch you over to the main office, groundside."

A low whistle drifted from the intercom. Golescu, posted at the engine, had heard. West came in the door, puffing from the climb up the companionway. He was a large man, his hair grizzled, face and stomach sagging a bit with middle age. But he was still highly able, Storrs admitted, and decent for an Earthman. To be sure, it helped that he was British. The revolution had been fought mostly against North Americans.

"Must be something big, eh?" West said. "Headquarters and all that." He settled himself in the navigator's chair.

"Hello, *Merlin*," said a new voice on the radio. It was a deep baritone, clipped but heavy with authority. "Evan Bailey speaking, assistant director of ISCC's Bureau of Safety." This time it was West who whistled. A message from so high an official of the World Interplanetary Commission, relayed straight from his personal desk—!

"A serious emergency has come up," Bailey went on. "There's no time to lose. Calculate an interception curve for sailship number one hundred twenty-eight, that's one-two-eight. Assume that you start acceleration at maximum thrust in, well, fifteen minutes. As soon as possible, anyhow. Is there by any chance another craft like yours reasonably near? We have no record of one ourselves, but there might have been some filing error. And you'll want every piece of help you can get."

"No," Storrs answered. "Nothing. The herdships are few and far between. You're lucky we happen to be this close to you right now."

That was not entirely coincidence. The orbits of the maintenance craft were planned to keep them never too distant from the great vessels of the Beltline. Some of the best mathematicians in the Republic had worked out the formulas for optimization of paths followed by sail and power craft;

an intricate, forever changing figure dance across half the Solar System.

Storrs sat up straight. "So what's the trouble?" he finished.

West's fingers had been playing a tattoo on the keys before him. A tape popped out with the information he wanted. "One-two-eight," he murmured. "Yes, here we are. Cargo of . . . I say, this is an odd one. She's carrying eight hundred metric tons of isonitrate from the Sword's Jovian-orbit plant. Right now she's approaching Earth, only about ten thousand kilometers away, in fact. There were no indications of trouble during her passage."

"Isonitrate what?" Golescu inquired over the intercom.

"An important industrial chemical," West explained. "Alkali complex or 2,4-benzoisopro——"

"Never mind," Golescu said. "I'm sorry I asked. Uh, everything's okay with our engines, if the gauges aren't liars."

Bailey had hesitated a while at the other end. Storrs could visualize the man, plump in a lounger behind several hectares of mahogany desk, sweating with fear that something might happen to interrupt his placid climb through the bureaucracy. His words, when they came, wavered slightly.

"The sun is going to flare."

"What?" Storrs jumped to his feet. An oath from Golescu bounced through the intercom. West paused at his work, hands frozen on the keys. After a second he grunted, like someone struck a body blow, and went back to setting up the computation of thrust vectors.

"No!" Storrs protested. "Can't be! This is a clear weather season." His eyes went past the stars, sought the one blank port, and clung there.

"My office issues more storm warnings than you perhaps realize," Bailey told him. "The big flare cycles are predictable far in advance these days, but indications that a small, shortlived one is going to occur are often not observable more than forty-eight hours ahead." His tone grew patronizing. "'Clear weather season' means only a period in which there will be no major flares and the probability of minor ones is low. Still finite, however. You asterites don't have to worry about solar radiation, out where you are, so perhaps you forget these details. Around Earth, we're highly conscious of them."

You smug planet-hugger! Storrs hung onto politeness with both hands. "I know the details well enough," he said stiffly. "After all, Mr. Bailey, every man aboard a herdship holds a master's certificate. I was only shocked. It seemed unbelievable that a cargo of isonitrate would be shipped, if there was any measurable chance of a flare while the vessel was inside the orbit of Mars."

The beam went forth. While they waited for reply, West said in a mild voice, "Call it an unmeasurable chance, then, Sam. The chap's right, you know. Solar meteorology is still not a completed science. It's either assume the hazard, knowing you'll lose an occasional ship, or else have no space traffic whatsoever. A coincidence like this one was bound to happen sooner or later."

"But for crying in the beer!" exclaimed Golescu from aft. "Why couldn't it have happened to a cargo of metal?"

"It does, quite often," Storrs reminded him. "Metal isn't hurt by radiation. Remember?" Sarcastically: "I've heard you gripe so often about how dull these cruises are most of the time. Well, here's your chance for some action."

Bailey had hung fire again. A rustle, penetrating the dry star-whisper, suggested he had been searching through a report prepared for him. "The flare is expected in about twelve hours," he said. "Predicted duration is three hours. Estimated peak radiation rate in Earth's vicinity is four thousand roentgens per hour. As you know, that will cause the isonitrate to explode."

Storrs exploded himself. *"Twelve hours!* You must'a known about it at least two days ago! Why didn't you alert us then? It'll take us two of those blithering hours just to make rendezvous!"

"Take it easy there, Sam," West said *sotto voce.* "Some of those high-caste officials are even touchier than that isonitrate."

As if in confirmation, Bailey's words turned hard. "Kindly watch your language, Captain. The delay is unfortunate, I admit, but no one is to blame. The prediction was issued in the usual way, and records were checked as per regulations. The nearness of one hundred twenty-eight was noted. However, it is an unmanned craft. You can't expect an ordinary clerk to know the danger involved in its particular cargo. That was only pointed out when the data reached my office for the routine double check. And then a policy decision had to be reached. We haven't the lugger capacity to unload so much material in time. It would have been simple for us to send a crew out to bleed off the gas and thereby save the sailship from being destroyed. But a staff physicist showed that this was impossible. I was informed of the dilemma the moment I came back from lunch, and immediately ordered that contact be made with the nearest herdship. What more do you want, man?"

Storrs choked. *Though I should have expected this*, he thought in a distant part of himself. *There isn't a government of any importance on Earth these days that isn't based on some version of "social justice." So of course independent thinking, conscientiousness, ordinary competence have gone by the board.*

He unpinched his lips, sat down again, and said, "Well, Mr. Bailey, you might as well order that crew of yours to jettison. We can't do anything more than that ourselves. Or have you some alternative suggestion?"

Waiting out the transmission lag, he heard Golescu say, "Whoof! Looks as if there's going to be more excitement than I bargained for."

West uttered a small chuckle. "Weren't you caroling about the mad, merry life of a transporteer?"

"Shucks, Ed, I was only practicing my act. Those blooming glamour boys from the scoopships and the prospector teams have been latching on to all the girls back home. Something's got to be done for our kind of spaceman."

"That gas must positively not be released so close to Earth," Bailey stated. "It would contaminate the entire inner region, causing damage estimated at ten billion dollars. You may valve it out when you are no less than one hundred sixty thousand kilometers from Earth sea level and/or basic Lunar surface. That's a direct order, by my authority under this jurisdiction and the Interplanetary Navigation Agreement. Are you recording? I repeat——"

"Judas priest!" Golescu yelled. "You expect us to haul away a bomb?"

A humming silence fell over the ship. Storrs became acutely aware of how the stars glistened, the power plant and ventilators murmured, the deck quivered ever so slightly with energies. He felt the roughness of his coverall on his skin, which had become damp and sharp-smelling. He stared at the meters on the pilot panel, and they stared back like troll eyes, and still the silence waxed.

Bailey broke it. "Yes. Unless you have some other plan, we do expect you to remove that stuff to a safe distance. Under terms of your company's franchise for terrestrial operations, it is your responsibility to dispose of this object in a manner not injurious to the public well-being. What's the problem, anyway? According to your rated thrust, you should be able to get the sailship's cargo section far enough away in four or five hours."

"The hell you say," Storrs barked. "We can't use full power on that big an outside load. Too much inertia. We'd rip our hull open. One-third of max'll be risky enough. And we've got to uncouple the sail first, to get proper trim—at least two hours' work." Desperately: "You're giving us no safety margin. You know as well as I do, flare time can't be predicted much closer than an hour. If it happens sooner than you claim, and the radiation sweeps over us before we can disengage and get clear—and *that* takes time—the explosion will destroy us. And you'll still have space contamination. Plus a lot of ship fragments."

"Also people fragments," Golescu chimed in. "We got a legal right to refuse an impossible job, don't we?"

"But not an improbable one," West said. His gaze went to Earth. "I did want to see Blighty again."

"You will," Storrs said. "We're not going to commit suicide for the benefit of a lot of Earthlings."

"Like me, Sam?" West asked softly.

Bailey came back on: "You are not expected to act without due precautions. You can safely tow at the end of a cable several kilometers long, can't you?"

"Know how much mass that adds?" Storrs snapped. "But never mind. The fact is, our class of ship isn't designed for cable tows. We hook on directly by geegee. A cable 'ud tear us apart, just like hauling under max thrust."

"Wait a bit," West interrupted. He had skippered a European League ship before he reached compulsory retirement age and Beltline made him an offer. Asterite law based retirement on medical data rather than the calendar. "I know what sort of boat can do a cable tow. Not an ordinary tug—I mean the kind that starts a sailship off. It hasn't enough power, considering how fast we'll have to work. But a North American Navy tug of the *Hercules* class would serve. I should think four of them could be hitched on without their drive fields interfering. Or perhaps you can borrow some *Kubilai* types from the Asians. With that many engines at work, we can cover the required distance in ample time. Have 'em there when we arrive, will you? We'll make the attachments and supervise the whole job."

Again the wait was longer than transmission lag would account for. At last Bailey's voice came, so small and shaken that the noise of the universe nearly drowned it. "I . . . guess you don't know. Both fleets are out near Venus. Joint maneuvers."

After a moment, assuming briskness like a garment: "We'll do what we can—alert the International Rescue Service; commandeer whatever else we can find that may be of help. I can't make any promises, with so little time to go through channels. But I'll do whatever is humanly possible."

"Amoebically possible, you mean," Storrs said. He managed to keep it under his breath. Shaking himself, he answered aloud:

"We'll get started now. Have to fold our radio-radar net. Acceleration forces would wreck it otherwise. When we've made rendezvous with one hundred twenty-eight, we'll call you on the short-range 'caster. Stand by for that."

He didn't wait for a response, but snapped off transmission as if the switch were Evan Bailey's neck.

Once the web had been pulled in by the appropriate machinery and acceleration had commenced, there was little for men to do until the end of the run. But doctrine required that Storrs remain on the bridge during his pilot watch—in which time he was also the captain. He roused from a period of angry lip-gnawing and said, "How about fixing us some chow? God only knows when we'll get our next chance to eat, and He isn't passing the information on.

"Right-o." West heaved his bulk out of the navigator's chair and started aft.

His body dragged at him as he went down the companionway and along the passage to the galley. There was, of course, no sensation of the ten gravities under which *Merlin* hurtled Earthward. The Emetts acted equally on every object inboard, and normally to the internal gyrogravitic field which furnished weight. But sometimes he wished the latter weren't kept at the standard Earth g. One of the few things he really liked about the asteroids was the sense of buoyancy on a rock where pull generators had not yet been installed. It was almost like being young again.

Oh, stop kidding yourself. Also stop feeling sorry for yourself. He squeezed into the galley and got to work. Herdships always carried a gourmet assortment of food, as one means of keeping up morale on their long, lonely cruises. West enjoyed exploring the potentialities, whenever his turn came to cook. And he had the honor of his country to defend as well, against that ancient canard about English cuisine. Usually he built the sandwiches as elaborately as any Dane. But today his mind was elsewhere.

How much risk are we obliged to run?

Under the law, a transporteer crew had the right to refuse a task as being too dangerous. Afterward they would have to face a board of inquiry, and Beltline might well decide to fire them. *Would I honestly mind that?* In this particular instance, though, they'd probably be cleared. *Merlin* represented a considerable investment. The company's cost accountants would not be happy if she were lost. In fact, if the isonitrate was simply released into space, a moderately expensive sailship could also be saved.

However, that might well embroil Beltline in legal action, considering how much economic damage Earth ould suffer. No one could hold anyone responsible for the sun's picking this day to flare. But a lawyer could argue that Beltline's agents had made no effort to rescue the situation, and therefore a whopping claim should be paid. Earth's SCC might be put under pressure to rescind the terrestrial franchise. A protracted court battle, even if won, would doubtless prove more costly than two ships and three men.

West shook his head. *That's another thing I don't like about the Republic. They can brag as much as they want about free enterprise, but it still amounts to the rawest, most cold-blooded kind of capitalism. Maybe the welfare states on Earth have gotten stuffy and overbureaucratized—nevertheless, we don't let the devil take the hindmost!*

He put the food and a pot of coffee on a tray and went forward. Storrs was busy with a slide rule and some bescribbled sheets of paper. He grabbed a sandwich with an automatic "Thanks," and chewed as he worked on. Rations, to him, were only fuel; West and Golescu never looked forward to his turn in the galley.

"What're you doing?" the Englishman asked.

"Trying to figure if we can't boil off some of the liquid as we tow, so gradually that it won't affect space too much, so fast that we'll shed noticeable mass. But hell and sulfur! I don't have the thrust parameter. Not knowing what sort of tugs we'll have available— How about hitching that Bailey character to the load and cracking a whip over him? A big wire whip hooked up to five hundred volts A.C."

West achieved a smile. "What'd he push against?"

"Hm-m-m, yeah, that's right. Okay, we'll get extra reaction by cutting Bailey into small pieces— very, very small pieces—and pitching him aft."

West's look moved out to Earth. The half disk was becoming a crescent as *Merlin* approached the spaceward side, but it was also rapidly growing. He traced bands that were clouds, white in a summer sky, the mirror sheen of ocean and the blurred greenish-brown coast of Europe.

"Don't be too hard on the man, Sam," he said. "When a world gets as crowded as that one there, you have to operate by a rigid system. Within the system, I presume he's doing his best."

Storrs spoke an obscenity. "A machine is judged by its output. How's your precious system performing in this mess?"

"Oh, forget the political arguments. There's England."

Storrs's features softened a trifle. "Kind of tough, huh? Passing this close to your wife and not getting a chance to see her."

West thought of the little house in Kent, where the hollyhocks would now be in bloom, so tall that they overshadowed the windows. He shrugged. "I knew what I was letting myself in for when I signed up as a transporteer." *Five years on the Beltline. I've waited out not quite three of them so far.*

He stared spaceward. Illimitable emptiness gaped at him, from here to the frost-cold stars. Out there plodded the sailships, unmanned, driven by the sun, slowly but cheaply carrying nonperishable cargo from the mineral-rich asteroids and the chemical-rich Jovian atmosphere to an Earth grown gaunt in natural resources, returning with such manufactured goods as the Republic had not yet gotten around to producing for itself. And there, too, flitted the herdships on the interweaving orbits, *Apollonius of Tyana, Simon Magus, Hermes Trismegistus, Morgan le Fay, Gandalf,* a score of them with radio webs outreaching, listening until an automaton cried for help. It was a chilly concept, somehow. He shivered.

Two more years.

After that, the real retirement, with Margaret in

flowering Kent. He didn't yet know if his decision had been right. Gardens, green hills, four-hundred-year-old homes were not anything a man could afford on a space officer's pension. Not with today's land values and taxes. But the pay scale in the asteroids was fantastic, the Republic did not levy on income, and Earth needed out-planet exchange so badly that every terrestrial government also exempted such earnings from impost. The house would be mortgage free by the time he came back to Margaret, and there would be enough in the bank as well for them to do everything they once promised themselves.

On the other hand, they paid for it with five years when they might have been together.

And if he got killed, they never would collect the goods. Margaret would have to move in with one of the kids, and—

West picked up the tray. "I'll take Andy his lunch," he said.

Storrs nodded absent-mindedly and returned to his calculations. No doubt they were his form of escape.

Passing through the tiny saloon, West heard the plink of Golescu's guitar. Words bounced after:

George Washington was a transporteer, he was, he was.
George Washington was a transporteer, he was, he was.
　He paddled across the Delaware
　To find the buck he'd shot-put there.
Bravo, bravo, hurrah for the transporteers!

He entered the workshop just forward of the bulkhead which sealed off the nuclear generator. A man was always supposed to stand by here under acceleration, in case of trouble. But *Merlin* had yet

to develop any colly-wobbles, and Golescu was
sitting by. His chair was tilted back against the
big lathe, his feet on the rungs and his instrument
on his lap. He was a squat, dark young man with
squirrel-bright eyes.

"Hi," he said. "Also yum."

West set the tray down and poured two cups of
coffee. "By the bye," he said, "I'm not too well up
on American folklore, but wasn't it the Potomac
that Washington threw the dollar over?"

"Don't ask me. My parents came to Ceres direct
from Craiova."

"Wherever that may be . . . .D'you want to go
back and visit there some day?"

"Whatever for?" Golescu rose. "Hey, those sandwiches look great."

"Thanks. I'm afraid my heart wasn't in them,
though."

Golescu made a face. "Yech! I should hope not."

"I mean I had the wind up so about this con-
founded affair——"

"Wind up?"

"Forget it. A Briticism." West shook his head.
"D'you know, I can't help pitying children who've
never felt wind or rain."

"Everything I hear about weather makes it sound
more dismal," Golescu said through a mouthful.
"Me, I feel sorry for kids that never get to ride a
scooter with the whole universe shining around
them."

He chewed for a while, then blurted, "Hey, what
is this problem of ours, Ed? There's no hazard in
jettisoning boiloff cargo, not to anybody except
the insurance carrier. Is there? It's not like when
forty-three's sail rotation went crazy. I still get
nightmares about that one! Why can't we just valve

off the isowhatsit, adjust the sail to whatever new track is right, and get back inside *Merlin*'s rad screen field long before the sun burps?"

"Space contamination," West said. "Weren't you listening?"

"Yeah, but I didn't get it. Eight hundred long tons of gas aren't going to make any dent in all that hard vacuum."

"The devil they aren't. You'd still need instruments to detect the difference, but—well, let's figure it out." West extracted paper, pencil, and a slide rule from a workbench drawer. "At a distance of ten thousand kilometers from sea level, Earth has an angular diameter of, um, call it forty-three and a half degrees. Adding in the surrounding volume of space that concerns us, we can say about fifty-seven and a half. If we jettison, nearly all the gas will arrive there; the molecules have an Earthward component of velocity. Between the upper atmosphere limit and, say, a twenty-five-hundred mile radius from the surface, the concentration of matter will go from about ten molecules per cubic centimeter, if I remember the figure rightly, to . . . good Lord, I have trouble believing this myself! Over fifteen thousand per cc!"

"And so? That's not going to cause any friction worth mentioning."

"We'd actually do better to let the ship blow up," West mumbled, still bent over his work. "In that case the gas will scatter every which way, and maybe only two percent or so will come near Earth. That's still intolerable, though."

"Hell, it'll dissipate again."

"Not for months, I'll bet. Remember the trapping effect of a planetary magnetic field. But even a few hours of that kind of contamination means the biggest economic disaster since the Nucleus failed."

"How come?"

"The equipment in orbit, man! There're a couple of hundred assorted devices near Earth these days. Photocells, for instance, directly exposed to space. Monitoring instruments. How d'you think solar meteorologists get their data? One of the primary sources is a set of ultra-clean metal surfaces with characteristic responses to various radiations— automatic spectrometers sending continuous information to the computers Earthside on the relative output of UV, X-rays, the whole band of solar emission. What do you imagine bombardment by so many metallic-complex molecules, and adsorption, are going to do to the work function of these metals? How about the weather satellites, with their electronic insides open to space, shielded against ions but not against vacuum? Or any cybernet constructed along those lines, controlling some such elaborate apparatus as a radio relay or a Mössbauer clock—or even a manned station." West slapped the bulkhead so hard that it rang. "Bailey said the loss would be ten billion dollars. But I don't believe he was counting in the indirect effects. He probably hasn't the nerve!"

Golescu put down his coffee cup with great care and jammed hands into pockets. A muscle jumped at the corner of his jaw. "I get you," he said.

West discovered that his appetite was gone. *You know*, it occurred to him, *the economic repercussions might even be such that my own government will have to put a surtax on everyone who has any money left, simply to feed the unemployed. Margaret could lose that house yet.*

"Remembered an errand," he said thickly. "I'll

be back later to fetch this tray." He left fast, stumbling at first.

You don't scramble into a full suit of space armor, no matter what the hurry. You wriggle and grunt your way in. Helping Storrs secure a knee joint, Golescu remarked, "And to think, when I was a kid, I figured it would've been real romantic being one of King Arthur's knights."

"Shut up and keep going," Storrs answered.

Maybe I am, though, in a way, Golescu's mind continued. *Or at least it's a line to feed the ladies. That dragon outside is fixing to spew some mighty hot fire.*

The intercom speaker in the locker room resounded with West's voice from the bridge: "*Merlin* calling International Space Control Central. Come in, Central."

The reply was abrupt. "International Space Control Central acknowledging call from *Merlin*. Stand by for relay from Earthside office."

"So they finally woke Bailey up from his nice nap," Storrs said.

"Nah." Golescu finished assisting and went back to clamping his own boots. "He finally came out of conference. Formulation of policy directive in re Cigars, Standard Officers' Issue of and Correct Angle in Mouth of."

"Relax, you chaps," West said. "You ought to know how hard it is to raise a spaceship of some given type on short notice."

"You mean they don't keep Rescue Service craft in orbit, with full crews?" Golescu asked, astonished.

"Oh, they do that much," Storrs admitted grudgingly. "But——"

"Bailey here," said the speaker. "That you, *Merlin*?"

"No, just us chickens," Golescu muttered.

"West speaking, now in command," said the Englishman. "We're near rendezvous with one hundred twenty-eight. I haven't picked up anything else on the radar. You do have tugs here, don't you?"

This close to Earth, there was no time lag that human senses could register. "I'm sorry, no," Bailey said. It was hard to tell whether his tone was curt or merely defensive. "Unfeasible."

"What?" Storrs cried. Golescu watched the shallow face turn quite bloodless. His own heart skipped a beat or two. He got violently busy with his armor. Above the clatter of metal, he heard West:

"But the Rescue Serivce has tugs."

"I know," Bailey said. "Believe me, Captain West, this decision was not arrived at lightly. The unfortunate fact is, as I told you before, every ship that could tow your load on a cable at a high enough acceleration to give us any chance is out on maneuvers. You must be aware that a standard rescue tug does not use cables and is not built for them. Just like your own vessel. A cable would add a great deal of dead weight, for no purpose when it is so easy to clamp on directly with a gyrogravitic grapnel. Nor do the tugs have more power than your type. It isn't necessary, in any foreseeable situation. A disabled ship need only be gotten into a stable orbit to wait for a repair crew. This merely happens to be so improbable a situation that it could not be foreseen."

"But three or four to help us——"

"How will you attach more than one hauler by geegee to a load as small in volume as this? If we had a ship available, so big it could take the container aboard, there would be no problem. Its radiation screen would protect the cargo. But we don't. The Navy transports are gone. So is the *Lunar Queen.*" Bailey's voice turned cold. "With the asterites taking over so much interplanetary shipping, and with so much terrestrial bottom destroyed during the war, those are the only such craft left to us."

Silence extended itself. Golescu could imagine West, alone before the pilot board, his sad eyes resting on the stars and unreachable Earth, methodically trying to think his way out of the trap.

"Build a frame around the gasbag, you Oedipal clot-brain!" Storrs snarled.

"Sam, please," West begged. To Bailey: "Forgive us. We are rather overwrought here, you understand. Er . . . what about it, though? A skeleton of girders around the bag, giving a large effective surface to which several tugs could grapple."

"How long would it take to build?" the man on the ground countered. "You know how ticklish and specialized a job construction in orbit is. The sun would flare hours before any such project could be finished." Something like eagerness came into his speech. "The Rescue Service is prepared to take you aboard one of its own units. You need only detach the sail and other excess mass, hook onto the cargo section, and operate your ship by remote control from ours. Quite safe."

" 'Fraid not," West said. "Herdships don't include equipment for unforeseeable cases, either. All we could do by remote control is turn the Emetts on and off. Which is insufficient. A ship coupled to an outside mass makes a highly unstable system. We'll need a pilot on deck, to correct every time it starts hunting."

He sighed. "Bring your ship around, though. Only one of us has to be aboard."

Storrs's face had gone from white to red. "Why one of *us*?" he shouted. "It's your problem, Earthling!"

There was a thump that might have been Bailey's fist striking his desk. "Yours, sir, yours," he threw back. "Read the Interplanetary Navigation Treaty, or your own franchise. Beltline sent that cargo here, and until delivery has been made, Beltline is responsible for the consequences. If someone has to risk a ship and, yes, a life, why should it be this Earth you despise so loudly?"

"Gentlemen—" West expostulated.

Bailey's tone smoothed over. "I agree. This is no time for recriminations. Do understand that our decision was a hard one. I sympathize with your feelings. We shall all pray for you. And don't forget, if the, um, the outcome is unfortunate, my own position will be seriously jeopardized."

Storrs swallowed something and clanged his faceplate shut.

"Very well, then," West said tiredly. "We'll proceed as best we can. Dispatch that ship of yours. Maintain contact with us. Let us know if you come up with any better ideas."

"Certainly. Good luck, *Merlin*."

"Roger and out, Earth."

Golescu's earplugs registered Storrs's suit radio: "I don't want that bastard's good wishes."

"Me, I'll take every scrap of luck that's offered me," Golescu said. "I'm not proud." To the intercom: "How long till rendezvous, Ed?"

"About ten minutes," West answered. "Better run off your suit checks fast."

"A checked suit . . . in space?" Golescu closed his own faceplate.

By the time he and Storrs had verified that everything was in order and had clumped their way to the airlock, deceleration was ended. They stood unspeaking while the chamber exhausted for them. The outer door opened a cup that brimmed with stars.

Golescu touched the controls of his geegee unit and went forth. Suddenly he was no longer encased in clumsiness, he flitted free as an Earth-dweller can be only in dreams. *Merlin* dwindled to a toy torpedo. Blackness surrounded him, lit by twelve thousand visible suns.

He did not look at his own sun. It could have struck him blind before it struck him dead. And Luna was occulted from here. But Earth lay enormous to one side, a dark ball with one dazzling thin edge and a rim of refracted light. There was not much poetry in his makeup, but he found it hard to remove his gaze from the planet.

Storrs's broadcast voice sounded in his receiver. "We're clear, Ed. Stay where you are till we finish."

"Right-o," said West. "Your velocity relative to target is . . ." He reeled off the figures.

There was scant need. As Golescu swung about, the sailship, which had been at his back, loomed like another Earth.

He had snapped down his glare filter. The stars vanished; he could now have stared Sol in the eye. The disk of the sail reflected with nearly the same brilliance. Protected, he saw it as a great white moon, growing as he sped across the few kilometers between. The suit radar controlled a series of beeps to inform him of vectors and distance. It made a dry, crickety music for his flight. Not exactly the Ride of the Valkyries, he thought—scarier. He found himself whistling soundlessly, the words running defiant through his head.

Chuck Lindbergh was a transporteer, he was, he was.
Chuck Lindbergh was a transporteer, he was, he was.
  His lonesome song was in the news:
  The Spirit of St. Louis Blues.
Bravo, bravo, hurrah for the transporteers!

"Hey, Ed," Storrs called. As an afterthought: "You, too, Andy."

"Yes?" West replied.

"I've been considering. The way this job has developed, it's most likely an impossible one."

"We must try."

"Sure, sure, sure. But listen. It won't do us any good to watch telescopically for the commencement of that flare. The highest energy protons don't travel at much under the speed of light. And there's that whopping probable error in the time prediction. One hour in advance, let's cast off, and to hell with those precious satellites."

"Sorry, old chap, no. *Merlin*'s going to stay coupled and hauling till the end of the run . . . or her. I'll pilot. We can dispense with the engine watch. You and Andy wait aboard the rescue ship."

"Stow that," Golescu said. "What kind of guts do you think we have?"

"You're both young men," West said dully.

"And you're a married man. And I got a reputation to keep up."

"Ease off on the heroics, you two," Storrs said. "If it comes to that, maybe we can cut cards. Meanwhile, every meter we can drag that canned stink spaceward will help some, I suppose—so let's get on with it."

The sail now nearly bisected the sky. Seven kilometers wide, the foam-filled members that stiffened it marching across the field of view like Brobdingnagian spokes with its slow rotation, that disk massed close to a hundred tons. And yet it was ghostly thin, a micron's breadth of tough aluminized plastic, the spin as necessary as the ribs to keep it from collapsing backward under the torque at its edge.

For while the pressure of sunlight in Earth's neighborhood is only some eighty microdynes per square centimeter, this adds up unbelievably when dimensions stretch into kilometers. The sunjammers were slow, their shortest passages measured in months, but that vast steady wind never ended for them; it weakened as they drove starward but so did solar gravity, and in exact proportion. They cost money to build, out in free space, yet far less than a powered ship; for they required no engines, no crews, simply a metal coating sputtered onto a sheet of carbon compounds, a configuration of sensors and automata, and a means to signal their whereabouts and their occasional needs. Those needs rarely amounted to more than repair of some mechanical malfunction. Otherwise little happened on the long, blind voyages. Micrometeoroids eroded the sails, which must eventually be replaced; cosmic rays sleeted through the carrier sections, unheeded by unalive cargoes . . . .

Or solar flares blow them to hellangone, Golescu thought.

First time it's ever happened, he reminded himself, *Probably the last time, too. Unique event. I'm priviledged to be on hand for it. What'm I offered, ladies and gentlemen, for my share of this unique privilege?*

He noticed, with a slight surprise, that he wasn't afraid. Well, nothing very dreadful was going to take place for several hours yet. Except a lot of hard work. Dreadful enough. *I should'a tried for scoopship pilot. Still, you got to make your money somehow, and the pay here is good, to compensate for having nothing to spend it on. A few more cruises, and I'll have me that stake to go prospecting. Now,* there's *the life!*

Passing near the middle of the disk, he noticed the hub in which the sunjammer kept its transmitter and its navigational sensors. Then he had slipped around behind. The monstrous moon turned black for him. He raised his filter and saw it become dim blue with reflected starlight.

Carefully, he moved with Storrs toward the opposite hub. It was linked by a universal joint to a large, dully gleaming cylinder which held the motors. Those drew their power—they didn't need much—from solar batteries in the sunward hub, and used it to control rotation and precession of the sail according to instructions from the pilot computer. For the sunjammer must tack from orbit to orbit, across the ever-radial energy wind. Gravitation helped only on a trip from the outer to the inner system; and even then the reduction vector was a continuously changing thing.

Golescu felt the slight jar as his boots made contact with the precessor hull. They clung, and he rested weightless. The motors beneath had been turned off on radio command from *Merlin*. He stood for a moment letting his eyes complete their adjustment to the wan illumination.

Storrs landed beside him. "Come on," said the impatient voice. "Get the lead out of your rectifier.

We'll need every bit of two hours to unhitch the cargo section as is."

"Yes, sure." Golescu began unstrapping the collapsible tool rack from his shoulders. He and his companion were hung about with equipment like a robot family's Christmas tree.

"I haven't worked on one of this type very often," he admitted. "You'd better be straw boss." He grinned. "I'll be the straw."

Storrs made a sour noise.

The gas carriers were a pretty special model at that. Their cargoes must be shaded by the sail, lest temperature go above critical, the liquefied material boil and the containers rupture. The standard form of sunjammer used a curved sail controlled by shroud lines, which pulled rather than pushed the load. Such an arrangement permitted a considerably larger light-catching area and proportionate freight capacity. The drawback was that maintenance crews on a standard vessel had to begin with erecting a shield between them and the reflector—if they didn't want to be fricasseed in their spacesuits.

West called: "Ed speaking. I had to drop behind. The sail was screening me off from you. Everything in order?"

"Just fine," Golescu said. "Apart from having an itch on my back that I can't scratch, and more work ahead of me than I'd dare load on any machine, and a prospect of getting blown to nanosmithereens, and no women in sight, and hell's own need for beer, I can't complain. Or, rather, I can, but it wouldn't do much good."

"Don't you ever stop chattering, Andy?" Storrs grumbled.

"Let him be, Sam," West advised. "We each need some outlet."

"Well . . . yes. Mine's hating Earth, I suppose. North America, anyway. You Britishers are still human." Storrs carried his tool rack to the farther end of the cylinder and set it in place with what should have been a crash but naturally wasn't. "Those Americans—the muckheads don't even have their regular gas boats out here unloading some of this cargo."

"They can't," West said. "Remember what Bailey told us. They haven't the capacity. Once the container was put in orbit, two or three luggers would have spent a couple of weeks shunting the contents groundside."

"Still," Golescu said, "seems to me that every kilo they can save right now would help. Make matters that much less serious if this thing does blow."

"Wouldn't make any significant difference, in the short time available," West said. "And it'd hamper our operations."

"But doesn't the consignee want his stuff? I checked, and this load is worth eight million dollars F.O.B. That works out to quite a bit per kilo."

"I just told you, Andy, salvage would interfere with the really important job—keeping those satellites functional." West's tone became thoughtful. "Y'know, if we do succeed, there ought to be rather a nice bonus for us."

Golescu snorted. "That's about as likely as the Milky Way curdling. Beltline ain't gonna be happy. Sure, they'll have gained good will Earthside. But they'll have lost a sunjammer and a shipment. Somebody'll have to make the loss good. If it's an insurance company, as I suppose . . . well, imagine what the premiums are going to go up to!"

"We might get a pat on the back," Storrs agreed, "and then the Old Man will call us in privately and tell us that the next time we do so poor a job of chestnut pulling, he'll put us on portside duty, latrine detail."

West sounded shocked. "Are you serious?"

"Uh-huh," Golescu said. "Asterites can't afford excuses. If you don't cut the mustard, you're apt to be dead, and so are your mates."

"But I have to cut it for Earth," Storrs said between his teeth.

Golescu's frame was now also in place. He flitted "up" to install a battery of floodlamps, "down" again to plug them in. Light glared, harsh and undiffused, on the spot where the work must be done.

That was the heavy U-joint connecting precessor with cargo section. The latter was also illuminated in part. Hitherto it had appeared only as a circle of blackness. Now, beyond the framework that held it in place, ponderously counterrotating, the translucent bag glimmered a deep, angry red.

It was not very large to contain so much hell . . . or so much money, Golescu reflected. Space-cold and liquefied under high pressure, the isonitrate occupied a sphere only some ten yards in diameter. Its substance, even the metal atoms, had been reaped from the atmosphere of Jupiter—a chill great star shining in Gemini, two firefly moons visible beside it, treasure house and grave of more asterites than Golescu cared to think about. They were brave men, too, who manned the orbital station where the Jovian complexes were processed into isonitrate. An accident there would not be quite like a nuclear warhead going off, but the difference was academic.

Yet Earth needed those energy-crammed molecules as the starting point for a dozen chemical syntheses. And Earth was willing to pay. Demand evoked supply, including a supply of men to keep production and the Beltline moving.

Golescu began to unclip his tools and hang them on the rack where they would be ready to hand. A sense came to him of his own muscles, not merely in arms but in legs and belly and neck, constantly interplaying with centrifugal and Coriolis forces to hold him in balance on this free-falling shell. That led him to notice how the breath went in and out of his nostrils, tasting of recycler chemicals, and how his heart pumped the blood slowly around the intricate circuit of veins and arteries, and how that made an incessant tiny throb in his ears. He was getting hungry again, and had not lied about wanting a beer . . . ah, cool tickling over his tongue, yes, that was why the asterites must sell to Earth, they hadn't yet succeeded in brewing decent beer themselves . . . .

"Sam," he said, "I've been thinking."

"About time," Storrs grunted.

"No, really. I never wondered about it before. But if this junk is so irritable, how come we can ship it at all? Why doesn't cosmic radiation set it off?"

Storrs sighed. The lamps threw the lean features behind his faceplate into highlights and black gullies. "If you'd spent more time in school learning your science, and less chasing women and beating that guitar—oh, well." He relented. "I'm no chemist myself, but it's fairly obvious. Isonitrate complex is actually quite reasonably stable. It's plain to see that X-rays and electrons don't bother it. And the probability of a high-energy nucleus breaking up enough molecules to start a chain reaction must be extremely low. Trouble right now is, we're due for one all-time concentration of high-energy nuclei."

"Uh, yes. If we could screen them off—maybe mount a field generator on the frame——"

"Where'd you get hold of one that puts out the right size and shape of field, in the time we've got? I daresay they'll be provided in future. Hindsight versus foresight, as usual. Now hurry it up there."

"Wait a bit," West hailed them. "Just got a signal from the Rescue Service ship. Want me to relay to you?"

"Might as well," Golescu said. "For the laughs."

A new voice, accented English: " 'Allo, *Merlin*. International Space Commission Rescue Service cutter *Rajasthan*, commanding officer Villegas speaking. Come in, *Merlin*." Golescu searched for the newcomer, but it must still be only a spark, lost among the stars.

"Acknowledging," said West curtly, and identified himself.

"We 'ave your position and path, *Merlin*. Do you plan to maintain same for t'e present? Yes? T'en we will adopt t'e same orbit, with thirty-kilometer lag. Unless we can do something to 'elp."

"Tell him to send over anybody he's got along who has sailship experience," Storrs said. "With an extra man or two, we'll finish sooner."

West passed the idea on. Villegas hemmed for a moment before answering, "I am most sorry, but we 'ave no such persons with us. You should 'ave asked for t'em before."

"We assumed you weren't infinitely dunderheaded," Storrs bit off. "Our mistake."

"Don't blow your gaskets, Sam," Golescu counseled. "Sunjammers are oddball craft. Earth hasn't got any. How could they know?"

"Beltline's got offices and personnel on Earth! Didn't that Bailey snerd even consult them?"

"Maybe no one was on hand except a secretary. This boat wasn't due to make final approach for another two, three weeks. Maybe all our people who could be of any help are out fleshpotting around Earth and not tuning in any newscasts. I hear they've got some mighty fine places there for that sort of thing."

The byplay had not been relayed. Villegas was saying: "No use to send any of my engineers, yes? T'ey 'ave not t'e special skills. By t'e time t'e men you want could arrive, yours will 'ave finished uncoupling and you will be under acceleration, I trust."

"Well, you'll take mine aboard first," West said. "We only need a pilot here for that maneuver."

"I never thought of Ed as the hero type," Golescu remarked. He squatted to fit a wrench around a bolthead. "Shall we oblige him?"

"What a dilemma," Storrs said acridly. "If I do, I'm a coward. If I don't, and we cut cards, I might end up risking my neck for Mother Earth."

"Come off that shtick, Sam. The war's over, or hadn't you heard? Besides, we may reach jettisoning distance before the flare pops. It's just as likely to be later than prediction as earlier. Or . . . you know, in armor, with a strong metal shield around him, a man might even survive the explosion. There's no air to carry blast. When *Merlin* breaks apart, he could be tossed into space in one piece."

"Sure. Into four thousand roentgens per hour. That means nine minutes for a lethal dose. The other ship isn't going to find him in any nine minutes, chum."

"Hm-m-m . . . true. Damn! What we need is a pocket-size rad screen generator. Or something very thick to hide behind—"

Golescu's words cut off. He stared before him, into the icy light of Jupiter, until its after-image danced through his vision.

All the stars danced.

"What's eating you now?" Storrs growled. "Get to work."

Golescu's yell nearly shattered his own eardrums. Its echoes were still flying around in his helmet when West cried, "What is it? I say, what happened? I'm coming, be there in a few minutes, hang on, boys!"

"No . . . wait . . . hold everything," Golescu stammered. "Not so fast. We're okay. Better than okay."

Storrs closed gauntleted fingers on the other man's shoulder-pieces and shook him. "What's the matter, you clown?"

"Don't you see?" Golescu howled. "We can save the whole shooting match!"

Words flew between sunjammer and herdship. The decision was quickly reached; a spaceman who could not make up his mind from a standing start was unlikely to clutter his profession very long. West called *Rajasthan*. ". . . Send us every hand you can possibly spare," he concluded. "I'll raise Bailey and have him rush us more crews from your service's fleet in orbit. But they can hardly arrive for a few hours yet, and we've got to make what progress we can meanwhile."

"Um-m-m . . . *nombre de Dios* . . . no, Captain,"

Villegas said. "I am sorry, but I 'ave no authority to do t'is."

"Eh? You're in command of your own ship, aren't you?"

"Yes, but my orders were only to——"

West surprised Storrs and Golescu with a choice recital of Anglo-Saxon monosyllables. "Very well, we'll get your orders changed," he said. "Hello, hello, *Merlin* calling International. . . ."

On the sailship, the asterites were hastily clipping tools back onto their armor. They didn't bother with any they didn't expect to need. Those could be collected afterward, if there was an afterward.

"Craziest thing I ever heard of," Storrs panted. "It *ought* to work, but—why didn't anybody think of it on Earth?"

"Same reason you and Ed didn't, I guess," Golescu said. "It's so crude and obvious, only a low wattage brain like mine 'ud see it. At least see it quick-like. I suppose somebody would've hit on it eventually."

"That would have been too late." Storrs's gaze traveled across the awesome blue plain that wheeled before him, curtaining off half the universe. "May be too late already. Hell's kettles, what a huge job!"

"Don't remind me. I got troubles of my own. Ready? Okay, let's stop rotation."

Storrs opened the shield over the manual controls, made several adjustments, replaced the cover, and used the handle of a small crescent wrench to push a deeply recessed button. At once he leaped back, off the cylinder. Golescu went simultaneously.

They were none too soon. Gears meshed, flywheels began to spin, the motor and cargo sections took up the angular momentum which was being removed from the sail. At the same time, the disk was precessed to face the sun directly.

So great a mass could not be stopped fast. Storrs and Golescu flitted clear, out into the fierce light. Their thermostatic units began to labor, converting heat into electricity and storing it in the suit capacitors. That energy would be needed; the men were going to be at work for quite a spell.

"You know," Storrs said, "you weren't right about saving everything. The sail will be lost."

"So?" Golescu returned. "The kit is what matters. A couple of hundred thousand bucks' worth of caboodle is cheap for salvaging the rest."

"If we do."

"Talk about pessimists! Sam, I'm surprised you don't wear a belt and suspenders both . . . .At that, come to think of it, the pieces of sail ought to command fancy prices as souvenirs."

West contacted them: "I'm having a bit of a tussle with Bailey. Let me cut you into the circuit." A pause. "Here they are. You'll have to argue with them as well as me. Equal ranks."

"Ridiculous arrangement," Bailey said.

"Not in the least. Each of us has to be able to do any task that comes along. But let's not waste time. What precisely are your objections to our proposal?"

"Why, the whole concept is fantastic."

"Look," Storrs crackled, "this is our line of work, not yours. We know what's possible and what isn't."

"Eight hours—less than that—to handle forty square kilometers of material?" Bailey protested.

"One micron thick," West pointed out. "A hundred square meters masses only about half a kilo. It's not like building a frame for tugs to grapple.

This job is elementary. Any spacehand with a geegee unit on his suit can do it."

"But—no, you can't."

"Not if you don't send us a swarm of men to help," West admitted. "And soon."

"If you think I'm going to authorize that kind of expense to the taxpayer, think again. I forbid this lunacy. You're hereby ordered to carry on with standard procedures."

An inarticulate sound vibrated in Storrs's throat. Golescu said bad words. West spoke with complete calm:

"You can't forbid it, or issue any order except for us to do our best. Please read the texts you've been citing to me. If Beltline is responsible for this operation, Beltline's agents have to have authority to decide how it shall be carried out. And our decision is to go for broke, as I believe you Americans say. Without your cooperation, we are bound to fail. And what excuse will you offer then? I respectfully suggest, Mr. Bailey, that you get cracking."

Stillness hummed, except for the noise of the crowding, flashing stars. Earth rolled tremendous against an ultimate dark. The sail began to bend at the edges as centrifugal force waned. Had it not faced the sun head on, it could have buckled into a hopeless tangle. As matters stood, when rotation ended it would approximate a section of a sphere.

Bailey's gulp gurgled in earplugs. "You win. I'll get several crews to you within a couple of hours, and meanwhile tell Captain Villegas to put his men under your direction. What equipment will be needed?"

"Torches, mainly," West said. "Quickest way of slicing up that stuff. We have metal rods aboard, so I can construct a frame to hold the whole mess in position myself, rather fast. Your gang will also want . . ."

Golescu signaled Storrs to switch bands. *"Whew!"* he said. "That was a nasty minute. I didn't think old Ed had it in him."

"Ed's a good fellow," Storrs said. "Uh, we'll still only require one man aboard *Merlin*, but——"

"Hell with that bleat. We're in this together. I'm sticking with him when the time comes."

"Right. Me too."

It was necessary for the herdship to grapple and apply power, lest spin expose the bag to the radiation storm. Golescu should have been at the pilot board then, but he and Storrs were too exhausted. The work had been brutal. They sat in the saloon with untasted mugs of coffee, staring emptily at the bulkheads, while West rode the controls.

Outside, Lucifer ran free. Coughed from the sun, ions with energies in the millions of electron volts flooded all space. Down on Earth, tourists in the Antarctic lodges crowded into the observation domes to watch the winter sky come alive with vast flapping curtains of aurora. Elsewhere, men who had heard the news huddled near their 3V screens, waiting for word. Reception was poor. The nuclear generators of ships beyond the atmosphere poured power into screen fields, deflecting that murderous torrent from their hulls. The engineers' eyes never left the gauges.

Merlin throbbed. Now and then, as she moved to keep the load at the end of her grapnel on an even keel, her members groaned with stress. That was the only token granted the men in the saloon. They dared not interrupt the pilot with questions.

"It's got to work," Storrs said stupidly, for the dozenth time. He rubbed his chin. The bristles of beard made an audible scratching.

"Sure it will," Golescu said. "My idea, wasn't it?" The cockiness had left his voice.

"Well," Storrs said, "if it doesn't . . . if that cargo explodes . . . we'll never know." He laid his fist on the table and regarded the knobby knuckles. "I'd like to know, though. How I'd laugh at those fat Earthlings."

Golescu reached for his coffee. It had gone cold. "They aren't that bad. And if you've got to be such a hot-bottomed patriot, don't forget that trouble on Earth would affect the Republic. We need them, same as they need us."

"Bull. I can show you economic statistics—damn and double damn! It isn't right! How many men's lives is it proper to risk, to save ten billion or so lousy dollars?"

"That dinero represents a lot more man-years than we three will rack up, even if I achieve my ambition to become a dirty old man."

"Work years. Not deaths."

"Scared?"

Storrs spat in the ashcatcher. "No. Tired and angry. This means one thing to Ed. Economic breakdown on Earth would hurt him directly. But you and me——"

"You didn't have to be aboard."

"I sure did."

"Oh, fork all those fancy moral issues," Golescu said. "This is what we get paid for."

"Hm-m-m . . . yeah . . . .Another half hour to go, by the clock, if the prediction is right. I hope Ed can stand the strain."

"He'd better. That's the real chance we take. We

knew right along the shield would be more than ample. Well, I saw him swallow a whole medicine chest full of antifatigue pills and psychodrugs." Golescu stirred in his seat. "Feel like a game of rummy?"

"No."

The sun's arrows rushed on through vacuum. Where they encountered *Merlin*'s screen, they swerved, with a spiteful gout of X-radiation that her internal shielding drank up. Where they struck at the cargo section—

They hit a barrier of plastic and aluminum: the sail, cut into fifteen-meter squares that were layered within a welded framework. The shielding factor came to about fifty grams per square centimeter. Light metals and hydrogen-rich carbon compounds are highly effective stoppers of stripped small atoms like the hydrogen and helium ions which make up nearly the whole of flare emission. For example, 32.7 grams per square centimeter of aluminum will halt protons of 200 million electron volts. The recoil characteristics are such that secondary radiation is not a serious problem—at least, not to isonitrate, which is only touched off by a nucleus plowing into its giant molecule.

But the whole clumsy ensemble of shield, cargo section, and herdship must be kept facing directly into the blast. And gravitation kept trying to swing it into orbit, which brought gyroscopic forces into play. Control was exercised at the end of a long arm; the mass had considerable turning moment, nor was it perfectly balanced. Compensation could become overcompensation with gruesome ease.

"If we ride this one out," Golescu said, "we really will get that bonus Ed was faunching for."

"Uh-huh." Storrs raised dark-rimmed eyes. "Andy,

you're a good oscar and I hope we can ship out together again, but right now I've got some thinking to do. Keep quiet, huh?"

"Okay," Golescu said. "Though thinking's the last thing I want to do."

He prowled aft to have a look at the engine-room meters. Not that he could improve matters much if anything was going awry, in his present condition. Why had not one single man, out of the scores who divided the sail, volunteered to ride along and help? Earthlings, of course, had no great cause to love asterites. Golescu caught himself wondering if the revolution had really been justified—if anything ever was that raised such bitterness between men. *Now stow that! Break out the guitar and —no, it'd bother Ed. Sam too, I guess.*

I should'a taken a sleeping pill—uh-uh, none o' that, either.

His bleared vision focused on the bank of indicators. Everything operating smoothly—good ship—wait a second! The external radiation count—

"Yi-yi-yip!" he screamed. "She's going down! The flare's dying!" And he did a war dance around the workshop and up the length of the corridor beyond.

Slowly, slowly, the storm faded. Until at last West said from the intercom, "It's over with. We're alive, boys."

Storrs began to dance, too.

After a while West reported, "Earth called in. Congratulations and so forth. They'll send a tug at once for this cargo, and hold it in the moon's shadow while they unload. We're invited groundside for a celebration." Wistfulness tinged his voice. "D'you think the company would mind if we accepted?"

"They better not," Storrs said.

"We need a checkout anyway, after putting the ship to so much stress," Golescu added. "And they'll have to compute a new orbit for the rest of our mission. We're bound to have a few days' layover." Exhaustion dropped from him. "Fleshpots, here I come!"

He snatched up his guitar and bellowed forth:

Ol' Einstein was a transporteer, he was, he was.
Ol' Einstein was a transporteer, he was, he was.
His racing car used too much gas;
It shrank the time but it raised the mass.
Bravo, bravo, hurrah for the transporteers!

Now he had a story to embroider for the girls in Pallas Town.

Interlude 6

Amspaugh, whose official position at the time provided him with many details that didn't get into the news, finishes the story.

"And the moral of it is?" Lindgren sounds a trifle sardonic.

"That there isn't any moral," McVeagh says.

"Or else that there're as many different morals as persons who want to draw one," I complain.

Dworczyk claps his hands down onto his knees. "This isn't helping us launch," he says. "I repeat, our business is not to make some pompous 'interpretation' and stuff it down the throats of the young. They'd regurgitate it anyway. We're simply choosing what facts, what actual events, every educated individual aboard this ship ought to know. Along with what aspects of political background, technology, economics, manners, morals, and so forth, at any given time, are worth remembering."

"Of course," Missy nods. "Our problem, though, is to find a basis on which to select what information should be included."

"But it's so simple!" Dworczyk exclaims.

We regard him. He drops his eyes momentarily sheepish; then he stiffens in defiance. "Okay," he says. "You want my specs. I'll give 'em to you. How's this for a broad outline of postwar history?"

He takes a few more seconds to arrange his words, then:

"In spite of everything, old grudges did tend to die, especially as prosperity grew and spread. The nations of Earth came to like the Republic, and many sold what asteroids they still had to its government. Their traffic with it was making them steadily more comfortable, as material resources flowed in from space. They didn't mind that per capita wealth was increasing faster—much faster—among the asterites. After all, the typical asterite worked a lot harder, often a lot more dangerously, than the typical citizen of a welfare state. Technological progress made it easier and easier to do things. The average Earthling took advantage of this opportunity to relax, to enjoy more leisure and security. The average asterite used the new capabilities to accomplish more. That made him richer yet; but from the Earthling's point of view, we weren't allowing ourselves a decent amount of time for enjoying that money."

"Besides," McVeagh comments, "Earthlings got—still get—vast satisfaction out of decrying the crudity and materialism of the space dwellers."

"It's too bad so many of the younger generation in the Republic are taking the Earthside criticism seriously," Amspaugh says.

"Oh, I don't know," Lindgren replies. "The end result may be just to polish some of the rough edges off our people. That, for certain would be no bad thing. Anyway, it's not our problem aboard this ship."

"Let me finish my outline, please," Dworczyk says. "I realize I've been using stereotypes. A book would have to show it was more complicated and interesting than that. Um-m-m . . . Plenty of Earthmen were explorers, pioneers, innovators, entrepreneurs. And plenty of asterites were scientists, artists, poets, philanthropists. Especially after a large economic surplus became available, private foundations and consortiums undertook nonprofit enterprises—like building a ship to reach the stars."

He stands up. "That's a rough sketch of what I have in mind," he says. "I really don't understand what the fuss is about. Let's lay down a truthful outline of what happened. The writers can fill it in with significant and entertaining details. And there you are. Now, either we cut this meeting pretty soon so I can return to my lab, or I'm going to pour me a drink and forget about working today."

"Bring me a rum and grapefruit juice, then, while you're at it," Amspaugh smiles. "You've hit the nucleus of our real problem."

"Which is?"

"Look, we want the youngsters to get a balanced account of the events that led to their being aboard— that made us determine the course of their lives. We want them to become neither nihilistic cynics, such as Colin pretends to be, nor unrealistic ideologues, such as Conchita pretends to be." Amspaugh wags his pipestem in the direction of those two. "You grapple my meaning, I hope. You're sincere in your basic views, and we want you to express them so we can get as wide a variety of opinions as possible. But in a discussion like this, everybody tends to overstate his own case." To Dworczyk: "You included. Tom."

"Okay, I'm off to the bar." Dworczyk continues talking as he moves. "Tell me how I exaggerate."

"As regards the possibility of a simple, straightforward account of happenings that were anything else except that. Oh, yes, it can be done for the earlier days. No great harm in ignoring certain complexities and failings among our glorious ancestors. However—" His humor departs Amspaugh. He becomes occupied with his pipe, knocking out dottle, refilling, relighting, "However," he says slowly, "we can't hide what is in this ship. She's not that big; and the children will have eyes to see what's around them. How shall we teach them to understand, and forgive, the raw truth?"

"Why . . . that wasn't supposed to pose any grave difficulties, was it?" Dworczyk reaches his destination and gets busy. "Had it been, this expedition would scarcely have started off."

"True, true," Amspaugh says. "Nevertheless, it's one thing to decide in theory that such-and-such a human situation ought to work out as planned. It's quite another to try it in practice. That's why the Board—very rightly—ruled that we should decide our own educational policies, after we'd had some direct experience. And my impression, on the basis of that experience, is that the decision's no easy one to make."

"Correct," Missy says. "The kids won't have known any world except this ship. They'll take for granted that the order of things here is right and normal . . . until their school history teaches them that it's exceptional, that other orders exist which are entirely different. The shock of learning this, if it isn't taught with care, could be badly unsettling."

"I can bear witness to that from the opposite side," I remark.

"How so?" Echevaray asks.

With hundreds aboard, *Astra* hasn't been under weigh so long that each of us in this room has had a chance to become familiar with the past life of everyone else. This is the more true when the experience I am thinking of was never made public.

"I didn't know what the setup was when I first came here," I say. "Believe me, it rocked my back teeth to find out."

"How could you not have heard?" Echevaray wonders. "With the years she was a-building, the thousands of books, 'casts, news stories, debates——"

"But I wasn't in the Belt," I explain, "or on Earth, Luna, Mars, the Jovian moons, anywhere in easy contact. I'd spent the previous five years on Triton, helping construct the city there for Nasty."

"For what?"

"Neptune And Satellites TYcoons. Not the official name of the outfit, nor the acronym we used when a big jet came visiting from headquarters." Nor was this the acronym we used when ladies weren't present. "Anyhow, my contract expired before we got the maser receiver built, so word from the inner System while I was there depended on an occasional supply ship. No doubt the reading matter that came in held some scatty accounts of *Astra*'s personnel difficulties. But I didn't happen to see them. After a tour of work"—in rock wastes, the night upon them hardly touched by a sun that was hardly more than the brightest of the stars, their sky dominated and saddened by Neptune's dim gray hulk—"a chap wants a nice piece of . . . of escape fiction, that is, not serious news analysis from worlds that almost don't seem real any longer. Or he'll go for games, sports, chasing the few unmarried females, and other hobbies. All in all, I came back with no idea of the truth about this project."

"You must have picked it up quite soon," Dworczyk says.

"Sure, I would've," I reply. "But don't forget, by then the policy decision had been made. The subject had stopped being news; everybody took for granted that everybody else knew the facts.

"That certainly was the case in company HQ on Ceres. I checked in with the idea of drawing my back pay and bonuses and really doing the planets on the year's leave I had coming. But they requested me rather urgently to handle one more job first. As you probably know, they were the prime contractor for this ship's internal power grid. It'd tested out well, but had suddenly been reported as giving bad trouble. Nobody aboard seemed able to find out what was wrong, and every qualified engineer on the company's rolls was busy elsewhere. And the system was similar to the one I'd been concerned with on Triton.

"Well, what the deuce, why not? I was interested in seeing the vessel anyway. They sent me in one of their speedsters. That didn't give me much time to study the technical setup; *Astra* happened to be orbiting fairly close to Ceres just then. So I had no conversation with my pilot. I arrived totally unprepared for the kind of men I'd meet. Talk about getting rammed in the rear by a comet!"

Recruiting Nation

At first she was only another spark and would have been lost in the star swarms did she not show the flicker and twinkle of an irregular body rotating in spatial sunlight. But the boat closed swiftly in. *Astra* swelled to a globe, to a city of clustered domes and turrets and housings and machines, to a world filling nearly half the sky. I leaned back in my safety harness and watched the play of radiance and shadow across that medley, as we spiraled toward rendezvous. The low power-hum vibrated in me like the beat of my own blood. The words that came to me from the forward section, where my pilot spoke with a traffic control officer, were laconic; but bugles have sent less of a shiver along my skin.

Here was the ship that would seek new suns.

Not at once, I reminded myself. *At least two years' worth of work—basic work, not the improvements that the crew can make during her long voyage—remains to be done. Including this debugging job of mine. And didn't Garrett drop some remark about recruiting troubles, about there not yet being a minimal complement committed to go? I can't understand that. When did a splendid vision ever lack for followers?*

An entry port gaped before us. I felt the slight,

elastic impact when the mesh field took hold on our hull and eased it into a cradle. The lock closed and air brawled in to repressurize the chamber. My pilot checked his gauges, uttered a final sentence to the control office, opened a master switch, and started unharnessing. "Here we are, Mr. Sanders," he said.

"Well, thanks." I undid my own webbing. "You bound straight back?"

"Oh, I may have a cup of coffee first somewhere, if I can find somebody worth talking to. But otherwise, yeah, no reason to stay." He yawned. "You'll probably be around for days or worse. I do sympathize. Mase us a call the instant you're through, and if it's me that's sent to fetch you, I'll cram on every *g* this boat has got."

It puzzled me. True, he must have visited the ship fairly often; but weren't she and her folk inexhaustible? I didn't inquire, because the chamber was now airful and the inner gate had swung wide. Two men waited. The pilot opened a valve for me and I clattered down the cradle stairs and across the deck to greet them.

One was grizzled and portly, his most conspicuous feature a rose nose, his garments a zigzag of reds, blues, and yellows so bright that my eyes hurt. He grabbed my hand and pumped it as if hoping I'd spout water. "Winston Sanders, hey?" he boomed. "Welcome aboard, welcome aboard! I'm your friendly chief engineer of interior power; Hodge is my name, Hodge Furlow, that is. When I heard you were making approach, I came right down to meet you personally. Have a nice trip?"

Slightly deafened, I contented myself with saying, "It was okay, thanks. Er—" My gaze went to the other man, who stood or rather loomed behind

Furlow. He was a conspicuous object. Though his enormous shoulders hunched forward, he was a head taller than me, and the beer belly that strained his slovenly coverall didn't make him appear less formidable. His face did a little: coarse features stubblefield jaw not much forehead, but at least a vacant grin. "Uh, Mr. . . . ?"

"Oh. That's J. P.," Furlow said. "My special assistant. You have baggage?"

"A fair amount. I brought my basic gear, instruments, tools, standards . . . you know."

Furlow looked hurt. "I assure you we're well supplied in my department, Win."

"Where you're going, you'd better be," I said snappishly. I don't like hearing my first name on first acquaintance. "However, I'm used to my own kit. And you've not had any dazzling success with yours, have you?"

"True, alas, true." Furlow dropped his tone to a dull roar. "Well, J. P. will bring it to your quarters." Turning to his companion. "You read me, J. P. ? Go in that boat. Ask for Mr. Sanders' baggage. Put it on a carrier. Take it to Suite Forty-six on M Deck. Got it?"

"Baggage," the giant replied. His voice was surprisingly high. "Suite Forty-six. M Deck. Okay." He slouched off.

Furlow linked arms with me. "Let's make for my quarters, Win. You must be tired. We'll chat over a drink and a smoke till lunch."

Perforce I accompanied him, into a corridor so long that its ends were hidden by the curvature of the ship. Nothing relieved it except doors and side passages. No doubt the decoration of its metal harshness, and that of hundreds like it, would help occupy the man-years of an interstellar voyage. At present it lay eerily empty and silent. I heard pumps throb, I caught gusts of warm, oily air, but chiefly I was conscious of how loudly our foot-falls echoed.

"I'm not tired," I said. "Slept well last nightwatch. Shouldn't I pay my respects to the captain?"

"He's not aboard," Furlow answered. "Seldom is. What would he be doing? The senior officer on duty in the executive department—um, I can't think who that'd be, but it doesn't matter. Some fourth- or fifth-level stripling. I'm sure I rank him, whoever he is. And he's probably still in bed—not necessarily alone, haw!"—a thumb nearly stove in a rib of mine "—and wouldn't appreciate having to act official. If he wants to see you, he'll let us know."

Oof! my mind exclaimed in its shock. Before me rose the image of every other spacecraft I'd ever been inside, and unterraformed asteroids, unearthly planets, moons of Neptune. The ultimate thin wall between men and raw space was discipline. *Do they figure to reach Alpha Centauri in this condition?*

"Well," I said harshly, "in that case, let's take a look at the system. The sooner I get to work, the sooner I can hope to crack your problem."

"Are you the solid-state citizen!" Furlow shook his head and clicked his tongue. "As you wish. To be frank, I doubt if you can accomplish much. No reflection on you, my boy. But your old Uncle Hodge isn't a complete fumblethumb, if I say it as shouldn't. No, he's not quite ready for the last orbit, these old brain cells still have some juice in them—and I've been working for months, Win, months, without getting into trajectory. With my whole team, remember, and a holdful of apparatus. I probably should have hollered to your company earlier, but I thought and I think, if we couldn't track down the cause, nobody can. You see, I don't believe the trouble has any simple cause."

He showed me to a lift shaft. Actually, we floated down, though that took me by surprise for a moment till I realized what it meant. Unlike more conventional vessels, this one imitated a terraformed asteroid in having Emetts at the center which generated a radial weightfield. The heart of the interior power complex was many decks inward from the hull.

Most of the levels we passed were deserted; nobody was living there yet, or nothing stored, or nothing installed. In a few, workmen were busy. It pleased me to glimpse their clean, efficient movements. "Any of those fellows coming along on the trip?" I asked.

Furlow guffawed. "You have a great sense of humor. Win. I like you. I really do. Tell you what. We'll stop at the Pallas Palace, it's right on the way, and I'll buy you a drink. Don't refuse. Man needs a quick drink, this hour."

"The Pallas Palace?"

"Our bar. The one that's open, I mean. Goes without saying, we'll need more en route. It's a long dry way to Alpha C, hey?"

We swung ourselves out into a section that looked more cheerful than what I'd seen hitherto. Corridors were painted and padded; an occasional door stood ajar, showing a piece of room and furnishing. Evidently this was where some of the crew—those whose jobs already kept them in the ship part of the time—resided. Probably the work gangs, who'd return home when their tasks were done, used unoccupied cabins elsewhere. Single men in temporary housing wouldn't fix it up this elaborately. We met a number of dwellers as we walked, male and female, moving along the halls or in and out of the apartments. They hailed Furlow, who seemed popular, and he made jovial response. The place might almost have been a small new settlement in the Belt.

Almost. Not quite. The difference, the wrongness grew on me with each step I took.

There were no children; that was to be expected at this stage. But there were too many old people. Nearly half of those I saw were wrinkled, white-haired, worn down by time. They kept their vigor; decks have been mopped with more than one Earthside tourist who referred to an aged asterite as a Senior Citizen. But they had spent most of their years.

And their briskness was lacking in the young. With few exceptions, those in the prime of life sauntered rather than strode, loafed around in a park circle through which we passed, sat slackly behind half-open doors watching 3V. Unlike the old, they tended to be pale and soft.

I did spy one good-looking group of youngsters, bounding along in a cloud of laughter. But they weren't on duty. The apparatus they carried was for a game of spaceball. And . . . I'm no prude, but some of the boy-girl antics weren't seemly . . . in public . . . on a ship!

"Haven't they anything better to do?" I exclaimed.

"Why, no," Furlow said. "Isn't it common knowledge? Part of the eventual crew are already aboard because they're concerned with preparations or maintenance, like me. But a larger part is simply here for the free food and lodging. How else could we attract them?"

Awhirl with bewilderment, I barely noticed his continuing talk while he hustled me onward:

"Getting back to our trouble, I'm sorry to say it of your outfit, Win, but I'm certain the fault is lousy design. No blame on you; you didn't draw the plans. And the components are okay. You know your company doesn't make but a few of those. It buys units from specialist manufacturers and fits them together. The black box principle, hey, boy? When something blows, you don't muck around trying to find one transistor or whatever the little dingbat is, one out of maybe a million, and fix it or replace it. No, you see right away on the meter which sealed unit isn't taking in the input or putting out the output. You yank that whole unit, plug in a fresh one, and repair the damage at your leisure."

I thought, vaguely, that he didn't mean to insult me with a kindergarten lecture. He merely suffered from logorrhea. Perhaps he wasn't even listening to himself. I tried not to. The thunders rolled remorselessly on:

"Well, now. Our power grid worked fine at first. Just fine. But then, several months back, it started going floomp. Irregular intervals, no predicting when. Nor any predicting which boxes would blow. They might be in the voltage regulation, the phasing control, the amplification, anywhere. Suddenly, boom, several units stop operating. Alarms sound, ring-ding-ding, poor Uncle Hodge got to tumble out of a sound sleep, like as not, and come fixee-fixee. We've got bypasses and standbys, sure. Nothing bad happens, no shutdown. But you don't like being without plugged-in spares, not in space you don't, hey? So you replace the blown units.

"Then you try to figure out what made them blow. I took charge of that. Opened each one myself. That was another reason I prevailed on the Foundation to delay calling in the contractor. We have to be absolutely certain that we can make every repair ourselves. You can't trot across any four and a half light-years to lend a hand, can you, my boy?

"In every box, the inside components were fused, so badly that it wasn't worth repairing, not even worth removing the parts that had escaped damage."

I grew alert. He hadn't told me anything I didn't know, but he sounded as if now he might. "I'd like to check those boxes too," I said.

Furlow raised beefy shoulders and let them fall again. "Sorry. I only kept one to show. For the rest, well, you realize how it is, Win. Skilled labor is worth more, by a good big factor, than the machine time it takes to make new units like these. So, like I said, repairing them wouldn't pay. However, each one *is* pretty damn expensive. Think of those rare elements and special isotopes that have to be put into the crystal structures just so. They don't come cheap. In fact, the Foundation's getting awful worried about these losses.

"So, trying to save the project what money I could. I've been shipping the ruined units to Mountain King Electronics on Hebe. They buy 'em to salvage the valuable nuclides. That way, a little of the cost gets returned to the Foundation. Not much, but a little."

I hadn't known that, though it was obvious that continual replacement of sophisticated black boxes would in time become financially murderous. My concern had been with the functioning of the system itself. Furlow was right; once the ship was off in interstellar space, he couldn't order supplies or bring in consultants. And what *Astra* could carry was limited.

And without interior power—for light, heat, ventilation, weight, bionics, utilities, a thousand different and essential machines—her people were dead.

"You have kept a spoiled unit, you said?" I asked.

"Yes, sure, sure, I expected somebody'd want to see one. It's from a six-way junction-point current distributor. You can take my word its condition is typical. . . . But here we are. Here's the dear old fuel tank."

A racket of voices and boom-boom music had been growing around us. Turning a corner, we saw the Pallas Palace. It was a sizable cabin with a vitryl bulkhead fronting on the hall. A bar was to the rear, tables to the front, a small dance floor on one side. Despite the early hour, it held a score or so, and saxophones were moaning out of a speaker. I don't like saxophones. My boyhood was misspent on a farm asteroid, and I got tired of listening to lovesick cows.

We made our way through the air, which was smoky enough to cut, among beer-wet tables and past squirming dancers, to the bar. It had live service. That didn't surprise me; why haul the mass of needless automata out of the Solar System? What did surprise, and dismay, was that crewfolk— they could only be crewfolk—were behaving like this.

"Morning, Ed, morning!" Furlow bellowed above the noise. "Double bourbon, straight, and what'll you have, Win? On me."

I tried to refuse, but he was so insistent that finally I took a soft drink. I also hate soft drinks.

We were standing there sipping, Furlow hailing everybody in sight and occasionally reaching out to paw some giggling girl, when a hand closed around my arm and a voice said, "My God, if it isn't Winston Sanders! Hoy, lad!"

I turned, and choked. The man was slim, dapper, sharp-featured, with slick black hair and snapping brown eyes. I knew him of old, a college chum. We'd seen each other infrequently since I became an engineer dispatched from world to world and he settled down in an insurance agency on Juno; but our reunions were good. It had saddened me two years ago to see, in a letter from a mutual acquaintance, that Jake Jaspers had been convicted of embezzlement.

"Son of a bitch!" The traditional spaceman's oath sputtered out of me. He grabbed my hand almost as energetically as Furlow but, somehow, more warmly. After a second I put aside both astonishment and moralism. We pounded each other on the back and I ordered a beer after all.

"What're you doing here, Jake?"

"Oh, passing the time. I'm in the steward's department, accounting office, but till the next load of gear arrives, I've nothing to account about, and my wife—say, I bet you don't know I'm married. Can you come to dinner? Have you signed on with us?"

"No, I'm troubleshooting. But, uh, that is, I heard——"

Jaspers laughed, entirely at ease. "That! My sentence was suspended on condition I join this ship. We've got quite a few like me."

I was glad for his sake. You can debate whether the Republic is right in rejecting Earth-style psychorehabilitation as an insult to the individual and a menace to liberty. But you can't blink the fact that our labor bases are pretty bleak. Not inhumane, of course; most have facilities for recreation, conjugal visits, spare-time education; and the work done is socially useful; but I'd hate to spend several years in one, and it'd have been worse for a *bon vivant* like Jake Jaspers.

Nevertheless—a starship with criminals in the crew?

"Sure, I'd be happy to come eat," I mumbled. He told me his apartment number, we set a time, and then I managed to detach Furlow from the bar.

He guided me through several deeper levels. Near the axis of the vessel, we stopped. Here was the core of the complex over which he presided: control rooms, workshops, the great central computer and its satellites scattered through the whole ship. On the way I had mentally reviewed the schematics.

The energy source was the same set of fusion reactors that activated the gyrogravitic drive. There was no reason to install another set for Furlow's department. If either engines or interior grid failed, the ship was equally doomed. But naturally, this mutual use complicated an already difficult problem.

The reactors had given no trouble. They continued faithfully furnishing as much power as desired. What kept breaking down was the distribution of that power.

"I take for granted you've run independent checks on the computers," I said.

"Independent and exhaustive, my boy. On the main one, on the auxiliaries, and on the lot of them in every combination and permutation. Look over my results if you want. Nothing came out less than magnificent." Furlow puffed himself up. "If I couldn't make sure of that, I shouldn't be in this job, hey?"

I nodded irritably. It was a duck-billed platitude.

The chief electrical engineer had to be good in all specialties that concerned his work, but first and foremost he had to be a computerman.

The schematics went on running through my brain. Counting the square kilometers of inside space—cabins, holds, corridors, shops, machine sites—*Astra* had the dimensions of a large city. And her power requirements were more, in volume as well as intricacy. Life might flourish aboard her, balancing its intake and outgo as automatically as life does on the mother world. But maintaining an environment where this was possible—in a hull alone for decades in airless, sunless, radiation-riddled space—took a network of artifacts whose complexity approached that of a living organism. And every one of those artifacts drew the energy that ran it from the electrical web which, simultaneously, linked them all together.

Here a heater, there a cooler; here a light, there a stove; here a cybernet requiring EMF exact to the microvolt, there a superwaldo drawing five hundred amps; here a radiation meter detecting single electrons, there a screen field which, created in an emergency, sucked megajoules in its first few seconds of buildup; and on and on, endless kilometers of wire, millions of transformers, transducers, electronic valves, amplifiers, regulators, generators, motors. . . . The human mind could no more visualize this creation of the human mind than an embryo can imagine the adult into which it will change itself.

"Okay," I said, foreseeing the answer, "what do you think is at fault in these breakdowns?"

"I told you," Furlow stated. "Rotten design. Maybe no one could've done better than your company did. Nothing quite like this has ever been made before. But the upshot is, the system's unbalanced. It's liable to violent surges, where positive feedback sets in—not throughout the whole, which'd at least trip circuit breakers, but locally. Before safety devices can operate, a number of components have gotten more juice than they can take."

"But the computers," I objected, "especially the main one, the computers are supposed to keep track of the current flow and vary it according to capacity as well as demand."

"Yeah, they're supposed to. Only they aren't doing it, my boy, they aren't doing it. Now and then they lose control. Right away you get a situation like a power blackout in an old-time interstate grid."

"What would cause the loss of control?"

"Probably inadequate monitoring. The instruments which keep the computers 'aware' of the state of the system at every point and every instant—well, my theory is that sometimes those instruments get 'confused' and send false information. This makes the computers order some very wrong shunting, which bollixes the monitors still worse, and so it goes. In a few milliseconds, you've built up bad trouble. Then after the damage has been done, when the standbys and bypasses cut in, the coefficients change and you get proper operation again—for a while."

I scowled and tugged my chin. "As for what starts the 'confusion,' " I said, "you feel that the system itself does?"

"Yeah. You can't expect monitors, computers, and regulators to do everything when a grid is this size and this complicated. The grid has got to have some inherent stability. True?"

"Uh-huh," I agreed reluctantly.

"Well, this one doesn't seem to."

"If you're right," I said, "the whole works will have to be ripped out, redesigned, rebuilt, retested——"

"Well, nobody's going to travel with a power system we can't trust."

"You might not get the chance to quit," I told him. "You may simply get laid off when they abort the project. My company contracted to put in a grid according to an agreed-on design. Our warranty only covers workmanship. It has to be that way; it's normal practice, in a largely experimental job like this. We're not obliged to do it over from zero, for nothing, and we won't, because we can't afford to. And the Astra Foundation doesn't have infinite money, either."

Having already faced on my own account the possibility of a total abort—since Furlow's diagnosis was bound to occur to any person who dealt with this kind of layout—I spoke in sadness rather than dismay. Also, I noticed, in puzzlement more than sadness. Because damnation, the grid ought not to be unstable! It wasn't that different from the ones in places like Tritown.

So maybe the trouble was in a key subassembly; or maybe Furlow had been mistaken when he gave the computers a clean bill of health; or maybe— whatever the truth was, I might well be weeks about tracking it down: especially if the grid was so impolite as not to misbehave while I was here to observe at first hand.

And double damnation, after five years under Neptune I *needed* the pleasures of Ceres, Odysseus, Mars, Luna, Earth . . . urgently!

We entered the first of a series of offices between us and the nearest control chamber. Through their transparent walls I could see the banks of meters, displays, blinking lights, switches, buttons, and induction plates which I must master. A low hum filled the air. So did a smell of incense.

Incense?

I glared wildly around. A few rooms held engineering types. They didn't seem to be working especially hard; in fact, I saw one man catching a nap. But where we were, the occupant sat on his desk in the lotus position. He wore a yellow robe and a beaded headband. A joss stick burned in a holder before him. His eyes were closed and his lips moved soundlessly.

"What the devil?" I started toward him.

Furlow halted me. "Better leave him alone. He's, uh, what he calls contemplating the allness of immanence. Or is it the other way around? I keep forgetting which."

"You let him say his prayers on watch?"

"Not prayers, exactly, I'm told. He's a Reformed Pantheist, Arkansas Synod. He doesn't go into these trances too often, Win. You should see some of our real nut cultists." Furlow put his mouth to my ear and whispered: "We got to take what staff we can get, you know. I'm afraid you'll find, even in this department, most of them aren't worth diddly-squat."

I arrived late for dinner. "Sorry," I apologized at the door. "I got so dirty I had to stop and bathe as well as change clothes."

"A man of your rank, crawling around in machinery?" Jaspers marveled. "I thought that's what the junior grades are for."

"So did I. But except for Furlōw, the gang's as dreadful a clutch of routineers and outright incompetents as I ever had the misfortune to wade through."

My friend sighed. "No surprise, is it? Well, come on in."

The apartment managed to be both vivid and home-like. Anne Jaspers was a small, pert woman whose figure reminded me acutely of how overdue I was for some R & R. We sat down over large martinis, in an aroma of roasting meat and the frolicking of a flute concerto.

"Good to see you again." Jaspers clinked glasses with me. "How's the universe been treating you?"

"Not often enough." The ancient joke didn't stretch to cover my embarrassment. "Uh you. . . ?"

Jaspers struck a cigarette. "Ease off, Win," he smiled. "You know, Anne knows, I know I made a mistake. It was my good luck that I could bug out of the consequences by taking a berth here, and my incredibly good luck that this girl did the same." He patted her hand. She purred. He added quickly: "Not that she signed on for any of the usual reasons. She truly wants to reach Alpha Centauri. She's a biologist, you see, and the latest probe data prove there's at least one planet similar to Earth, complete with life. By now, she's got me eager, too."

"But how many aboard are like you, Mrs. Jaspers?" I asked.

"Anne, please," she replied. "The answer is: our top-echelon officers and scientists. They're going for the sake of discovery."

"Maybe ten percent of the total crew," Jaspers estimated.

"But what about the other ninety percent?" I persisted. "Clods, cranks——"

"Crooks," he finished. "Sure. What else did you expect?"

"What *else?* My God, the greatest voyage in history, and . . ."

They studied me till Anne said: "You know, I don't believe you've heard about the recruitment problem. The ship was in an early stage of construction when you left . . . five years ago, was it? Nobody had yet made a serious attempt to collect personnel. The difficulty didn't become plain till, oh, three years back; and the solution wasn't accepted for several months after that."

"Could that be right, Win?" her husband said. "You never got the news, and nobody's thought to tell you?"

"Seems like it." I sat back grimly, and don't tell me that isn't possible. "Proceed."

"Well, it should've been foreseen," Jaspers said. "I've read a number of sociological treatises demonstrating the inevitability. Wonderfully sharp hindsight. The matter crystallizes out to something very simple. Who wants to leave Utopia?"

"I don't track you."

"Who abandons a life he enjoys for one where the only certainty is that it'll be different? A few will, scientists, idealists, dreamers. But those are rare. The average man, even the average gifted man, sees no benefit.

"Think. How many noblemen and rich merchants went from Europe to colonize the New World or Australia-New Zealand? Not many! The immigrants were the poor, the persecuted, the malcontents, the criminals—in short, those who couldn't make a proper go of it at home. Same thing happened when space was colonized. That was partly masked by the fact that, in the early days, you couldn't survive without a technical education. Still, you didn't see any noticeable outflow of the genuinely successful from Earth, did you? What incentive had they?"

"Achievement," I said. "Research. Adventure. Glory."

"That drew some," Jaspers conceded, "just as it did to the New World. But they were exceptional. By and large, Americans are descended from the failures of Europe, and asterites are descended from the failures of Earth. A comparative term, to be sure. You might be making a fairish living at home, and simply failing to do as well as you could if you emigrated."

"The starship is in a still worse fix," Anne said. "You can't go to Alpha Centauri in the hope of amassing a fortune—or becoming famous—and then returning. If you leave, it's forever. And who leaves Utopia?"

"I'd scarcely call the Solar System that," I protested.

"Another comparative term," Jaspers said. "However, wouldn't you include a wide range of individual options in your definition of Utopia?"

"Well . . . yes, I suppose so."

"Okay." He talked with the eagerness and stroboscope rapidity I remembered from earlier times. "You've got it, these days. No wars or pogroms going on, are there? Some governments are kind of arbitrary, but none forbid you to leave if you don't like them. Everywhere on Earth you can enjoy economic as well as physical security, a peaceful, orderly existence. If that starts feeling too stuffy, you can move into space. There the boom guarantees you can find work at high pay, and offers you some chance of getting rich. If you want, instead, to be an explorer, a scientist, a builder, a pusher-back of frontiers—why, the opportunities are crying out for men!

"So, barring a very few persons with very special interests, who has any reason for going to Alpha Centauri?"

A tingle went along my spine. I let the martini slide cool over my palate before saying slowly: "I begin to get the point. And it's on the end of a shaft. You need capable men and women for the expedition; and they're happy where they are."

"Right. Remember, they'd have to spend a substantial part of their lives in transit—in a placid, isolated environment where the only challenges are those they make for themselves. That's a tall barrier for the sort who might otherwise be afire to start off."

"So the Foundation ended up taking what was available," I said.

"Right," Jaspers repeated. "The third-raters. The failures. The loafers. The wastrels. The clunkbrains we've begun breeding again, now that conditions are easy on the terraformed asteroids. The cranks hoping to found their special paradises or find their Lost Galactic Empire or whatever the nonsense chances to be. The handicapped. The crooks."

Anne said in haste: "Conditions aboard, and at destination, will be rather special. Don't forget that, Winston. For example, a compulsive gambler might ruin himself in the Republic. But what can he bet away that matters between the stars? It'll be his salvation."

Jaspers chuckled. "Or what can a guy like me steal? How do you forge a check or water a stock issue? You'd be surprised how many nonviolent criminals are coming with us. Excellent people, too, by and large."

Wanting to change the subject, Anne said, "We've another important source of able personnel, especially officers: the aged. Too old to compete effectively at home any longer—but still alert, still with an eye for fresh horizons, plus the wisdom of their years—yes, I think the eventual governors of this ship will mostly have passed the century mark."

I scowled into my glass. "Look here, though," I said. "En route you can get by with inadequates. But what happens when you arrive? The reason for such a big crew is that it'll be needed on the Centaurian planets. Do you seriously think a mess of . . . of human messes . . . can survive, let alone accomplish anything worthwhile on totally strange worlds?"

"They don't have to," Jaspers replied. "They'll have bred a new generation while they traveled. Those will be the explorers, maybe the colonists."

"There was a terrible controversy when the idea was first broached," Anne said. "Wouldn't they be just as hopeless as their parents? But the argument was from pure snobbery. The equilibrium concentrations of good and bad genes won't differ significantly between the ship's population and the Republic's. And proper upbringing will prepare the children to cope with Centauri."

Jaspers leered. "It isn't mentioned—you can't tell your crew straight out they're a bunch of bums—but I feel sure the planners expect to make use of normal adolescent rebellion," he said. "In this case, it'll be against laziness, sloppiness, hedonism, and the rest. I imagine the kids will grow up almost Spartan, chronically appalled at the behavior of their elders."

"Of course," Anne said, "we must have a nucleus of first-class people to run things during the

voyage. Not only the machinery and the biosystems
. . . no, they have to steer the human development
onto the right course and hold it there."

"Why don't you join us, Win?" Jaspers suggested.
"We'll be a goodly company, we select few. Plenty
of work to keep us amused, including the work of
human development Anne mentioned. And afterward, given antisenescence, why, we won't be too
feeble to tramp across that living planet, fight its
dragons and rescue its princesses. Hell, no!"

Unhappiness rose in me. "I hate to dampen your
pleasure," I said, "but the expedition may never
come off."

They regarded me in silence. At last, softly and
flatly, Jaspers said, "The power grid problem is
that serious, eh?"

"Well, I don't know yet," I answered. "Probably
won't know for some while. As nearly as I can tell,
from a general survey today, Furlow is right in
claiming the computers are functional. But I had a
look at the blown-out unit he'd saved. It wasn't
repairable. You can't carry enough replacements,
if these breakdowns continue at their present rate.
And if it turns out that the whole grid has to be
done over—well, I'm not certain the Foundation's
funds will reach."

"Can't you find a simpler solution?" Anne's tone
was low but desperate. Her man was at stake.
"I've talked with Hodge myself. He thinks the
grid is inherently unstable, doesn't he? Couldn't
that be compensated for by adjustments to the
computers?"

"Perhaps," I said skeptically.

Jaspers tried to lighten the atmosphere. "I don't
care who writes the nation's laws," he misquoted,

"if I may program its computers. Say, love, isn't the food——"

The drink leaped from my hand and splashed across my lap.

Physically, events climaxed one week afterward.

I am no actor. As the days went by, I noticed Furlow's small pale eyes resting on me ever more often. My tests and tinkerings were simply motions. My conversation was brusque. I avoided his company as much as I could. In particular, I declined repeated invitations to dinner in his bachelor quarters, though he was said to be a gourmet cook; and when we happened to meet in the bar, I wouldn't let him stand me a drink.

Also, no doubt, I asked certain questions in a manner too elaborately casual.

On the evenwatch when the charge exploded, I'd stayed after hours. (While the ship idled in orbit, there was no point in manning a post around the clock.) The pretense was that I wanted to finish whipping into logico-mathematical form a notion that had occurred to me about how feedback might become positive in the monitors, so that we could have a computer check whether the notion had any merit. The fact was that I had no such hypothesis and the symbols I scrawled on paper were merely impressive doodles. My plan was to snoop around. I knew better than to try burgling Furlow's cabin or the like; but maybe, somewhere in the files or among the stored tapes . . . .

Quietness encompassed me. Only the slight pervasive hum, the breathing of ventilators, the soft fall of my shoes, touched my eardrums. The primary control console of the main computer filled two sides of a spacious chamber, from deck to overhead, with blinking, flickering, quivering intricacies. The rest was ancillary machines, desks, cabinets, everything clean and metallic and unhuman beneath cold white fluoropanels. I felt that chill in myself, and a trickle of sweat down my ribs. Its odor was sharp in my nostrils.

A card catalogue listed the programs that had been taped and kept for reuse. They numbered well over a hundred. These computers did more than ride herd on the power grid; they performed calculations relevant to it. For instance, one of them might determine where in the network a large geegee oscillator could safely be connected. Also, a number of separate control programs had been prepared in advance. Special circumstances, like the changeover to the Bussard mode of fueling between stars, would require special approaches to the task of stabilizing the current flow.

Purloined letter, I thought. *Maybe what I'm after is in plain sight in some cabinet, listed here under a misleading code——*

"Winston, boy."

I whirled. My heart slammed. Furlow stood in the doorway. Clifflike behind him was J. P.

They moved toward me. Furlow's affability was extinguished. "You're supposed to be in your office," he said.

"I—well—that is, it occurred to me, uh, somewhere we might already have a formulation—" My voice dried up.

"And you couldn't wait till tomorrow to ask me." Furlow halted a few meters off. His gaze was unblinking upon me. "I've been wondering about you. I really have."

"What—" My tongue felt like a strip of sandpaper. "What's the matter?"

"I want to find that out. I guessed you would—no, stay where you are! Grab him, J. P.!"

The giant came across the deck faster than I could scuttle. He caught one of my arms, spun me around in front of him, and applied a hammerlock. Pain shot through my joints.

"Don't break him," Furlow said.

We stood for a moment, I panting, he brooding, J. P. robotic at my back. "What's got into you?" I finally groaned.

"I have the floor." Furlow took a cigar out of his tunic and struck it on a desk. Lounging back with one fat thigh on that surface, he drew smoke into his throat and streamed it out again.

"I suspect you suspect me of wrongdoing," he said. "When you behaved so eager tonight, I thought it'd be smart to come check on you."

"Let me go!"

"Not till you tell me things, Win."

"If you use force on me, you're convicting yourself."

Furlow shook his head. "No. If you've been acting paranoiac, my duty is to restrain and interrogate you. I've got to make sure you're no menace to the ship. If it turns out I'm mistaken, why, I'll apologize. But I'm in my legal rights as ranking officer aboard. What do you suspect me of, Win?"

I glowered.

"A little twist, J. P.," Furlow said. "Not too hard."

I couldn't help yelling. When the hands stopped racking me I hung on them. Darkness closed in.

It faded. "Sorry," Furlow said. "He gets a mite overzealous sometimes."

I decided that heroism was all very well in its place, but when it gained nothing except the risk I'd be crippled or killed, this wasn't the place.

Bracing myself against the fires that licked in elbow and shoulder, I said:

"Okay. I'll tell you what I think. Nothing's wrong with the grid. No unit was ever ruined, except the sample you prepared. You wrote a special program and substituted its tape in the main computer whenever you got a chance. It makes various boxes cut out as if they'd been overloaded. Your underlings being a clot of drones and nincompoops, you get away with it. You send the 'spoiled' units off for 'salvage.' Actually they're resold. You and your confederates in Mountain King pocket the difference. The scheme doubtless wouldn't work on Earth. This is the Republic, though. The asteroids are scattered across millions of kilometers; the government is committed to noninterference in private enterprise; most transactions are not a matter of public record. Eventually, I suppose, you'd've quit this job on some pretext and gone off to spend your loot."

"Not nice," J. P. piped. He started to take me apart. A shout from Furlow stopped him in time.

"Let him go," the engineer ordered.

"He don't like you," J. P. said.

"Let him go, and fetch the whisky from my office."

The moron grunted, released me, and shuffled off. I collapsed into a chair at the desk where Furlow rested.

He looked down on me, not unkindly. "What a weird obsession you've picked up," he said.

"Proof—" I breathed deeply until a measure of steadiness came. Rallying my nerve, I met his eyes and said: "I blundered tonight, but I was never so stupid as to try playing solitary detective. Did you notice Jake Jaspers requisitioned a boat several

days ago and left for Ceres? He claimed he wanted
to discuss some anomalies in the manifests. We
weren't sure we could trust the ship's communications. He's gone to see the authorities. A squad
with a warrant ought to arrive soon."

"Let them," Furlow shrugged. "They won't find
anything. Won't be anything to find."

"No," I said bitterly, "now that you're warned,
you'll destroy the tape. Are you considering destroying me?"

"Why should I? Even if I were a murderer, which
I'm too squeamish for. Hell, I'm sorry you were
roughed up. I didn't intend J. P. should do more
than throw a scare into you."

"Do you admit here in privacy, what you were
doing?"

Furlow laughed. "I don't admit one damn thing,
my boy. When the police come, it'll be your ground-
less accusations against my blameless record."

"Investigation elsewhere, like at Mountain King,
ought to furnish evidence."

"It ought to, assuming I m guilty, which is your
assumption and not mine. But do you seriously
expect the police to bother? This is the Republic,
my boy, not Earth. The police are spread too thin,
they have too much important work like rescue
operations, to spend time sniffing out petty pecu-
lations. They won't act on those unless the case is
open and shut—and I assure you this one isn't."

"I know. That's why private detectives do so
well in the Belt. If the Foundation hired men to
dig up the proof of your carryings on. . . ."

Furlow looked smug. "It won't," he said. "I've
got more experience than you with the Foundation,
and it won't. Among other things, it's terrified of
scandals, after the fuss about recruitment. I pre-

dict it won't even fire me on suspicion—after *I* report I've licked the power grid problem. This boat has such a shortage of people who know their jobs." He blew a smoke ring. "If anything, Win," he continued, "you're the one whose paycheck is in danger. Telling fantastic slanders to cover the fact you were failing in your assignment—tsk, tsk. But I feel generous. Let's get together and work out how this whole miserable business can be smoothed over and hushed up."

An answer hit me, hard as the original solution had done. I sat straight in my chair and barked a delighted oath.

"What now?" Furlow's calm was the least bit rattled.

It had cause to be. "My boy," I said, "you're not merely going to confess your misdeeds to the Foundation's representative, you're going to describe your modus operandi in loving detail."

"Why in cosmos—? I mean, that is, there isn't any!" he bellowed. "Explain yourself!"

I leaned back, cocked my feet on the desk, waved in lordly style the arm that wasn't sore, and told him, "I prefer to wait till the whisky arrives."

So much for that small melodrama. The real climax came later.

Jake Jaspers and I sat in the office Joseph Amspaugh had taken when he came with the police. He had assumed responsibility rather than Captain Davidson, whose concern lay more with operating the ship than the folk inside. Already we expected Amspaugh's election to presidency of the civil government, once the expedition was fully manned. The cabin was austere, but champagne goblets bubbled in front of us.

"Do you really feel we dare keep Furlow on?" Amspaugh inquired.

"Oh, he'd better be demoted," I said, "but he's too useful to let go. As he pointed out to me, competent officers are precious jewels in this vessel. And any expert who checks the false tape he prepared will agree he's downright brilliant where it comes to power grids—as well as being liked by the crew and rascally enough to spot anyone else's chicaneries early in the game."

"But what he's cost us——"

"He'll make restitution of most of the money," Jaspers said, "and he expects Mountain King will come through with a large donation to the project if we don't hurt their good name by pressing charges."

"Doesn't he feel any shame?" Amspaugh's tone was indignant.

I grinned. "Who cares? If it'll make you happier, sir, he is chagrined at the way we've trapped him. He never intended to go traveling."

But I had explained to him that a third party was concerned which could not wink at this affair like police or Foundation—my company, the contractor. It would have to protect its own reputation by showing there had been nothing wrong with the grid it built; and this it could best do by putting detectives on the trail of Furlow and his confederates. He would have ended in a labor camp.

His alternative was to show us the tape and thus demonstrate an ability which made it worth our while to forgive and retain him.

"I feel somewhat like a blackmailer," Amspaugh fretted.

I lifted my glass and sipped. The wine was tart, the bubbles tickled my nose. Fine stuff; and from this ship, too, where a vineyard had already been started. "Would you rather be vindictive and get him jailed, sir?" I asked. "Or let him go to pull another crime somewhere else? He'll be all right here. Once under weigh, he can't do any harm and in fact, with his own dear hide to worry about, he'll be valuable."

"Till we do start, what about him?"

"Well, I did say he'd better not remain in charge of the department. We can keep watch on him."

"We?" Jaspers murmured slyly.

Amspaugh's eyes kindled. "Then we shall need a new chief power engineer," he said.

Epilogue

Polaris lies behind us; the star by which we steer is Alpha of the Centaur leftward of the Southern Cross.

Conchita says "We don't want the schools to hurt anyone's feelings. Let them, the majority of the present generation, let them play their pathetic little game of being bold pioneers. By now most of them believe in it. I only hope their children won't be too brutally frank ... after seeing through them."

"That's good of you," I say to her. Leaning close: "And very like you."

We share a smile and a fleeting touch of fingers, *Yes,* I think, *I'm glad I decided to come. Excellent company, indeed! And fascinating work; and at the end, whole new worlds to wander across with my sons.*

"I still don't see where it matters exactly what goes into the texts otherwise," Dworczyk grumbles.

"I must concur," Echevaray says in his diffident manner. "What is important is how we train our young to meet the demands that will be laid on them at journey's end."

"Why, that's known," Missy says. "We planned it along with the ship herself."

She doesn't need to recite the possibilities. This

mobile planetoid has ample room for athletics, even for camping and hunting in the forests we have planted. Besides formal education, we will develop elaborate ceremonies for the children. Those will do more than fill time; they will inculcate discipline and a sense of belonging to each other.

She does comment: "It's happened in the past, the evolution of a personality type that can live an easy life without going soft, without losing the ability to meet trouble. Think about, oh, to name one, Earth's Polynesian islanders. We might borrow from them, at that. It may seem a little odd, extra-Solar spacefarers going in for tattoos of rank, and ritual dances, and gorgeous feather cloaks—but why not?"

"Remember something, though," Orloff cautions. "A major part of their culture, of any culture, was their stories about the great ancestors. And that, Tom, is where our history books come in. They will create our myth. Its truth or falsity has nothing to do with its function as a myth—a narrative embodiment of those things, those beliefs, those chosen destinies by which men live.

"What shall we choose for our children?"

I have finished my drink and rise to fetch another. But my gaze falls on the stars, and for a while I lose myself among them. When I return, everyone else is looking at me.

"Oh." I shake myself and laugh. "Sorry. Got to thinking." I point out, into the illimitable night which is not night at all, being filled with suns. "Isn't that, the real universe, isn't that enough? What more do we need?"

"Do you mean," Lindgren asks, "that we may as well tell the undisguised truth about what brought us here?"

"Yes," I reply, "because the only thing that matters is that we *are* here."

My attitude alone does not decide them, yet I have spoken the idea toward which we have been groping together. One by one, they begin to voice agreement.

Missy Blades clinches it with a word which is not really cynical, but smilingly affectionate. "Sure. Go ahead. Let them have the truth. When they grow up, they'll gloss it over anyway."